SENTINELS: JAGUAR NIGHT

BY
DORANNA DURGIN

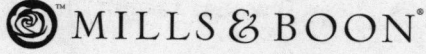

First published in Great Britain 2010
Harlequin Mills & Boon Limited,
Eton House, 18-24 Paradise Road, Richmond, Surrey TW9 1SR

© Doranna Durgin 2009

ISBN: 978 0 263 87912 4

46-0310

Harlequin Mills & Boon policy is to use papers that are natural, renewable and recyclable products and made from wood grown in sustainable forests. The logging and manufacturing processes conform to the legal environmental regulations of the country of origin.

Printed and bound in Spain
by Litografia Rosés S.A., Barcelona

Available in March 2010
from Mills & Boon® Intrigue

Doranna Durgin spent her childhood filling notebooks, first with stories and art, and then with novels. After obtaining a degree in wildlife illustration and environmental education, she spent a number of years deep in the Appalachian Mountains. When she emerged, it was as a writer who found herself irrevocably tied to the natural world and its creatures – and with a new touchstone to the rugged spirit that helped settle the area, which she instils in her characters.

Doranna's first fantasy novel received the 1995 Compton Crook/Stephen Tall award for the best first book in the fantasy, science fiction and horror genres; she now has fifteen novels of eclectic genres on the shelves. Most recently she's leaped gleefully into the world of action romance. When she's not writing, Doranna builds web pages, wanders around outside with a camera and works with horses and dogs. You can find a complete list of her titles at www.doranna.net, along with scoops about new projects, a lot of silly photos and a link to her SFF Net newsgroup.

Dedicated, of course, to the critters in my life –

Jean-Luc, Cheysuli Jean-Luc Picardigan
OJP NAP OJC NAC, CGC

Belle, Cheysuli's Silver Belle
CD RE MXP3 PAX EAC EJC, CGC

Connery, Ch Cedar Ridge DoubleOSeven
CD RE MX MXJ EAC EJC, CGC

and Kacey, Xtacee Carbon Unit, CGC, who was still
with me when I wrote this book, and Strider the
WonderHound, who was there when it all started.

But especially to Duncan the Lipizzan, aka Pluto
Gladys, who has resisted critical injury, extreme
distance and lengthy separation to always fulfil the
task of keeping me humble.

And with thanks to Tashya Wilson and Tara Gavin,
for giving me a chance at all this fun!

Prologue

Meghan crossed her arms over her flat ten-year-old's chest and gave her mother a defiant stare. "You never listen!"

Her mother smiled. Her mother *always* smiled. Sometimes her smile hinted at a joke not yet discovered by anyone else…sometimes it was a cleverness she'd seen in the world. Sometimes it was just because. Thus was the coyote shape-shifter—hard to pin down, cheerfully unpredictable.

Tonight, that smile broke Meghan's young heart. "The animals are worried! Listen to *them!*"

"Ah, my sensitive girl…connected with us all." Margery Lawrence sat right where she was, cross-legged there on the ranch-house porch, and pulled Meghan's resisting body into her arms. Lanky, coltish Meghan didn't quite fit there any longer, but her mother appeared not to notice. Her mother ran a hand along Meghan's hair, smoothing…petting.

Meghan wasn't fooled. She didn't relax into the embrace. "You shouldn't go," she muttered. It sounded sullen even to her own ears.

"Meggie," her mother said, making the word a caress. "I won't be alone. There's someone coming to help, a fine young man who takes the jaguar when he shifts. He'll watch for me."

The demand burst out of her. "Then why doesn't he do all of it? Why make you go out?"

Her mother laughed in genuine amusement. "Because he's big and brawny, but he's not half so clever as this nimble coyote…and he's got no nose for the tricky things. Besides, he doesn't know this land the way I do. The way *you* do."

But Meghan sat, stiff and resistant and still unable to keep her lip from quivering.

Her mother pressed a quick kiss to her forehead. "I might not really be one of them, Meggie, but I don't need the Sentinels to tell me how important this is. Neither do you. The animals wouldn't feel it, otherwise—or the land. Or even you, for that matter. So the fine young man will meet me here, and we'll go take care of things. And then the animals won't feel this way to you any longer, and neither will the land."

More words burst out, even though she knew better. "But it's not fair! They don't pay any attention to you at all, not until they want something! They don't even think you're good enough to be one of them, but they still—"

"Shhh," her mother said, a firmness in her voice. "You know that's not true. It's my decision to stay apart from them, as much as is allowed. This…this is something I have to do. It's my legacy…and in some ways, on some day, it'll be yours. Now give me a kiss and a hug, and let's make sure the dogs are put up and won't bother our jaguar visitor."

But the jaguar never came.

And Margery Lawrence left anyway.

Chapter 1

Dolan knew where to find her—or at least, how. Her scent was all over this mountainous "sky island" territory, the fat junipers and sage and high ground. The hint of her ancient Vigilia nature tingled beneath, along with the sharp smell of the occasional pine.

The daughter. The one who'd grown up apart from them…who barely realized what she was. If anyone could help, it was her. *Meghan Lawrence.* Child of a Sentinel who'd died for the cause.

A woman who'd long ago rejected them all, just as they'd rejected her.

On the eastern horizon, menace loomed in a long, hazy cloud that had no business in this southwestern spring sky—the Atrum Core, keeping track of this area, their dark presence a constant itch between his shoulder blades. For all he knew, they and their twisted prince sought the very same trail he now followed.

He'd have to get there first.

Nearby, an ATV crawled clumsily over fragile soil, chewing up plant life. Dolan veered off in annoyance, a silent snarl on his lips. The rider—oblivious beneath a helmet—crept forward in jerks and stops, challenged by the rugged nature of the protected ground. This, too, was why Dolan was here. Sentinel of the earth in all ways.

He eased back down to ghost along behind and above the man, taking up a loose-limbed trot. Biding his time. Controlling the thrill of the hunt that made his ears flatten, his head sink lower. This wasn't the hunt. This was the job. *His life.*

And so when the time was right, when the ground slanted sharply away but not too sharply, when the creosote and scrub oaks offered uphill cover, Dolan coiled himself on powerful legs and freed his ever-simmering anger, leaping to smack the ATV rider right off his machine and tumbling down the slope.

He almost couldn't control the impulse to follow *the hunt, the kill, the satisfaction, strong jaws crunching bone;* he took his ire out on the machine instead, shredding the plastic and cables and vulnerable exposed guts. Even as the rider lifted his head, Dolan whirled and bounded into the brush, surging with instincts and impulses that wanted to stay. *To kill.*

A mile away he stopped, crouching into the wispy grasses and rough ground, panting. Leaving the man behind to return to his own forbidden quest.

He wasn't supposed to be here. He was supposed to

have waited in Sonoita for orders, for a team. *Waited until too late.* Just as his brother had.

He folded his whiskers back tight with disdain, crouched down close to the earth and dismissed the Sentinels from his thoughts. He closed his eyes, opened his nose and rediscovered the trail. The woman. The dark quest he'd been following before he'd indulged himself.

No. It's part of the job. Of protecting this territory. Not just from the evil that menaced it, the Atrum Core, but from the mundane things as well. The man would think twice before returning here, embroidering the story of his brush with death until his friends ceased to truly believe him—but they, too, might also think twice the next time they went four-wheeling on protected lands.

And the man might have seen a flash of black, might have felt the brush of fur and whisker and massive paw…but nothing more. For all he knew, he'd been nailed by a desert Bigfoot.

Not a huge, sleek and healthy black jaguar with startling blue eyes and a man's thoughts.

Meghan saw him coming. She knew him instantly for what he was; her mother had taught her that much before she'd died. *Vigilia. Sentinel.* Those who had failed her mother. Those who had sent her out to die alone.

Another couple of steps and it hit her in a literal gasp of realization—his other nature.

…a fine young man who takes the jaguar.

Jaguar. In every step, emanating from his very being…as clear to Meghan as if he'd stalked up to her in form, just as her mother's coyote had always glimmered clearly to Meghan's younger eyes.

The horse knew what he was, too, and she barely managed to secure the side rein snap before he leaped away, pulling from her grasp to gallop in panicked circles at the outside edge of the training pen. Around and around, flashing repeatedly between her and the approaching man, tail clamped tight and ears back, side reins flapping.

She walked toward the man from within the pen, her stomach already churning. Never mind the way he moved—fluidly, each step deliberate and yet barely contained. Never mind his expression—so alert, so intense—or the very direct way he approached her. She could have closed her eyes and still known him as Sentinel. *As a jaguar.*

That was one of her mother's legacies. The connections, whether she wanted them or not.

He was close now, close enough to see that his eyes weren't black at all, but a deep, startling blue. Close enough so the terrified gelding fled to the opposite side of the pipe panel round pen, snorting and grunting his fear.

She slipped between the metal rails and straightened as he came to a stop. She didn't give him time to speak. "I know what you are. *Who* you are." She felt it in every fiber of her being, a strange reverberation that raised the hair on her arms. "You're not welcome here."

He lifted his chin ever so slightly. Instead of resentment or disappointment, interest flickered in those eyes. "You *think* you know what I am."

She fought the urge to take a step back. Nothing but cold metal pipe behind her. "I know enough." She wouldn't make the mistake of listening to Sentinel words—to Sentinel requests. Especially not from this man.

He eased closer, off to the side, as though looking at
her from a slightly different angle would somehow
improve his perception of her. "I didn't know your
mother." The morning light flashed against his eyes,
bringing out their clarity; it skipped along the angles of
his cheek and jaw and got lost in the gloss of thick black
hair. All black, so wrong for this climate…black jeans,
black leather biker jacket. "But I know *of* her. We all do."

She snorted. It wasn't delicate. "Right, because she
was your patsy. She let you talk her into dangers she
shouldn't even have been near."

At that he shook his head, short and almost imper-
ceptible. "Not I."

"As if it matters," she said, bitterness leaking through
along with disbelief. The noises of the ranch folded in
around her—horses calling to each other in reaction to
the gelding's fear; human voices raised as they queried
each other, pausing in chores. *They* were her family
now, the people who worked rescue with her. And they
didn't need this interference any more than she did.
"You know what? I'm busy. And you're scaring the hell
out of this horse. Go away, Sentinel."

"He'll get used to me," the man said absently. "They
do." He shifted again, still watching her. Still giving her
that shivery feeling, the same one she'd felt all morning.
He'd probably been watching her that long. Abruptly,
he crouched, resting his elbows on his knees to look up
at her. Damned well settling in. "I haven't yet done
what I've come for."

"You probably think it's important, too." Something
to do with saving the world. With asking too much, just
as they'd asked too much of her mother—whatever it

had been. Some vital mission. Something impossible that her kind, life-loving mother had no chance to survive. "But I won't. So, seriously. Go away now." With someone else, she might have hidden her irritation, taken the blunt edge out of her voice. But this man...

She felt as though she already knew him. As though he made no attempt to hide any of himself from her, and as though she had no need to hide herself in return, not even to soften that bluntness.

And so when he started, "The Atrum Core—" she didn't let him finish. She knew the Atrum Core organization held the bad guys; it seemed as though she'd always known. They were ancient power mongers, sucking energy from the land to use for themselves, never heeding the cost to the earth or individuals. She didn't need to be told again, and she especially didn't need to hear what he wanted her to do to fight them. The Atrum Core had been out of her mother's league; they were far, far out of hers. She held up her hand, and he stopped. He didn't like it, but he gave her that much— here on her own land, her own turf.

"I," she said, each word distinct, "do not care. Do you really think there's more to it than the little incestuous battles between the Sentinels and the Core? Do you think it matters to the rest of the world? Because if so, you need to get out more often."

She expected to make him angry, to set those eyes flashing. She expected a retort...she'd even hoped to send him stomping off in reaction. But he only watched her for a long moment, hands relaxed.

She didn't expect him to say, so quietly, "Your mother was not a patsy. She was a hero."

Unexpected tears prickled at her eyes and nose; her throat tightened. Ten years old she'd been when her mother died. *Ten.* And she still didn't know what had happened that night. Only that her mother had been wearily satisfied with what she'd accomplished—and then she'd gone off to lead the Core astray. *Alone.* "Yeah, well, guess what. I'm *not.* Not a patsy, not a hero. Your people are users and liars, and they're not getting both of us."

His hands tightened briefly into fists, then opened again, a deliberate effort. He stood, abruptly enough so she stiffened in response. "You're right. They can be both of those things." He looked at her as though she weren't wearing old jeans and scarred boots and plenty of barn dirt, her dark hair escaping from its sun-streaked ponytail in spite of the ball cap she wore. He looked long enough that she suddenly wondered what he saw. He added, "But I'm not."

Not like that. Sure.

Her throat hadn't loosened yet. Her words came out hoarse and a little desperate even to her own ears, though every bit as intent as they'd been the first time. "I want you to go."

He eased back a step; in some odd way it seemed like advance instead of retreat. He lifted his chin slightly, acknowledging her words. "Leaving now," he said, "would waste your mother's sacrifice. You don't give her enough credit…. Neither did we. But I'm beginning to understand just what happened here fifteen years ago. I thought you would want to know, too…to help preserve what she accomplished."

She barely had time to process that this man knew

what she didn't—knew what her mother had done, and why she'd died. And then, quite suddenly, he was looking at her from beneath a lowered brow, the kind of look that seemed charming on Clooney and yet downright dark on this man. "I'll go," he said, forestalling the deep breath she nearly took to repeat the demand. "But I'm not *leaving*. I'm not done here, Meg."

"Meghan," she said. "Not Meg. Not Meggie. Not anymore."

He acknowledged that with the slightest tip of his head. "Meghan. Before I go, I need to warn you—"

"The Atrum Core," she said. "Yeah, yeah."

He moved so quickly she didn't realize until too late that he had trapped her against the round pen pipe panels. Just suddenly…he was there, taller than she'd thought and closing her in an intimate cage, his hands gripping the top pipe on either side of her shoulders. There was a growl low in his throat; her whole body clenched in response to it—a fear and flight response, as well as the recognition of what he was. "Don't," he said, and stopped, closing his eyes to take a deep breath. *Control.* In that moment she heard nothing but the galloping pace of her own heartbeat, loud enough so surely he must hear it, too. He released his breath through flared nostrils and opened his eyes to pin her with his gaze, direct and inescapable. "Don't take them so lightly," he said. "You may not count yourself as one of us, but you can be sure that they do. That Fabron Gausto does. If he finds you here, death will be the least of what your people will suffer."

She didn't have time for a response before he tore himself away, heading back to the ridge that rose up to the south of the ranch buildings. Even if she'd found the words, she wouldn't have shouted them at his back. She stood, shell-shocked, right where he'd left her, staring dumbly after him with just enough presence of mind to realize she was trembling.

He stopped his ground-eating pace and turned to look back at her, so deliberately she thought he might even return. But instead a sudden strobe of intense blue light scattered and fractured, startling her eyes. She blinked, and that was all the longer it took for him to change. To become *other.*

Knowing it was one thing. Seeing it was another. One moment a man, the next...black and low and lithe, staring back at her with intelligence. Jaguar. As she'd thought...only deep, dappled black, not gold and rosette. The jaguar once native to this area, stronger and heavier of bone than a leopard, imbued with power. He hesitated there, tail held low and twitching, as if waiting for Meghan's response.

But Meghan stood transfixed, pinned by both memories and unwilling awe. Behind her, the gelding stamped a foot and snorted, a high blast of alarm that would carry across the whole ranch. The black jaguar turned and bounded away, effortlessly scaling steep ground into the cover of juniper, oak and pine.

And Meghan sagged against the metal pipe behind her, cursing his presence here—cursing the Sentinels, cursing the Atrum Core...cursing the jaguar who'd finally shown up. Hearing his words echo in her mind.

You may not count yourself as one of us, but you can be sure that they do.

Chapter 2

Dolan surprised himself by returning to the slopes above the Lawrence ranch. He'd let the jaguar have the night, submersing most of his humanity until sunrise. He hadn't expected to find himself here come dawn, with the hard glint of light skipping over the tops of the opposite ridge. He squeezed cat eyes closed against it—and opened the eyes of a man. Colors brighter but not quite as crisp, movements dulled from sharp clarity to mere smears.

Below, the ranch spread out in a series of outbuildings, paddocks and a main house with a satellite casita. Still sleeping, all of them. Even the horses were silent, slouching in the sunshine to shake the chill of the high desert night.

He wondered if his brother had made it this far.

Leave it alone. You'll never know.

He shouldn't have come back. He could do nothing

more than draw attention to her, and he'd seen how unprepared she was, how resistant to warning—how reactive to his very presence. But here he was, sitting on the crest of a ridge with his legs crossed and his hands relaxed on his knees, watching for the movement he already knew as hers.

He'd come here the day before, too. *Fool.* Lured by nothing more profound than her very presence, the tangible self she'd imbued into this land along with her love of it—just as her mother had. Lured by the hope that she might change her mind, if he could find the right moment to approach again. *More fool yet.*

He'd known her just as surely as she'd known him. He hadn't needed the research, the driver's license photo from sources that didn't know they'd been tapped, the old online yearbook from her high school. Glossy dark hair, wiry form with a scarcity of curves, a narrow-chinned foxy face and almond eyes, so heavily lashed as to look sooty. He'd known her, all right. And he'd—

He lifted his shoulders, tensed, and let them drop—literally shrugging away the memory of his unexpected response to her, the ache he could still feel.

Or trying to.

Best not to go down there again in any event. He didn't have the time to convince her to delve through painful memories in hunt of the tiniest clue. He definitely didn't have the time to sort out his response to her—a stupid, foolish response from someone who had every reason to know better.

He'd have to hope that the remains of the fading wards on this land were strong enough. They'd already failed in the untamed areas, but here, right around the heart of the ranch, they held. "You're on your own, Meghan Lawrence," he murmured out loud, and then wondered whom he was trying to convince.

Knowing the answer just made him mad.

He came to his feet in one swift motion, turning his back on the sharpening sunlight. Too bad it couldn't burn away the persistent ethereal haze of the Atrum Core's presence—he knew he'd see it out there again once the sun rose high enough, hovering over the spring dust devils of the lower grasslands. They wanted what he wanted, and they wanted it badly: the indestructible *Liber Nex*. They'd wanted the ancient manuscript since they lost it, back when the Spanish conquistadors were foolish enough to use its recipes and wisdom against a new land, stealing ancient native strengths, twisting power they hadn't understood.

That particular expedition had consequently destroyed itself, leaving the *Liber Nex* on its own among the land's own people, obscure and mostly forgotten, but recognized as an object of great evil by those with the vision to see. The most recent rumors of its existence— from the eighteen hundreds—placed it in northern Mexico. And nearly twenty years earlier, talk of it had revived, making its way into the Sentinel archives on nothing more than the whispers of hope growing in the Atrum Core. Whispers grown loud enough to act on, however belated. *Fifteen years ago.*

Dolan didn't have any trouble believing the *Liber Nex* had made its way just north of the border. Or that it had even somehow been found during the mess of an operation that followed. Found and hidden again, by someone who didn't live to tell of it.

Such a person would have to be tricky of mind…
would have to enjoy puzzles. Not necessarily a powerful
Sentinel, not necessarily even a proficient one. Just good
at mind mazes, and good of heart.

Just like the coyote shifter who had once lived on this
land.

And the Atrum Core had finally figured it out, first
chasing the whispers, then infiltrating Sentinel intelligence, and now, finally, racing Sentinel reaction.

Well. Racing *Dolan*.

As far as he knew, the brevis regional consul still
debated over the best team to send, no doubt cursing his
willingness to act without them. His brother had taught
him that—not to count on them. He'd learned it again
when the local Core *drozhar* had gotten his hands on
Dolan, and the Sentinels had assumed Dolan dead…
leaving him to escape while they pondered the most
politic response to the situation.

Hard lessons, well learned.

Dolan's gaze flicked to the horizon. There was the
haze again, thicker than ever, right where it had been
during the two days Dolan had hunted the manuscript.
Margery Lawrence had died on this land; the manuscript
couldn't be far if she'd truly been the last to hide it.

And Meghan Lawrence might know of it, and yet he
was supposed to sit in Sonoita and wait as the Core
closed in, led by Fabron Gausto…a man with a grudge.

He wished truly that he believed Meghan knew of the
manuscript, though he feared she didn't. But he did
believe she knew her mother's ways better than any of
them, and that she might hold latent, buried clues to the
manuscript's location. He took a sudden deep breath,

beset by the urge to return to the ranch, to talk to her…to convince her. But there was no time for that, so instead he let that breath go in a harsh gust, giving the ranch one last lingering look before he turned away. "Be careful, Meghan Lawrence."

And Meghan Lawrence lifted her face to the still air of the morning, standing in the eastern doorway with the sun streaming over her hair and face, warming the huge old flannel shirt she'd thrown on over her skimpy night tank top. Cold desert nights, welcome dawn. A faint contact brushed over her skin, as subtle as the sunlight— but it tingled over her entire body, including the skin well hidden in flannel. Without thinking, she followed impulse; she ran out into the hard-packed dirt and dust of the yard, bare feet a stupidity in this climate of things that bit and stung and pricked. She couldn't have said why she searched the steep slab of ground west of the ranch, but search it she did.

And far up the slope, gliding upward with power unhindered by the steep, rocky ground, she saw the sinuous black shape of a big cat.

She wanted to say *good riddance* or *get lost* or *don't come back*. She wasn't sure why she instead murmured, "Be careful, you." Or why she stood bare-legged in the yard watching for a black form long since gone, her fingers clutching the flannel shirt closed and Jenny's dog investigating her toes.

"Meg, you all right?"

Meghan looked at Jenny in surprise, then down at the rubber currycomb and stiff rice-bristle brush in her hands. The horse cross-tied before her—a sweet little mare still regaining her health after her former owner nearly neglected her to death—had obvious swirls of curry pattern in her shedding spring coat, not yet brushed smooth. It was a task Meghan should have finished half an hour earlier...if she hadn't been staring at the oddly hazy nature of the eastern horizon.

That tingle between her shoulder blades...she wasn't sure, any longer, that her Sentinel visitor had caused it. *The Atrum Core uses many forms,* her mother had once said, patiently teaching a young girl what feeble wards she could muster, what faint healing skills. *They are just people, but they do things that would horrify you and me.*

It had been too much for her at six or eight or ten, but now that she was twenty-five, those words lived deep within.

And warned her.

Meghan gave Jenny a little smile, full of sheepish chagrin for a job half finished and hiding thoughts she could never share. "Woolgathering," she admitted.

"More than that." Fair Jenny had a knack for seeing through those little white lies, even the ones people told themselves. She also had the knack of seeing through to the heart of a horse, and she took charge of their problem rescues. Now she leaned against the aisle rail of the open-air mare motel, crossing her arms. "You haven't been yourself since yesterday morning. Not since Starling lost his wits in the round pen. Something's got you shook-up."

Everyone at the rescue ranch knew when someone rattled up that long rutted driveway, and no one had; she could hardly say a visitor had rattled her. Meghan went for a half-truth. "Got a call from an old friend of my mother's."

Not hardly. The man who'd let her mother face the Atrum Core alone.

Jenny winced in sympathy. "Stirred things up, I'll bet." But as she gave the mare a pat and pushed away from the stall panel, she added, "It's more, though. There's something...else." She shrugged. "Won't pry. As long as you're dealing."

"I'm dealing." Meghan rubbed a cheek against her upper arm to dislodge flyaway winter horse hair; her hands were already covered in it. "Listen, you and Chris gonna be here this afternoon to take in the drop-off? I want to get a good start with this one—I think we've got potential for a therapy horse in the turnaround."

"Nice change of subject," Jenny said, and then she let it go. "Chris has something at home." Their teenaged young man currently playing jack-of-all-trades had nothing if not a turbulent home life. "Anica will be here." Anica did the on-site nursing work and had been with Meghan the longest. Rescue work...it tended to burn people out. Meghan was grateful to have Jenny and Anica and Chris, not to mention their fund-raising wizards and the rotating volunteers who handled the necessary physical work involved with the rescue operation. Jenny and Anica both lived on the ranch, and plenty of others had overnighter kits set aside for the unexpected need.

Jenny had also been here long enough to know when to walk away from unanswered questions. She left Meghan to her grooming and her thoughts with nothing more than a parting invitation to talk if she wanted. Meghan returned to the currycomb with a vengeance, and the mare leaned happily into her hand. *Stirred things up.* That much was the truth. Stirred up her grief and her resentment and her anger, and brought out in the open the things she'd always tried to forget about her life.

That her mother wasn't like other mothers. That she had shifted her form. That along with her wicked sense of humor and gentle smile, she also occasionally wore fur.

That a man had changed to a black jaguar before her eyes, bringing that world rushing back to collide with her own. *A fine young man who takes the jaguar...*

Could he even be the same man who should have met her mother that night? Was he old enough? Certainty became less so as logic crept in. But then, she wasn't a big believer in coincidence.

She thought about their confrontation, about the moments he'd backed her against the corral. How she'd felt every inch of her body—the skin tightening down her back, the unexpected tremor in her legs, the very air on her face. Her skills were modest, would always be modest—and yet still she'd felt the power in him. She'd known then that he was a predator, but...also a protector, as her mother had been.

Too bad she didn't trust him.

Dolan found the land's abandoned old homestead in late afternoon, layered in so many wards that he wasn't the least surprised it had taken him two days, or that he'd been through this very area three times before noticing the old buildings. At least a century old, crumbling adobe and exposed wood framing, ocotillo cactus skeletons still lingering atop the porch to create scattered shade... Prickly pear clung to the corners of the buildings, struggling in this altitude. A lean-to shed for animals surrounded by the drunken remains of a corral, the tiny home, a chicken house, an outhouse and a shed that was now merely a trace of a foundation in the dirt.

He stood in the center of the yard for a long moment, on human feet with human senses attuned to the wards that had once been installed over this place. Layers and mazes and switchbacks, all set by a mind he admired anew. A natural trickster, one who could not only worry over the ends of a puzzle until it unraveled, but who could create her own. Her daughter might indeed have unraveled it all faster than he, but only if it wouldn't have taken too long to convince her to try. Now he searched the patterns of the wards, having long ago realized that there was no single bright spot, no obviously protected area—and he finally saw what he was looking for.

Surely it won't be this easy. Not a bright spot, woven into the threads of protections and the occasional glow of obscuring aura, but a blank spot. A don't-look-at-me spot. He opened his eyes and superimposed his inner ward vision over his outer, and found himself facing the old house. Right through the open, damaged wall to what remained of the old fireplace.

In the chimney of the old fireplace.

Not quite as tricky as he'd expected—not the location, not the process of navigating those ward lines. At least, not until he realized what she'd done by using the old homestead, for anyone who did happen to notice the lingering wards would think nothing of them. Many older dwellings still carried protections, especially in an area where they might be needed fast. Violent monsoon storms, cold desert nights at even colder altitudes…as wrecked as it was, this place was still shelter. Still worth protecting.

Dolan slipped through the warding on the house, leaving it as intact as he could—out of respect, and out of the need to keep things quiet. The Core was hovering too closely as it was. He thought briefly about waiting, of bringing Meghan Lawrence back here to take part in what had surely been her mother's greatest victory and greatest sacrifice....

Then again, maybe not such a good idea. He'd stop for a quick visit on the way out, letting her know her mother's legacy. She deserved that, and he...

Maybe he just needed to prove he could walk away again.

He flattened his ears in annoyance. Oh, maybe they were currently human ears and maybe they didn't truly flatten, but he felt it all the same, and knew it reflected on his face—annoyance at his own inability to let go of the woman who'd wanted nothing to do with him or his quest or his blood. Sentinel blood, like her own...but running too thick to dismiss.

Dolan glanced at the sky, at the sun about to go down, and shrugged off his distractions, a literal twitch of shoulder. He'd come here for a reason, and one reason only—and if Meghan Lawrence thanked him for anything, it would be that he achieved his goal fast enough to prevent the official team from descending on the area. So he quit hesitating in the doorway and crossed the threshold, hyperaware of the fresh breezes stirred by his entrance. Not physical breezes, but metaphysical disturbances just waiting for him to take a wrong step, to prove he didn't belong.

He didn't really want to find out what a trickster would do in retribution to a trespasser.

So he offered his respect and his caution, and he slowly progressed to the interior of the crumbling house, the single main room with its sleeping and cooking alcoves and the hand-formed fireplace still in near-perfect condition. He crouched beside it, hesitating long enough to check for traps and black widow spiders alike, finding neither. Just that blank space that had drawn him here, alluring…close enough to success to send tension zinging down his spine.

As dusk fell around him, he reached into the chimney and felt around until his fingers came to rest on crackling paper.

Yes. With care, he eased the manuscript free. It felt right in his hand—the expected size, the expected heft— if at the same time without the *presence* he'd expected. The weightiness.

He withdrew it from the chimney and set it on the hearth, a paper-wrapped package thoroughly secured with duct tape. More duct tape showing than paper, dammit. The stuff would be hell to cut through, even after all this time. He reached into his treated back pocket for his folding Buck knife—and that's when he realized.

Not dusk, this darkness. Not yet.

Atrum Core. Here. Now. In spite of his personal wards. Coming for the one thing he could never let them have.

The haze once restricted to the horizon now abruptly descended around him, saturating the air with an oily stench. He threw himself down on the manuscript, pulling the threads of his wards tighter even as he sent the most piercing Vigilia *adveho* call he could—the 911 incantation of a Sentinel in deepest jeopardy. By then he realized the haze wasn't mist, wasn't droplets of any sort, but had turned into infinitesimal insects, gnats almost too small to see—and that as they settled on the skin exposed at his wrists, they sank right into his damn skin, making it twitch with the sudden burning fire of their passage.

Can't be good. He instantly gave over to the jaguar, trading inadequate clothing for thick black fur, still crouched over the manuscript, ears flattened closed and eyes tightly closed, his nose tucked down between his front legs and his tail curled tightly to his side. *Expose nothing—and never stop reaching for those wards—*

Abruptly, the stench eased. The fiery burn beneath his skin eased, fading to an ache. The dusk—true dusk—enfolded him in silence. Dolan didn't move, not at first—he finished reinforcing his wards, not allowing himself to wonder why the Core had retreated when they—face it—they'd had the complete advantage. The Vigilia *adveho* hadn't yet even reached its target; the ward reinforcement hadn't been finished. His dappled black jaguar fur wouldn't have kept the invading gnats away forever, and the fire of them had been enough to fragment his concentration. And yet...

Gone. All of it.

Dolan slowly raised his head, a growl slipping out. He flexed his claws into the stone hearth—claws sharp enough to tear through duct tape as easily as a knife. He didn't waste any time tackling the manuscript wrapping, beset with the sudden urgency to see the thing, to touch it directly—to feel it. Beset with the sudden premonition that it—

That it wasn't the manuscript at all.

Dolan growled again—couldn't stop it, or stop from lashing his tail. *Decoy.* Paper encased in leather—a fancy journal of some sort, filled with the scripted details of daily life. The Core must have realized it, and they had promptly quit the field.

He'd been lucky in a backward kind of way—the Core shouldn't have been able to find him, shouldn't have been able to reach him…but they had, and only this decoy had saved him from that bafflingly successful attack.

But it left him with no manuscript and a cold trail.

And it left him with the need to return to Meghan Lawrence, to see if she could lend insight to his search. It left him with a biting inner self-scorn, knowing he'd underestimated Fabron Gausto and the regional Core.

A twinge shot through one front leg, involuntarily flexing his claws into the journal's leather binding; he stared at it without immediate comprehension. A spasm flickered across his ribs; he grunted in surprise, hissing as a contraction twisted his back leg hard enough to kick out across the dirt floor beyond the hearth.

And then he knew.

The Atrum Core had left not in retreat, but because they'd already done what they'd come for. Another twist of muscle down his back, a grunt of pain from deep within, tinged with annoyance and—

—yes, desperation.

They'd waited for his distraction and they'd somehow infiltrated his defenses, instilling sly dark poisons and now—

—fire traced down his back—now Meghan would be on her own—*a dry jaguar cough, wrenched from a body*

twisting around itself—and the real manuscript was still
out there for the taking—*consciousness fading, making
way for the fire and*—

Failure. Agonizing death and failure.

But he still held the threads of the unfinished call, and
he redirected it to a closer target, to the one he least
wanted to endanger and most wanted to help.

*Meghan. Sentinel unblooded. Daughter of the trickster.
Hope of the Vigilia.*

And the one face he wanted to see.

Meghan stiffened. Echoes of pain shot through her
body, trying to twist her—trying to take over. Without
thinking, she whirled to face the eastern horizon, which
was darkened by dusk...but no longer by the strange
haze of the past few days, the one she'd first thought was
an atmospheric oddity and then smoke from a distant
fire and then pretended not to notice at all.

"Meghan!" Jenny ran down the aisle of the open-
sided barn to reach her, hands closing over her upper
arms to turn her, to look her in the eye. "Meghan—?"

Meghan had to blink a few times before she truly saw
her friend—before she realized she'd dropped an entire
bucket of oats and psyllium, leaving the hungry gelding
in the end stall pawing in frustration. "I have to go," she
said, and the words sounded as if they came from
someone else's mouth.

"You—" Jenny dropped her arms, took a step back.
"You *what?*"

"Have to go." Meghan spoke more briskly, her mind
racing ahead—choosing a horse, listing supplies...
preparing.

She'd felt the pain. She knew who it was, if not why. She knew he was alone on her land.

She knew she had to go…

If not why.

Chapter 3

Meghan ignored Jenny's hovering presence as she grabbed saddle, bridle and the saddlebags set aside for trail emergencies. A quick side trip to the house and her bedroom, and a low storage bin bumped out from beneath her bed and across the braided rug to yield her mother's lore box with its precious herbs and powders.

Meghan dashed back to the barn, nearly colliding with Jenny at the threshold. Jenny did a double take, her gaze settling on the box tucked under Meghan's arm. Wooden, carved with loving but basic skills by an adolescent Margery Lawrence...the most meaningful thing Meghan had left of her mother.

"I'm okay," Meghan said, knowing how very much circumstances indicated otherwise. "But my mother... she may have left something undone. And I have a feeling—" She broke off. How she hated that phrase;

how she usually avoided it. How she'd been teased as a girl in school—

But this was Jenny, and her face cleared. Or nearly cleared. "All right," she said. "But is it *safe?*"

Meghan hesitated long enough to shrug. Safe? Not in the least. That somehow didn't, at the moment, seem relevant. "Grab Luka for me?" she asked Jenny, and pulled a floppy camp bag from the small tack room opposite the saddles.

"Luka," Jenny echoed. "You're going into rough country?" But her feet were already moving for the gelding's stall.

Because Luka would get her there. Wise, once mistreated into a man-killer, the aging gelding had finally found a rider who understood his mighty Lipizzan spirit. He still suffered no fool gladly, but he'd given his heart to Meghan—and now his sure feet and still-powerful body would take her anywhere.

A mount she might well need, since she had no idea just where she'd end up. She only knew she'd follow—

Wrenching pain, fracturing thoughts...

And a sudden brief clarity, a presence so clear that it arrowed right through her. *Danger,* it said, and Atrum Core and *'Ware, Meghan Lawrence* and then more faintly, an entirely different tone behind it, something yearning, *Meghan...*

Meghan blinked. She scrambled to her feet, having found herself on her knees in the aisle—and just in time, for here came Jenny with Luka, and in what possible way could she explain her reaction, explain why she still had to go?

Still reeling from the touch of him—the dark presence,

the faint, sharp spice, the hint of something deep, untapped—she wondered quite suddenly if the jaguar had touched her mother like this. If he'd warned her.

If she'd gone anyway, as Meghan intended to do.

"You're sure?" Jenny asked, dropping Luka's lead rope beside the gear; it was as good as tying him. But she didn't wait for an answer; she said, "Let me grab you a couple of jackets, then." Because the temperature would drop fast on a crystal-clear night like this one; already Meghan's sweatshirt didn't seem quite enough to keep the goose bumps away.

Or maybe that was the lingering touch of his presence in her soul.

She shut him out as best she could, just so she could think. She quickly saddled Luka, stroking his noble baroque nose when he turned to inquire of her hurry, but swiftly turning to tighten the girth on the lightweight synthetic Aussie saddle, adding a breastplate, strapping the bulging saddlebags in place...and turning to find Jenny proffering not only an armful of easily layered jackets, but pommel bags stuffed with trail food. She gave Meghan a quirky little smile and said, "I had a feeling."

Meghan gave her a quick hug while Jenny still had her hands full, and then pulled on a Windbreaker and vest and strapped the remaining two jackets over the sleeping bag. "*That's* why I choose my family."

"Oh, pshaw," Jenny said airily, but her eyes had a glint in the sallow mercury light of the barn aisle. She double-checked the straps and girth as Meghan slipped a practical trail halter bridle over a head almost too dignified to carry so much. Luka chomped the bit and waited patiently, nothing like the mount he'd be once Meghan swung her leg over the saddle.

"I've got my cell phone," Meghan said, though she knew she wouldn't use it even if she managed a rare connection. There was no way she'd lure her unsuspecting chosen family into the thick of this mess. They knew of her *feelings,* of her connections…in truth, there was a little of it in all of them, that common thread that drew them here. But they had no idea her long-dead mother had shifted to a coyote any time or place that pleased her. They had no idea such organizations as the Sentinels and the Atrum Core even existed.

And if Meghan had anything to say about it, they never would.

Once mounted, Luka transformed—no longer a stocky, aging gray-to-white gelding, but a creature of movement and air, dancing his way out of the ranch yard and heading toward familiar trails. Meghan allowed him to pick up a power trot, propelling them along the steady incline of a trail. He stretched into the generous rein she offered, arching his neck like a young stallion, and took them up into the darkness.

As the trail turned twisty and tricky, Meghan gave him his head and turned inward, bracing herself, and cautiously opened the connection she'd shuttered away. Sensations flooded in, swamping her. She reeled in the saddle, dimly aware that Luka deftly shifted beneath her, balancing her again. *Black fur and clawed dirt and burning lungs and the fiery agony of spasming muscles* and again, that briefest instant of awareness—this time with a hint of puzzlement, as though he perceived her approach. *Meghan?*

She might have answered, had that awareness not
shattered into a stuttering fugue of pained disorientation.
She clutched Luka's thick white mane, struggling to
control the connection, to keep from drowning in the intensity of those shared impressions.

Nothing had prepared her for this...not her mother, not
her mother's death. Not her guardian aunt's uninterest in
the shape-shifter skills that touched their lives. Not even
this man's sudden presence in her life two days earlier.

Jaguar.

I'm supposed to hate you.

Maybe she did. Maybe that's what had created the
strength of the thread between them. The clarity. And
even the tears running unchecked down her face as she
absorbed the smallest fraction of his experience.

Beware, Meghan...

"I'm coming," she told him, out loud into the night.
His protest beat against her—but only for a moment
before pain swept him away. Setting her own jaw, she
shifted to follow the sensations; Luka willingly took the
next chance to turn uphill, scrabbling between a batch
of tightly bunched oaks, his big unshod feet biting into
the scrabble-rock hillside. She balanced lightly over his
withers, giving him freedom to move. Soon enough
they'd reach the high ponderosa pines, leaving Luka
more space—at least until they hit the canyon that di-
vided her land from Coronado National Forest.

But as they reached the pines, as the feel of the Sentinel
began to fade—weakening—she found herself turning
directly toward that canyon, leveling off their progress.
Luka moved out strongly beneath her, as if he knew where
he was going—and suddenly, so did Meghan.

The old homestead.

The first homestead took advantage of the canyon stream, the one funneling cold snowmelt down the side of the hill; it was tucked into the small natural clearing beside the stream, using a backdrop of pines and oak and the occasional creosote bush, with cedars creeping up the side of the hill. But even so, it was now only a wreck of disintegrating structures, barely enough for emergency shelter in the case of a sudden storm.

His thought, surfacing randomly against hers before sliding away again. *I thought it was here. I thought…*

Meghan stiffened in the saddle, causing Luka to hesitate for the very first time. *It.* Her mother had been dealing with an *it*—one she never would identify, not even in the most generic terms. An *it* that had killed her—if not directly, because of the Atrum Core's obsession with the thing.

Meghan had thought it destroyed. She'd thought it gone. And yet the jaguar had come back to hunt it?

For the first time, she truly hesitated. Luka, not quite willing to stop his energetic process, nonetheless scaled back to a cadenced, high-kneed trot. The trail unfurled before them in the light of the rising moon—coming on full, it was enough to light their way in these well-spaced pines. Enough, if she let him, for Luka to flow forward into a collected canter, perfectly balanced to avoid ruts and suddenly jutting rocks alike.

Sudden regret found her on a breeze. *His* regret—and yearning and *need* and a deep, bitter underlayer of…

Failure. Loneliness.

Meghan settled deep in the saddle, giving Luka the

faintest lift of thigh and seat bone to release him into
the canter.

I know where you are. And I'm still coming.

Failure. He'd come to put an end to this once and for
all…to secure the indestructible manuscript where it
would never be found. He'd come to involve the
daughter, as his brother had involved the mother. But
he'd meant to keep her safe…not writhe out his life on
the dirt floor of an ancient home while the daughter was
left to take the heat.

Like his brother.

Jaguar fur, scattered over the towering desert landscape. Gold and black rosettes, a claw…a whisker. No
more. Because the brevis regional consul had delayed
backup with scrying and warding and—

Whatever. *Too late.*

They'd be too late for Meghan, too.

Your brother? The thought had a light touch, gentle…and unfamiliar.

Hearthstone bruised shoulder and spine as his body
jerked uncontrollably against it, twisting so tightly he
couldn't find room to breathe. The world dimmed even
further, and still he recoiled inwardly in the alarm of
no longer being alone. His lips drew back in a snarl and
his whiskers quivered, and even blinded by pain and
his body's jerking dance, his slapping paw found its
target, claws clogged with dirt and blood but still able
to pierce skin.

He hadn't expected to feel the pain of it, sharp and
wounding; he froze. Only for an instant, and then the
poisons took him away, the world fading away to thin

nothingness. He barely felt the light touch on his head, around his muzzle—confident fingers lifting that frozen snarl and smearing his gums with a paste imbued with the feather-touch of incantations.

As fast as that, the rigor eased, his long and powerful body sagging back to dirt and hearthstone. And when the world darkened, it was as if he fell into himself, deeply into himself…back into the life of his beating heart and panting lungs and even that deep growl of feeble protest stuck in his throat.

And then, somewhere along the way, he fell *into* her. *Meghan.* Slip-sliding from one thought to another, from his to hers and back again. Through it all echoed his anguished backdrop of warning—*Atrum Core…Atrum Core…'ware. Meghan, Atrum Core…*

They'd come back if they knew she was here. They'd come back if they thought she'd become involved…if they thought she'd shed her noncombatant's role to join the Sentinels outright.

If they thought, as he'd thought, that she could help to find the *Liber Nex.*

'Ware, Meghan…

And then he lost himself to darkness, to sweet scents and blessed lassitude and the enfolding blanket of determination that he would not, after all, lose *himself* to the Core.

And Meghan followed him down to the darkness.

You shouldn't go…don't go—! Sweet little girl voice, gone reedy and thin with desperation, the recognition of futility.

The world skipped around memory turned into reality. Long coltish legs crossed on the bed, covers over her head…herbs pungent in their pinched little piles, arrayed directly on the sheets around her bare legs. *Breathe deep. Take them in, like Mama says. Transform them. Empower them.* They didn't quite have meaning, those words, but by God she *tried.* She built wards and she built warnings and she built safety.

Or she thought she did.

But she felt it happen. She felt the death…the loss. *Mama! Don't go, Mama! Don't—*

A whisper of goodbye, a scant caress of love—

You said there'd be help! *You said there'd be a* jaguar! *You said—*

Gone.

Scattered herbs, sheets damp from sobbing, heart broken forever. Little girl betrayed. By the—

Jaguar.

Older brother. Strong, golden, black rosettes rippling with the movement of bone and muscle beneath. Jared, who could do anything. Jared, confident in running point for the Sentinels, in assessing a situation, in doing what had to be done until the entire team arrived. Jared, steeped deep in Sentinel lore, Sentinel responsibility…utter faith in teammates.

Jared. Brother, father and mother in one package, enough years between them to make it work. Enough years before them to anticipate working together. *Sentinels.*

"Sure, it's dangerous—it's the damned *Liber Nex,* Dolan. But I won't be alone. Working point, yeah, but the team will be there. Making sure we're clear without drawing attention our way."

Jared.

Not coming back.

What do you mean, he didn't make it? What do you mean, you weren't there in time? *What do you mean, he's—*

Dead.

No jaguar. No Sentinels. Just Margery Lawrence, left on her own and now—

Dead.

Echoing wails, bitter, bitter grief, wrenching loneliness…resentment.

And childhood resolve, not quite as young and untouched as it had been only days earlier. *I'll rebuild my own family. My chosen family.*

And the Sentinels will have nothing of me. Not—

—ever.

They'd let him die. The Sentinels had tangled themselves in some dumb-ass protocol and they'd delayed and they'd left him out there to die.

Jared. His last thoughts had been for that woman, a single mother, a joyful coyote with no real place in fieldwork, no training, just heart. *His last thoughts—*

Bitter, bitter grief. Choking fury…

A young man's resolve. *I will never trust them. I will be one of them, but not* theirs. *Not truly. Not ever.*

For Jared, he would save the ones he could. Hard and independent and…

Rogue.

Chapter 4

Meghan sat back against the long-dead fireplace in dazed exhaustion, beyond thought. Beyond decision-making or reaction or feeling.

She stared through dawn light at the huge black cat sprawled on dirt and rock before her, instantly reconnected to the memories they'd shared. His memories, her memories…all the same now. She pressed a hand to the base of her throat where that hard ball of grief welled up so suddenly, so deeply.

Perhaps not beyond feeling after all.

Her arm protested the movement; she stretched it out, shoving back torn sleeves for a good look. Punctured, smeared with dried blood, swelling. She'd cleaned the wounds and covered them with an herbal paste—preserved with warding, enhanced with personal power—that would have them pink and closed by the time she made it home. After last night, Margery Lawrence felt…closer, somehow.

And meanwhile…she didn't understand it, but that blood…his blood…his saliva…they'd all mixed, somewhere along the way.

Made a difference. A connection.

Luka whickered. Hungry, no doubt, and thirsty… he'd waited, accepting the other side of the crumbling old house as his stall. She'd removed his tack and trickled water into the collapsible water bucket, but he needed more.

She wasn't ready to leave the jaguar. Not yet.

Dolan. She knew his name now. She wasn't ready to leave Dolan Treviño.

The darkness lifted, steadily brightening into a typical morning here on the Santa Rita sky islands. Crisp and bitter cold at night, the clear sky quickly turned from star-spattered ink to coral-rimmed cerulean and then to a blue so sharp it almost hurt to look at it. Even here, tucked away in the trees and shadows, the day warmed fast enough for Meghan to ease off her quilted, oversized vest.

Meghan regarded the jaguar for a long moment from her slumped seat at the hearth. His ribs rose and fell in a steady rhythm, and the growing light picked out the faintest dapples of the rosette patterns within black fur.

His tail twitched; a paw flipped and went still. Meghan crawled back over to him to rest her hand on his side, his shoulder—feeling for the spasms from the night before. She still had no idea what had happened—what had poisoned him so badly, or how it had gotten into his system. She'd only treated the symptoms—red clover, valerian, magnesium powder, all tied to infusions of power for efficacy—and she'd been lucky when it worked.

He'd been lucky.

Dolan Treviño, and not his brother Jared after all. Jared, golden and vibrant and dedicated…and every bit as dead as Meghan's mother. Killed on his way to her.

Meghan wondered again if he'd sent out a warning, just as Dolan had warned her. If her mother had *known* that last night…and gone out anyway, making sure she wasn't at home when the Atrum Core came after her. Came after the *Liber Nex.*

A forbidden book of the dead. An instruction manual for corrupt, death-based, power-wielding techniques, long-buried and long-forbidden. Great. And that's what Dolan was looking for now? That's what he thought her mother had handled?

His tail flicked again. A dream, maybe…or maybe a memory. His broad brow furrowed. "I'm sorry," she said, drawn back into their moments of sharing that which she'd learned of him. Of his brother. "I didn't know. But I still don't want anything to do with this." She hadn't grown up with it, not the way he had—and until now she'd had no idea of the deeply instilled obligations the shifters felt. Even Dolan, who blamed the brevis regional consul for his brother's death, still found a way to serve their cause. To remain Sentinel.

Well, Meghan had never *been* Sentinel. And her mother, tied to the Sentinels only by the virtue of her shape-shifter nature, had never been meant for field duty.

Jaguar fur lay warm beneath Meghan's hand, and she felt the massive weight of him as though somehow he lay on her hand and not the other way around. Glossy fur slid between her fingers—and then suddenly the lax muscle stiffened. Meghan felt rather than saw an impending flicker of blue light, and then it was too late to snatch her hand away, to leap away—

He changed, fur to smooth skin to leather-clad human, and there lay her hand through it all, flickering in the light and for the briefest instant literally a part of Dolan Treviño.

And, oh, God, she hurt and she couldn't see and she had two hearts, beating hard and fast, and four lungs, gasping for air, and nerves that sizzled and popped and *ached* to be every bit as connected as that one hand on that one shoulder—

She cried out, in fear and astonishment and denial, and the sound came from his mouth. And then the blue light slammed them apart with chastising whips of energy and Meghan quite suddenly lay at the hearth, sobbing for breath and barely able to lift her head to find Dolan coming up to his hands and knees, to his feet, and then down again, full length on the floor.

He looked just as she felt...stripped away, seared by another's soul. When he lifted his head he cried, "What did you do?" in a voice ragged and barely audible.

She heard him anyway. She heard him clearly.

She heard him within.

"What did you do?" He demanded it again, his voice hardly any steadier. Off to the side, a horse snorted in alarm and annoyance. Meghan looked as wild as Dolan felt, sprawled in front of the hearth with the look of someone who might just bolt.

No, not her. Not the woman who'd stuck with him

through this past night. Even now, her expression quickly sharpened. She looked at him; she looked at her hand. It gave him time to think, to realize how every bone and muscle burned and ached, to understand that the memories sitting so freshly in his mind weren't all his. Weren't all—

She'd been just a kid. She'd never known that his brother had died for the cause, trying to reach her mother. Her guardian, her father's sister, hadn't been a shifter, hadn't been Sentinel at all…and the Sentinels—as ultra-secretive, ultracautious as any clandestine organization over two thousand years old—hadn't told her a thing. They'd cut Meghan loose, knowing she wasn't a shifter and sacrificing what skills she did have—what she might have been nurtured into. More fools, they. She'd saved his life. What she might have done if fully trained…

"I'm sorry," he said, and his voice felt rough-edged in his throat. "If I'd realized they cut you off…I'd have told you what happened myself."

"Doesn't matter." She tucked back a loose strand of hair, tightening an espresso ponytail gone loose and sloppy, her expression turning her sharp features yet sharper. "The Sentinels let them *both* die. And you're still with them?"

Dolan managed to push himself upright, leaning back against the wall with one leg propped up before him. "You don't *leave* the Sentinels. Not if you're a shifter."

"Nice," she said, prompt and sharp. "They take lessons from the mob?"

Dolan laughed. Not loudly, not long, but as amused as he could be with his body still tasting an Atrum Core death. "Didn't your mother teach you anything about us?"

Meghan stiffened. "She taught me what she felt was important." She absently rubbed her arm, but stopped with a wince, pulling her hand away. At his frown, she held out her arm, displaying the ripped sleeves. "You weren't a grateful patient. At least not at the start."

"I—" Vaguely, he remembered it. Damn. "You'd best get it cleaned. Is it—" But he couldn't quite bring himself to ask herself if he'd hurt her badly.

"It's fine." She'd gone brusque on him, more like the woman he'd met several days earlier—if not altogether convincing, there at the corners of her eyes. There, he saw lingering grief, lingering puzzlement. She stood, slapping off dusty jeans more vigorously with one hand than the other. "I'll take care of it. First I've got to see to Luka. Since you're all right for a few moments?"

Luka. "Your horse," he realized. "He's done well with me."

"Luka has a noble soul," she said, simply enough so it almost hid her great affection. "But he needs water. Rest, and I'll be back in a moment—and then you can tell me just what happened here. *Before* I got here."

He'd damn well warned her away, that's what. Warned her about the Core. Not *called* her here. A sudden spike of annoyance made it through his pain. "And *you* can tell me why you ignored my warning—"

She laughed—short, no humor to it at all. And then she walked over to the horse—a luminous gray with great dark eyes and the baroque head from every old European statue Dolan had ever seen. He greeted Meghan with a gentle bump of his nose, and the halter lead rope between them was merely a token as she led him out of the house.

He was still absorbing the fact that she hadn't answered him when he fell asleep.

When he opened his eyes, it was to find her saddling the horse outside the house while the animal nibbled at last year's dry grasses and stripped the new leaves from a nearby ash. Sunlight played along her bare arms as she gave the horse a last stroke beneath his heavy mane, highlighting toned, lightly tanned muscle. She wore a T-shirt; the jackets were tied around her waist, an absurd tangle of sleeves obscuring her lower body. Her arm glistened with salve, and as she returned to the house, he winced at the bruising around the puncture wounds. Widely spaced, made by a huge feline paw. *His.*

"You shouldn't have been here," he said. "I warned you—"

She laughed again. "Right. And what was I supposed to do about *that?* If the Core wants me, it probably gets me. But you know…they could have had me any time in the past fifteen years. It's not like anyone was watching out for me."

"They were *here*," Dolan said, and his emotional hackles rose just thinking of it. "Last night. You would have played straight into their hands."

She shrugged. "You were the one who called me."

"I did no such—" But he stopped, and thought twice. He'd warned her. He'd meant to warn her…hadn't he? Surely he hadn't transmitted any of his…

Right. His dying man's desire to see the face that had haunted him for days.

There wasn't any way to finish what he'd started to

say, so he left it at that. He said, "So you came out to help the Sentinel?"

Her lingering humor dropped away; her chin lifted slightly. Sharp features; sharp-eyed glance. "I came out to help *you*." She sat quite suddenly on the hearth, a rise so short that she had to cant her knees together. Her voice was quiet with both wonderment and horror as she asked again, "How did they do that to you?"

Dolan looked away; his jaw clenched. "I don't know," he said. "They shouldn't have..." He took a deep breath and found the fortitude, somehow, to look her directly in the eye while admitting to the failure. "I dropped my guard. The Core got in. Isn't that enough?"

She tucked that wayward strand of hair behind her ear again. "I suppose it is. Now, do you think you can get on this horse?"

He blinked. He hadn't been expecting the concession—not from a woman who'd been so fiery, so opposed to him from the start. He wasn't sure what it meant—what she was really thinking. And so he was cautious when he said, "Brevis regional will be here in a couple of days."

"I can't stay out here that long," she said, quite sensibly. "And if you think I'm leaving you, think again. I know exactly what I gave you last night, and how long it's going to take to get over it. I doubt you can even take the jaguar."

And boy, wouldn't he love to prove her wrong! Except when he reached for the jaguar, just for the *feel* of the jaguar, he found a deadness he'd never experienced before. An emptiness. He fought a sudden stab of panic.

"Don't worry," she said. "It'll wear off. But until then, you need a place to stay."

And bring her more deeply into this mess, with the local Core, under Fabron Gausto's rule, more aggressive than he'd ever suspected? "I'll be fine here," he said. "They think I'm dead."

"Then there won't be any problem with having you at the ranch." She stood, stretching. Two of the three jackets slipped off; the T-shirt pulled high to expose a tight, smooth line of skin. "Look," she said, bending to scoop up the jackets. She rolled them lengthwise and shot him a direct, spearing look. "I've got a horse coming in this afternoon. I need to be there. Can we just do this thing?" As if she didn't have circles under her eyes and a certain grim determination to her movement.

And every moment he argued with her was a moment she wouldn't be on her way home. He nodded; it took her by surprise much as her own recent concession had startled him, and she relaxed visibly.

There were already saddlebags resting over the horse's loins; she tied the jackets over them and returned to the house, giving the floor and hearth area a careful inspection. "Can't have the slightest bit of the herb stuff left out," she said. "It'd kill anything smaller than a dog, with the whammy I put on it."

Whammy. Oh, yeah. The Sentinels would just love that.

Meghan pushed away the exhaustion of the night, the turmoil of the morning, the fears for the future—even the odd feeling in her bones. She focused on her hands, where they tightened the girth one more time for the rugged ride home with a rider who wasn't likely to keep his balance. "Have mercy on him, Luka," she murmured as Dolan finally made it to his feet, wobbled there a moment and pretended to have found his strength.

She would have believed it, too, if she didn't know what he'd been through this past night—or if she hadn't seen him in full strength only days ago, full of prowl and power in either form. He made it to the gaping doorway and leaned there, and somehow made it look casual. She knew better than that, too.

"I'm not sure about the wards," he said. "I thought I left them strong...but the Core followed me in without much trouble. I—"

"Can't see them," she said, only belatedly realizing she'd not only finished his sentence, but to judge by the startled look on his face, done it accurately. Or was that expression more properly called a glower? "I'll come back later and see what needs to be done." Not that the homestead often found use, but it still deserved some respect and protection. "I can do wards, but...not right now." She ran a hand down Luka's shoulder. "We're ready when you are."

He wasn't. And he wasn't going to be. She saw the flicker of despair on his face, there and gone again, right back to the tough-guy glower. For a scant moment, she wondered if it might not actually be best to leave him here. But even if the Core thought him dead, they might figure out they were wrong. And besides...she simply didn't want to leave him behind.

Not that she wouldn't have enough explaining to do when she got back.

She dropped the halter lead and went to him, where he pretended to stand in the doorway, and slipped in

under his arm. "Oof," she said, under her breath. And
then shrugged off the shiver that ran down her back.

Luka stopped his tree-grazing to regard Dolan with
a wary eye, pulling himself up with a high and warning
neck. "Not *now*," Meghan muttered. But still, she gave
the horse a moment to accept Dolan's nature. Dolan
leaned heavily on shoulders made strong from ranch
work and training—and she would have borne it easily
had not another shiver run down her back, following
each leg all the way down to the soles of her feet, to her
toes. And the flush that followed, and the empty ache,
building inside her chest.

Maybe just what she deserved for running out into
the middle of a Sentinel/Atrum Core squabble.

But surely it hadn't been *catching*. And she'd felt
Dolan's pain; she'd felt it clearly. This wasn't painful...wasn't even truly uncomfortable. Just...unusual.

Dolan's arm tightened around her shoulders—for-
bearance, she thought, as Luka offered a stretch of
his neck, a disgruntled but accepting snort. Dolan
reached out to the saddle, steadying himself that way.
She would have bent to lace her fingers together into
a "leg up" for him, but his hand fell on her arm,
sending tingles of warmth and demand through the
limb. Her jaw dropped; she looked down to his hand
in disbelief.

Quite suddenly that hand moved to the back of her
neck, half cradling her head. He pulled her to him—
right up against him, her head tipped back and that ache
nearly exploding inside her, separate pinwhirls of energy making her light-headed and joyous and terrified
all at once. She gasped, fighting it, and his hand tight-

ened behind her head, fingers catching in her hair. And when he asked, again, *"What did you do?"* this time there was a growl to it.

Except when she found his eyes, she found shadowed desperation.

What *had* she done?

She realized her lower lip trembled; she put fingers on it to still it, and the uncontrollable swell of emotions suddenly infuriated her as well. She tore away from him, losing half her ponytail but freeing her head, and she channeled all her fear into defiance. "I don't *know,*" she said. "And I don't *care*. It doesn't mean anything. It's just the aftereffects of—"

Of mingled blood and mingled memories and mingled pasts....

"It doesn't mean anything," she repeated, but her voice had lost its defiance. "It'll fade."

"You think so?" Hoarse and full of pain, those words. "Because I'm not so sure, Meghan Lawrence. I think there's more to you than you know. I think there's more to what's between us than you'll admit. And I don't think this is *going away.*"

The absurdity of his words put her back on solid ground...dampened the pinwheels. "Get real," she said. "There isn't anything *between us*. I met you once, three days ago."

"I know," he agreed, and when she tried to look away she found her gaze flickering back to his despite herself. Still full of that dark desperation, purest, deepest blue flaring bright in the rising sun of a desert sky. "It happens that way with some of us. But this...this is beyond." He closed his eyes, sucked in a breath.

He released her. "Some of *us?*" she said, stepping back. "I'm not *us*—and you know it."

He didn't open his eyes. "You've got the blood, whether you want it or not."

And the ache, which had intensified now that she no longer touched him, intensified and swelled in protest, but now…faded.

And like that, she shook it off. She took another step back, clinging to the absurdity of it all. Shape-shifters, coming into her life these fifteen years later. Her enhanced herbs and old wards and a night with a black jaguar trying not to die…and now she stood, flushed and unsettled, by Luka's head.

She straightened. She pulled the overstretched hair band free; she gathered her hair up and scraped it back into containment. "I think," she said, pulling the band into place again, "that you'd better get into that saddle on your own."

Chapter 5

Dolan managed it somehow, crawling into the saddle with all the grace of a bread pudding.

She might hope the connection between them would fade. He wasn't expecting it.

Hell, he didn't even want it.

She admonished him not to touch the reins, which she'd clipped to the saddle's grab strap. And she didn't bother with the halter rope, tied in a loop around the horse's neck. "He'll follow me," she said simply, and he did.

A man whom most horses wouldn't approach didn't get much time in the saddle. A man who could take the jaguar had little use for it in the first place. He clutched the flat swell of the pommel, and half the time he wished for a horn to grab and half the time, as he slumped and bobbed, he was grateful for the lack of it.

As they hesitated before the lip of a steep slope, she

advised him to lean back, but halfway down the slope she stopped them and adjusted his legs with the confident touch of an instructor—except she just as quickly snatched her hands away, glaring at him. "Figure it out," she said, and resumed her sliding, sideways progress down the rocky slope.

He didn't need to guess at her discomfort. He'd felt it, too, the moment she'd touched him. A flow of energy, something greedy and demanding...wanting more. *He'd* wanted more.

Luka followed Meghan in mincing steps, and Dolan did his best simply to stay out of the animal's way until they reached the bottom.

But *bottom* was a relative term...it simply meant the narrow trail now wound sideways along the slope. Meghan stopped again, patting Luka's sweat-soaked shoulder—for although ambient temperatures were still modestly cool, the high-altitude sun stabbed down hard.

Meghan hesitated, looking down the vista below them—the tiny dots of the ranch house and barn, the swell of the hill from which he'd once watched for her. She glanced back at him. "God, you're a mess," she muttered. "Maybe I *should* have left you..." But she didn't finish that thought. She took an audible breath and reached for him, steadying him; straightening him. She wound his fingers firmly around the grab strap. He knew she felt the surge of energy there—her hand tightened briefly around his. Not consoling, not reaching out, but a white-knuckled attempt to push through it.

"There," she said, and her voice was hardly steady. "We're almost there." Then she looked down the hill again and gave a short laugh. "Well, maybe not. But the hardest parts are over." Her hand, free of Dolan's, trailed down the horse's neck. Luka turned his head and tilted it just so, and Meghan gave a little laugh. "I don't have any. Get us back home again and I promise you a bucketful of carrots."

But as she stepped out in front, she hesitated, and said somberly, "It's never really going to be the same, is it?"

"No," he said, hating the weakness in his voice, the vulnerability it exposed. But she deserved an answer...she deserved the truth. "You know too much now."

"I've *seen* too much," she said, and glanced back at him—no recrimination there now, just sad awareness. "I'll have to lie to my people. My chosen family. Or not answer them. Either way, they'll know something's wrong. And changed."

"Don't think about the big picture," he said. "Screw the future. Think about getting down this hill. I know I am."

She gave a short laugh. "I'll bet. But you know...if you didn't find what you came for...if the Core didn't get it from you...then this has really all just begun."

And here he'd thought she'd been so deeply in denial that she hadn't been paying attention. *Wrong*. He reeled slightly in the saddle, caught himself and met her eyes one last time before she turned and led them back down the hill. "Yes," he said. "It's really all just begun."

"Meghan!" Anica ran from the casita at top speed, slowing only when Luka made himself tall in warning, raised neck and pricked, intense ears. A small, dark and well-rounded whirlwind of a vet tech who'd burned out of city life, Anica now focused all her considerable energies toward healing the rescued animals of Encontrados Ranch—and sometimes the people.

Not this one, Meghan thought. Anica would quickly pick up on Dolan's unusual nature. Not everyone who came to this ranch had their own quirks and sensitivities…but those who stayed? Yeah. They all found this place to be a haven, and some had stayed in this chosen family that Meghan found herself building.

"We were worried to death!" Anica said, running to meet them. "What were you doing out all night? What happened to your arm? You should have taken a cell phone!"

Meghan shook her head. "No reception that high, you know that. I ran into someone in trouble, that's all. We couldn't travel in the dark. And I'm fine."

Anica said flatly, "You ran into someone in trouble." She held her hand up in a dramatic gesture, her faint Latino accent coming out a little more strongly. "No. Wait. Don't tell me. You had a *feeling*."

Here came the evasions. "This is Dolan. Think altitude sickness. And unless I'm mistaken, he's about to fall off the horse."

"Right." Anica stood to the side, giving Dolan the once-over. Dolan, in his black leather biker jacket and his black jeans and booted feet, whisker-shadowed jaw and pain-shadowed eyes, barely sitting in the saddle at all. "A tourist."

Meghan swallowed back her new fears, knowing there was little she could do or say at this point; either Anica would accept Meghan's new understanding of her world, or she wouldn't. Just another way that Dolan's appearance had intruded on her life.

She led the horse toward the porch, with Dolan dipping and swaying over Luka's withers. One hand was still clamped around the grab strap; the other had found Luka's mane halfway up his neck. His eyes were clenched as tightly shut as his grip. "Dolan," she said, reaching to touch him—and then thinking better of it.

"He's really out of it," Anica said. "Maybe we should call 911."

"He asked me not to," Meghan said. She knew well enough that Dolan would prefer to stay out of the system—that the Sentinels would be coming for him. And that conventional medicine would be of little help anyway. But at the look on Anica's face, she added, "Don't worry—if he doesn't perk up with some liquids, we'll call."

"Okay, then," Anica said, tugging Dolan's foot from the stirrup. She went on to untie the jackets and saddlebags, pulling them off Luka's rump to splat carelessly against the dusty yard. "You ready?"

Oh, no. Not for the touching. "Come on, Dolan. We're home."

But when he looked at her, she wasn't the least bit sure he actually saw her—or anything, for that matter. There was no focus or recognition in those blue, blue eyes. Dammit. "Hold on," she said to Anica when the other woman would have shoved his leg over Luka's patient rump. Another deep breath; she flexed her hand, reaching out to his calf…hesitating with her hand close enough to feel the warmth of him.

"Meghan?"

Right. Best get on with it. Gently, she let her hand settle onto his leg. At first she felt only muscle beneath denim, lax with the herbal incantations she'd put into his system, warm and yielding. And then it started—a thrumming through her body, an aching awareness— awareness that this time pooled in sensitive places she'd very much rather not have respond to him at all.

Anica gave her a strange look over the saddlebags, and Meghan did what she hadn't even thought to do, but which suddenly felt altogether too natural after a night of swapping memories. She focused her thoughts and snapped *Dolan!* without ever opening her mouth.

He started slightly, looking at her with a confounded expression. Anica abruptly shoved his leg over Luka's rump and Dolan's eyes widened—and over he went, taking Meghan down with him in a tangle of arms and legs and the disgruntled snarl of a jaguar in the back- ground of Meghan's mind.

"Take care of Luka?" Meghan asked Anica, straight- ening Dolan's legs on the bed of the creaky-floored little box of a guest room and starting in on the leather laces of his boots.

Anica hesitated, still aware she hadn't been given all the answers here, aware that Meghan was giving off a muddle of mixed signals, and nodded shortly. "Call out if you need anything. I'll give Luka a good rubdown and get the quarantine stall ready for our newcomer. You'll be out?"

"That's the plan," Meghan said, doing her best to keep the *grim* out of her voice.

Anica hesitated in the doorway as if she might say something. When she finally murmured, "Call for help if you need it," Meghan knew those weren't the words that had lingered on the tip of her tongue. Those words would have been something more like *What's up with you, woman?*

Just as well Anica hadn't asked. Meghan had no answers.

She finished pulling off Dolan's boots and did her best to straighten the twisted leather jacket; then she grabbed a quilt off the foot of the iron bed frame and spread it over him, here in the cool interior of the house. All the while, her blood thrummed and heated, and she had a weird duplicity of perception, as though she felt Dolan's vague impression of the moment along with her own.

And even though she tried to busy her mind with such practical matters, she found herself lingering at the side of the narrow bed, watching the little flickers of movement in his face. At the moment she should have walked away, she instead crouched by the bed and watched her hand touch his cheek, trembling along the contours of his brow and the dark hair at his temple.

Not all of the shifters reflected their other form. Her mother hadn't. Her mother had looked like Meghan, all dark hair and dark eyes and sharp jaw in clean, exacting features. The coyote showed only in her laughing eyes. But Dolan…Dolan somehow looked exactly like what he was. Blue eyes, holding all the shadowed power of his past. Black, sleek hair, falling across his forehead just a tad too long. But mostly it was in the way he moved, the way he held himself…and now all the sinuous power hidden beneath the incantations she'd fed into his system with her herbs.

Her fingertips tingled. Her body throbbed. She touched

his jaw; she ran the backs of her fingers along the stubble there. She let herself feel what came from him.

Longing and need and...

He growled, deep in his throat; he tensed, a quiver passing through his arms and torso. She held her breath, startled as arousal reverberated through her, uncertain if it was him or her or both of them. She closed her eyes; bit her lip. She had the sudden, startling revelation that if she stayed here with him, if she kept the contact between them, she would quiver herself right into an orgasm, right here beside the bed with both of them fully clothed and barely touching and barely knowing each other at that.

She wrenched herself away, so hard that she lost her balance and tipped over to land on her butt. After that, she didn't linger. She climbed to her feet and marched out to the kitchen with long, deliberate strides, pulling chipped ice through the refrigerator door and grabbing a spoon. She returned to the bedroom and made short work of spooning a few chips into his mouth. And when the plastic tumbler was half-empty, she left it on the bedside table and marched herself off to the shower, shedding filthy clothes along the way.

A nice, cool shower. She might even be tempted to call it cold.

Chapter 6

Meghan strode out into the yard with purpose. Jenny's dog, a mixed cattle dog—all pricked ears and foxy face, mottled blue coat and short, stout tail—circled her with excitement, barking at the sudden energy and movement in the yard. Meghan hushed her with a gesture and stood in the center of the packed-dirt hub of the ranch, reassuring herself that some things were still normal.

The main house. All one floor, it had started small and grown over the generations. It had belonged to her mother's family...although Meghan knew little of them. Only her mother had manifested the coyote, after her grandmother's long-lost Sentinel lover had ended the happily-ever-after story of the ranch. Until then, generations of Lawrence ranchers had raised horses, grazed cattle and escorted tourists around the mountain ranges that formed the inviting sky islands of southern Arizona.

And then came Meghan's grandmother, who'd had Margery Lawrence and never married when her Sentinel lover didn't return for her. Margery followed Meghan's grandmother's path and loved a man who died before Meghan was even born.

So here she was, raised by her mother and then by her aunt, who hadn't taken to the Southwest and had moved back East as soon as Meghan came of age.

And so Meghan had decided to choose her own family.

The ranch house, tiny casita—Jenny's and Anica's— and storage shed made up the yard. There, where the cleared flatland elongated to a point, lived the smaller livestock, all damaged or behaviorally problematic or simply in need of hospice care.

The horses took up most of the space, occupying a long mare motel with covered, open-sided stalls, paddock runs, several communal paddocks and even a separate quarantine area. This generation, Encontrados was purely a rescue ranch, funded by donations, investments, volunteers and a grant or two. Never enough to get comfortable, but…

Successful.

And those who helped her run it…they were her people now.

People she intended to keep safe from Dolan Treviño and whatever trouble he'd brought with him.

She headed for the three-stall quarantine barn, the ranch barn, made of sturdy timbers and thick planking from rough-sawn wood. A detour through the mare motel showed her Luka, groomed, relaxed and happily munching on hay. One of a kind, her dangerous Lipizzan gelding turned indispensable ranch horse.

Inside the quarantine barn, Meghan found a wide-open stall filled with fresh, deep wood shavings and a welcoming flake of hay already shoved into the hay rack. The cool, dim light of the little barn made her realize how warm the day had grown. It might still be spring out there, but it was looking real hard at summer.

There was no sign of Jenny or Anica, but Jenny's dog had darted back toward the casita—Jenny, at least, was there. And all looked to be ready here, so…

It gave Meghan a moment to realize how tired she was. Bone-tired, after a night of no sleep, wrestling with the effects of a mysterious Atrum Core poisoning and sometimes wrestling with the jaguar himself. And fit as she was, the hike back to the ranch had been a long one. If she was lucky, she'd grab a nap before the new horse arrived—an event that could occur any minute now, or late in the afternoon. With a volunteer at the wheel, she wasn't inclined to nag.

She emerged from the barn, cast another thoughtful look around the place…felt another surge of protectiveness.

I shouldn't have brought him here.

He'd said the Core thought him dead. He'd argued it, even.

She hoped he was right. But she didn't think the only threat to Encontrados came from the Core. The Sentinels, too, knew how to focus on a goal…and how to sacrifice others along the way.

It made her realize just how very much she'd been taking the ranch's safety for granted. It had been so many years since her mother's death…so many years since she'd seen even a hint of Sentinel or Atrum Core activity.

Well, you've seen it now.

So she stood in the doorway to the barn, and she *listened.* She closed her eyes and tipped her head back, falling into unconscious habit. Sometimes she listened to a horse, sometimes to the land, sometimes to the true mood of those around her...sometimes she just listened to see what was there.

And this time she heard something.

It was small and slippery and whispery, a harsh and discordant sound. She tipped her head, followed it.

It moved.

From the outer edge of the property toward the center, it eased between strong wards. As if in response to having been noticed, its movements increased in speed; Meghan felt a hint of malevolence, and fury swelled within her. How dare anyone send such an incantation sneaking around her ranch? Trespassing, unwelcome...*malignant.*

She wasn't a prodigy when it came to wards, not like her mother. She didn't have the power. Still, she knew enough to find the nearest ward lines, to grasp those shadowed glow lines in her mind's eye and slam them together over that dark blot of unwelcome presence.

A sizzle; a pop. The presence vanished. The ward lines wavered, momentarily diminished—but they were tied strongly to the land, and the thin spots soon flowed back into balance.

Meghan let out a long, deep breath, finding herself with a small grim smile of satisfaction. "No trespassing," she murmured to the world at large, and went to take her nap.

Dolan opened his eyes to an unfamiliar room. His body continued the low-key background thrumming he now associated with Meghan, but was still plenty weak, muscles full of burning pain and lassitude. Unfamiliar panic surged within him—concern that Meghan, barely schooled and unpracticed, had truly done him harm. Had somehow locked him away from the jaguar permanently.

It's been only half a day. She said it would take time.

He smelled the water by the bedside and took solace. If he could smell the water, then the jaguar still lurked.

Not to mention he was damned thirsty.

He sat for a moment, checking his stability, taking in the details of this room. An old room, nothing quite in true any longer, everything worn around the edges… comfortable. It smelled of Meghan, gingery, and while at first he accepted the effect as a natural for her house, his gaze finally landed on the rocking chair in the corner. He realized that the bundle of light knit cotton throw was actually a bundle of Meghan beneath the cotton throw.

He watched her sleep for a moment, getting his bearings. The bedside clock said it was early afternoon; they'd only been here a few hours.

She'd said it would take time. Not a few hours, but *time.*

He quashed the flare of impatience and reached for the bedside pitcher—slowly, deliberately, taking none of his muscles for granted—to pour himself a full glass. He downed it in a few deep gulps, his eyes still on Meghan. She hadn't stirred. Exhausted…and with good reason.

He wondered about her arm. No cat's claws made a

wound to be so casually dismissed—too prone to infection, regardless of size. He should check…

And still his body urged him to return to sleep, a deep escape from pain. He found the glass still in his hand—and then he misjudged the distance to the serving tray. The tumbler clunked awkwardly into place.

Meghan's eyes opened at once. "You're awake," she said, voice a little creaky. "How are you?"

"I was wondering the same of you." He flung the quilt back and dropped his legs over the side of the bed, relieved to find himself still fully clothed. "Your arm?"

She pushed the light throw down; she wore a bright coral tank top under a white, gauzy tunic, spaghetti straps barely visible. His gaze got hung up on the strong, graceful lines of her neck and the sweep of her collarbones; she pushed up the tunic sleeve and held her arm out for inspection, turning it this way and that.

What he saw got his attention, all right. "That can't be the same wound."

Her face held the smallest of smiles. "My mother's herbs drove off the Core poison," she said. "You think they can't deal with a couple of scratches?" But she shifted so the window light hit her skin, and he saw the remains of the bruising, the clean red puncture marks. "It's still sore," she admitted. "But give it another day." She slid the tunic sleeve back into place. "There's a reason I don't use those herbs for everyday injuries."

So she thought like a Sentinel, even if she didn't want to. Low profile. "It would draw a lot of attention if you healed overnight from every bump and bruise."

She brushed a self-conscious hand down the front of the tunic. "Bad enough they'll wonder why I'm in town clothes with a horse coming in any time now." But of course a plain T-shirt or tank top would have revealed the wounds—and her healing rate.

She gathered the throw and draped it over the back of the rocker as she went to the window, looking over the back edge of the property, the intense blue sky filling the window. Light shone through the gauze tunic so the tank top outlined her spare shape in clear silhouette—strong shoulders, the nip of her waist, the flare of her hips and a tight, toned bottom.

Dolan scrubbed a hand over his face. It still felt like someone else's hand, not quite doing his bidding, tingling painfully in every joint. "I didn't mean to take your bed."

She turned, startled, a three-quarter view he found just as arresting. "This? This is the guest room."

Which would explain why it held so little of her personality. And yet…he gave the chair a pointed look.

She turned away again. "I headed for my room, and somehow I ended up here instead. I just felt…I just…"

"There's something," he said, realizing it himself as he watched her stiff back.

"From last night," she said, barely audible—but her resentment was clear enough.

He didn't answer. He didn't think he needed to. It was obvious enough to both of them. He turned to other matters from the night. "The Core came in on a sending mist," he said. His hand clenched into a fist—and that, too, felt like someone else's doing. "I don't know how. They shouldn't have been able to find me. And what they did with that mist…I've never seen anything like that before. The Core has some new toys. I need to warn—"

Her back stiffened even more; her head snapped around. Her hair, of course, had loosened in its pony-tail, and strands of hair fell at the sides of her face. Dolan felt a barely perceptible thrill of alarm…and he didn't think it was coming from within. No, it came from *her.*

"I almost forgot," she said. "I think they were here. Or not *them,* but…something. I just happened to…*look.*" She glanced at him, a question on her face—seeing if that was enough, if he understood.

He understood, all right. He understood that she used her skills on a daily level in ways she didn't even think about. "There was a…" She shrugged. "A grody spot. I've never seen anything like it. It came right through my mother's wards, too—good strong ones."

"And?" he demanded.

She laughed, but it had a hint of darkness in it. "You think I'd have come back for a nap if that thing was still heading toward us? I slammed it between two ward lines."

"You did *what?*" His explosion startled her—and then her eyes narrowed, her sharp jaw going hard. "You think they're not going to be just a little bit curious about who obliterated their little toy? You think they won't come looking? You should have led it astray, weakened it slowly—let them think their damn probe failed!"

"I shouldn't have brought you back here!" she said, just as vehement as he'd been. "The *probe* wouldn't have mattered if you weren't here. And you shouldn't have come in the first place!"

Astonishingly, he couldn't disagree. Not with the way things had turned out—the two of them, now tied by blood and incantation and a night of fighting death, and neither of them worth anything but trouble to each other.

Unless he could do what he'd intended from the start. Unless he could get her help—get her insight into what her mother had done with the *Liber Nex* all those years earlier. "Meg…"

"No. *Meghan.*" She turned away from the window; she turned away from him. "I'll protect this ranch," she informed him, on her way out the door. "And I'll do it *my* way. Because I already know where your Sentinel ways lead."

Space. A chance to take a deep breath. They both needed it.

Dolan let her go.

As hard as it was to think with Meghan's influence thrumming through his veins, as desperate as he was to find the *Liber Nex,* Meghan, too, struggled. Until the night before, she'd known only that the Sentinels had abandoned her mother…had let her die. And after all this time, she'd obviously thought herself completely free of Sentinel influence. Of the Core.

No, he shouldn't have come here.

But if it meant finding the manuscript…

Yeah, he'd do it again.

The front screen slammed shut. He made his uncertain way to the bathroom, and to the kitchen after that, skipping past a cozy-looking living room with deep leather couches and bookshelf-lined walls.

In the kitchen, the ceiling fan turned lazily overhead, doing little to dispel the warmth in this southern-exposure room. The deep overhang of the porch shadowed the two big windows of the southern wall; the others were wide open to the sun.

Dolan helped himself to more ice water, listening to the bark of a dog off by the barn, the rumble of a diesel pickup, the clang of a gate. A sudden spate of whinnying confirmed the arrival of the new horse, and Meghan was no doubt dealing with it.

Just as well. He had a phone call to make.

He found a couple of half-made sandwiches on the counter, lunch meat and thinly sliced cheese, and he took one for himself, sticking the other in a baggie for Meghan's return. So damned domestic he could hardly stand it, rambling around in her kitchen as though he might actually be welcome there.

You're not paying attention, he thought at her. *Not if you still think I'm Sentinel in anything but name.*

He hadn't been, not since losing his brother. He'd wanted out altogether…not an option, not for a powerful jaguar. So he did things his way…and he got away with it, precisely because he took the jaguar. Because he was good, and effective, and he made things happen.

But they were always waiting for him to stumble. To find a way to rein him in.

Or to try.

And that meant he had a phone call to make. Follow procedure…shift the problem back to the consul's shoulders. The man had been in position too long…his complacency and self-assurance had turned from asset to liability. *You could go down with this one,* Dolan thought at him.

He just didn't want to go down alongside the man. And he quite suddenly didn't want Meghan to go down alongside the man, either.

He helped himself to a shower, rinsed out his shirt and left a towel hanging around his shoulders. By then his brief burst of functionality had waned, and he promptly fell back to sleep before he could use the phone.

Fell asleep, and fell into nightmares—or maybe just memories. Even in the midst of them, he wasn't sure. Jared's death would always be a little of both—receiving his final message via the Vigilia *adveho,* the frantic rush to find help for Margery Lawrence, Dolan's own decision to bolt from their Sonoita home and out into the nighttime desert, cross-country on a dirt bike that could cover ground with more speed than his adolescent jaguar form.

He remembered the disbelieving anguish the most. His brother's Sentinel cohorts descending upon him, stopping him. Taking him down from the bike—*It's too late, you can't do anything* and *You'll die out there, you idiot!* and *Hold him,* hold *him*—and the physical agony as he fought them, grief and fury and determination, and yet unable to change a single whisker because of the wards they dropped on him—

It's too late, you can't do anything. You'll die out there, you idiot! Hold him, hold *him*—

He woke with a shout, his body caught up in the past. He fell back, rolling over to groan into the pillow. The scrape of damaged nerve and tendon in his shoulder—dislocated those fifteen years ago in his fierce, feral fight to escape and reach his brother's side—faded to the leftover damage of the Atrum Core's poison.

Already the grip of that poison had eased. He felt for the jaguar…and though he felt only a faint stirring, a flood of relief, warm and overwhelming, washed through his chest and filled his throat. A sudden gust of breath against the pillow, a sharp, reflexive inhalation—he forced himself to move past it. The jaguar was there, waiting. Not if, but when. It was enough, for now.

He rolled over and found that the shadows in the house had changed, their edges gone soft. Sunset, and a long southwestern dusk.

No sign of Meghan.

Carefully, he sat. He rotated the once-injured shoulder—habit now, to keep it loose—and he downed water gone lukewarm as he pulled the phone into his grip, dialing a long-memorized number. Sometimes the voice on the other end was familiar, sometimes not. But it always changed when the receptionist du jour realized who had called.

The troublemaker. The rogue.

And, not coincidentally, the Sentinel they sent out on all the impossible fieldwork, simply because he kept coming back alive.

This voice, as it happened, was one he knew. The consul's recently assigned adjutant. "Carter. It's Treviño. I need to talk to—"

"Talk to me," Carter said. An abrupt, efficient man was Nick Carter—he'd probably outlast the consul. Their styles clashed hard enough for visible sparks.

"I need Dane." The consul, dammit. Straight to the top

this time. "Unless he handed over leadership of the *Liber Nex* field team to you sometime in the past several days."

"Nations could rise and fall between your check-ins. The team is minus a crucial member, so is waiting for results from another lead."

"Results? I've *got* results—"

"Which we could have taken into account had you bothered to report them."

Deep breath. "First opportunity." The man knew well enough there was no cell phone reception out here. Not to mention that cell phones were incredibly unreliable around Sentinels in general. He gritted his teeth and added, "I need the team out here."

Since *keep them the hell away from me* was Dolan's classic reaction to field-team involvement, he wasn't surprised at Carter's momentary silence—or his question. "The Lawrence girl yielded clues?" Carter demanded.

"The Lawrence *woman*. And no. But I'm still convinced she will."

"We can't send an entire team out without more—"

Dolan didn't even wait for it. "The Atrum Core is convinced, too."

Carter's hesitation was so short that Dolan almost missed it. "Are you certain?"

Ah. No wonder he'd been left dangling after his call for help. "Didn't get my message, I take it."

"We've heard nothing." Definitely wary now—but not of Dolan. Of events.

"I sent an *adveho*." Dolan didn't hide his pointed response. There were people who should have been listening, who were *always* listening, who knew which teams were in the field and which were likely to encounter the most trouble.

"And yet, here you are." Carter, too, let the message come through in his voice. The *adveho* was only to be used under the most dire circumstances. Life or death.

Dolan laughed, the sound filled with pain. "No thanks to brevis regional. Let's just say that Meghan Lawrence isn't entirely what we expected. The consul should never have cut her off as he did—damned waste of talent."

"Are you still in the field?"

"I'm out of commission. Could be a couple days, could be a week. We need backup—they've already sent a probe looking for her."

"Or for you. Gausto wants you, and you know it."

"She found the probe," Dolan said, as if Carter hadn't spoken. "She destroyed it. She's completely untrained, and she destroyed a Core probe."

"Sounds as though maybe we should have a talk with her."

"I don't think so. The Sentinels screwed up when they let her go…you can't fix it now." Emphatic, a little too much so. But he couldn't tone it down. "She doesn't want anything to do with you." *She doesn't want* me, *for that matter.*

"Has she been initiated?"

"The Sentinels gave up the right to ask that question," Dolan said, as cold as cold. She hadn't been, of course… she probably didn't even know what it meant.

Carter cleared his throat. "You don't sound a hundred percent objective, Treviño."

Dolan had to stop himself from shouting. "Damned

right I'm not objective. You knew I wouldn't be. My brother died here, on this same mission—and you never cleaned up after it. So now here I am, doing the job for you. No, I'm sure as hell not *objective*." Maybe his voice had risen nearly to a shout…maybe it just sounded that way in his head.

Pointed silence filled the line between them before Carter said, "In point of fact, I wasn't on the rolls fifteen years ago. And you, my friend…if you're going to do any good—if you want to keep yourself and the Lawrence woman alive—you need to get over the blame game and focus on current events."

Dolan kept his snort to himself. Not as hard as it should have been…he felt his energy fading. *Dammit.* But he hadn't expected anything better from Carter— the consul's man, shrugging off responsibility for an event in which he had no investment. Typical. "Backup," he said, returning to the matter at hand, finding some fitting sarcasm. *"Now."*

"I'll pass along the word—the irony of it will help."

"Yeah, yeah, yeah. Dolan Treviño wants the Sentinels to step in. To quote you—more or less—*get over it.*"

Carter's amusement came through clearly enough, although it faded quickly with his next words. "They've shuffled the team. The right people aren't all local—and they aren't all here yet."

"Screw the *right team*," Dolan snarled. "Just get someone—" the room went dark and sparkly at the same time; he pulled it back into focus through sheer will "—out here!"

The unexpected happened. Carter said, "You okay?" and almost sounded as if he cared.

"No," Dolan snapped at him. Or meant to; he wasn't sure how it came out. "I'm not. And Meghan Lawrence won't be, either, if you don't get someone out here to *back me up*."

Maybe he hung up the phone; maybe he dropped it. He figured Carter would get the point either way.

Chapter 7

The new horse should have been trotting around the small run off his quarantine stall, head high and tail flagged, snorting and calling and investigating his new digs. Instead he clung to the corner, head hanging, giving his generous portion of Bermuda hay a dispirited snuffle.

"We had him down for Bermuda, right?" Meghan frowned at the dusty bay, frowning especially at the stocked-up fluid in both hind legs, at the jutting hipbones, the prominent spine. She leaned against the shaded barn and watched, determined not to think of the Atrum Core the Sentinels, the wards and the grody spot. And Dolan?

No. Not thinking about *him* at all—flat out in the bedroom, and still able to set her teeth on edge with the intensity of his purpose, that slight feel of him a sandpaper-rough presence floating against the borders of her mind and body.

Everyone else, quite appropriately, was thinking only of the horse. "I've got the vet coming out tomorrow to float his teeth," Anica said. "I think that'll help. I'll soak him up some hay pellets. It's too rich to give him much, but it'll get him started...I'll portion it out."

"Amazing how fast they can go downhill." Jenny rubbed her arms as if they were cold. "Those people... they signed him over and then dithered two damned weeks over the arrangements."

Meghan touched her shoulder. Jenny cursing meant she'd let the situation get to her, and she knew it; she took Meghan's concern with a quick, bitter smile. "He'll be okay," she said. "He's still the same horse we evaluated."

"Once he's moving around and gets a little muscle on him, that stocking up won't be a problem," Anica added. "Don't expect to do endurance trails on him...but I think the therapeutic-riding folks will be eager to have him."

Jenny rubbed her arms again, giving Meghan a wry, self-aware little smile. Anica turned to her with a canny expression that let Meghan know the subject under examination was no longer the horse.

Now it was Meghan herself.

"How's your visitor?" Anica asked. "I can't believe I let you talk me out of calling the EMTs this morning. I can't *believe* you poured him into your guest bed."

"He's better," Meghan heard herself say. "He'll be okay." Casual, as if she'd really just found a lost hiker on the trail. As if she'd somehow randomly bolted out into the night to do so.

"He's already *okay*," Jenny said, widening her eyes suggestively. But she quickly grew serious. "He's dark, though, Meghan. Be careful."

"It's too late for that," Anica snorted. "He's *in the guest bed.* And don't tell me there's not something going on. Not when you rush out of here onto a night trail and come back with someone else in Luka's saddle. And what happened to your arm? Did you really think we wouldn't notice?"

"You want to know what I noticed?" Jenny asked, not giving Meghan time to do so much as stutter a response. "I noticed that since you heard from your mother's *friend,* things haven't been right. Every time you think no one's around, you've got your listening face on." And she briefly demonstrated, tipping her head back, closing her eyes. "That's something you do only around the anniversary of your mother's death. But in the last three days? All the time."

"That's true." Anica crossed her arms beneath her breasts, a move that emphasized her well-endowed nature. When men came to the ranch, they looked at Anica, not at Meghan.

Except Dolan. He'd come for her; he'd never so much as glanced around for the others. "That was Dolan, three days ago," Meghan muttered. "And he wasn't my mother's friend. I misunderstood that part. He knew someone who…knew her." Boy, did that sound lame!

Lame enough so Jenny, gentle Jenny, snorted loudly. The horse lifted his head, swinging it around to eye her with his first real curiosity since arrival.

"Look," Meghan said, drifting out into the sunshine to lean her elbows over the stall run—ostensibly to see if the horse had enough curiosity to check her out, but mostly just to move. To give her body some thinking space. And to move her arm away from Anica, which was ultimately futile but might buy some time. "You know I was young when my mother was killed…I don't know a lot about it." *More than I'm telling.* "You know the people involved were never caught—not much chance of that, with the authorities calling it an accident. But the thing is…" Yeah, just go for it. "I think those people are back."

That got their attention. Anica's brows rose, dark wings against an olive complexion. Jenny, strawberry redhead and prone to flushing, instead went pale, stark against the shaded barn exterior.

Meghan cleared her throat. "And the thing is…I'm not really sure how safe it is to be here. I'm doing my best to keep it that way, but…I thought you should know that."

Anica nodded. "Yeah," she said. "I just wish we hadn't had to drag it out of you."

Guilt flashed over into defensiveness. "Oh, come on—it's not like I've had a lot of time to think about it—or that there's even a whole lot to say. Dolan has some concerns, that's all. He went to check them out. He got lost and messed up, and now he's here to recover. I'm sure once he feels better, we'll get some answers. Get this all sorted out." *Sure of it?* Maybe not. But hopeful.

Anica shook her head, her short, black hair stirring in a rising breeze. "That still doesn't explain what's between you and this guy. You know, the one you just met? Give me a break, I could practically smell the secrets between you. And did you see the way he looks at you? Even half-conscious, Meghan, my dear, he thinks you're his. Don't ask me how that works in this day and age, especially when you're the one rescuing his sorry ass from trails he shouldn't have been hiking unprepared. But damned if that's not what I saw."

Anica's language. Always frank, always a little earthy. Just like Anica herself. It didn't mean anything, not like when Jenny worked herself up to cursing. But Anica's *words*…those did. They made Meghan hot and uncomfortable, forced into looking at things she'd been trying very hard to avoid. She pushed away from the pipe corral, where the horse now lipped at a single stem of hay without any real intent. She said, "I don't have any more I can tell you right now. Dolan will check into some things when he can, I know that much. If you're not comfortable staying—"

"Oh, *right*." Jenny, that time, was as emphatic as she ever got. "Because the animals on this ranch will feed themselves, and train themselves and care for themselves. Have you looked at the volunteer roster lately, how many of us it takes? As if we're going anywhere because some incredibly hot guy shows up on your doorstep spouting doom. Me, I'm sticking around. I've got work to do."

Anica turned to Meghan, the same determined look on her face, one raised eyebrow adding a touch of sardonic *get real* to the unspoken commentary.

Meghan felt the unexpected prickle of tears and blinked against it, sunlight momentarily fracturing her vision into a dozen watery reflections. "Looks like I chose my family well."

Over the next few days, Dolan lurked around Encontrados. Not quite welcome, not the least bit understood, he stayed away from the various volunteers, mucking out stalls and paddocks and feeding the animals. He knew how to go unseen, even when his movement was hampered by lingering aches and unreliable muscles.

But it was getting better. Meghan had been right.

He avoided Meghan, too. Not because he wanted to…but because he wanted *not* to. And because without his full faculties, he couldn't sort out either his feelings or his reactions. So he lurked on Encontrados and he constantly tested his improving connection with the jaguar and with himself.

And in the meantime, he found the wards. He walked them, tracing lines in the dirt, avoiding the prickly pear cactus that appeared only randomly at this elevation, following the cottonwoods marking the steep seasonal stream—bone dry in the stark regional spring, but still lined by water-loving, desert-tough vegetation.

Wards were his strength, a skill that he'd shared, however distantly, with Meghan's mother. A skill that would have sent him into that desert to help the woman handle the *Liber Nex,* had he been but a few years older.

And then, instead of his brother, he would have died with her.

Dolan shook off the flattened-ears feeling, the impulse to growl to himself. That such impulses crawled so close to the surface told him both that the jaguar was returning and that he wasn't up to full strength. Shape-shifters who could not control their *otherness* were not tolerated.

Dolan turned aside thoughts of his brother, of Meghan's mother, and concentrated on the wards. Margery Lawrence, it was clear, had been a pure wizard with the lines and webs of protection. Then again, it was only to be expected from the woman who had created the decoy at the old homestead.

But maybe, while he looked for weak spots and planned the necessary steps to shore up defenses... If he could absorb the nature of this work, if he could take it into himself, then maybe he could find the manuscript when he once again prowled these hills as the jaguar.

So he walked the ward lines by feel; he slipped into ward view to study them, and then when he was able to visualize them, he sat in the shadows and traced them with his mind. Along the ground, through the air...a three-dimensional web of protective energies, largely untouched by time. Tangled and tight around the ranch yard, akin to personal wards and capable of keeping out amulets and Core workings. Loose grids around the ranch acreage, more of a warning system than anything else. That Meghan had been able to manipulate them at all only confirmed that the Sentinels had made a serious judgment error in cutting her free—leaving her uneducated, leaving the Sentinels without her services.

Not that he didn't think she was better off without the Sentinel yoke. But what she might have been...

That, he rued.

No doubt she didn't even know that the initiation process would take what she already had and mature it, enhancing her current skills, bringing new ones to the fore. But Dolan...

Dolan didn't want to be the one to explain that process to her.

He'd hoped he'd find something in her mother's things—not only clues to the manuscript's location, but any reference to Sentinel rites that he might point out to

Meghan. Let her learn these things from her mother, if she hadn't already done so. He'd even gotten permission to look through the storage tubs under her bed, although she'd pulled them out into the guest room rather than let him in her own room, and conspicuously made herself absent—not quite abandoning the house, but hiding away in the small room that served as the office.

He'd found nothing in the tubs, though. A respectful sifting of the contents netted him the same box she'd had at the homestead and several batches of paper. He found Margery's birth certificate, a lone letter from a man who must have been Meghan's father, a few early scrawlings done by Meghan herself and several notebooks that couldn't quite be called diaries but which nonetheless held Margery's dreams and plans and hopes—carefully envisioned improvements to the ranch, some of which had been carried out; scratched notes on the history of the place. Wish lists. Books she wanted to read, movies she wanted to see, inexpert sketches of plants she wanted to identify. There was one sketch of a grinning coyote, a rough few lines that somehow perfectly captured the creature's essence.

No casual name-dropping of the *Liber Nex*. No commentary about the Sentinels whatsoever. If Margery had kept any written record, any notes, any hints, about the Sentinels and her involuntary association with them, she hadn't kept them where they'd been found.

Yet.

With Margery's things returned to Meghan's room— left respectfully just inside the door, to be precise— Dolan had returned to prowling the land. Two days into his recovery, the jaguar lurked just beneath the surface, testing his control—which, it seemed, was distinctly lacking. So Dolan stalked the land until he tired himself, the ache seeping back into his bones, and then he dared to return to the house and to sit on the small, flat mattress of the guest bed and stare at the wireless phone in his hand, wondering if there was any point in calling brevis regional, wondering if the growing sensations within—a low vibration within his very bones, a warmth flushing across his skin—spoke of recovery or some lurking problem.

Either way, it was time to push harder. To go back out on the land and find that manuscript, hoping that his new familiarity with Margery's warding touch would be the piece he'd been missing. To go native, and leave this ranch alone.

Running footsteps slapped the dirt outside; the dog barked once, sharply, and then silenced. Meghan smacked the screen door open and came charging into the house, her face flushed and her hair contained only because she still wore her ball cap, a pale denim thing with *Boss Mare* embroidered on the front. She also wore a snug T-shirt with cutoff sleeves revealing a completely healed arm. By then Dolan stood in the doorway of his appropriated little room—but he stepped hastily aside as she barreled right on through. Spare, wiry, all lean muscle and bristling energy, she somehow managed to pull herself to a stop—a graceful one at that—and spin on the heel of her paddock boot to face him. "I found another one!"

He took a step closer to her and stopped, brought up short by the hum of response in his weary body. "Another—?"

She made an impatient gesture, pulling her Boss
Mare cap off to tug her hair back into submission. "A
spot! A *probe*."

Instant alarm spread false strength through his body;
it almost covered up his reaction to her presence.

Almost.

He turned to the window, looking out as though he
needed his eyes and not his mind's eye to see the ward
lines—lines he knew well by now. The back of the property spread out before him, the ground falling away in
a slope of thick junipers and cedars and clumps of
greasewood—but already he searched the layers of the
world that most people couldn't begin to perceive. He
felt the bright presence of Meghan beside him, and
looked farther—to the sizzling lines of energy encir-
cling this area, woven in neat patterns in some areas and
tangled spasms in others—but all deliberate, all as
Margery Lawrence had intended it to be.

But that, there…

A malignant blot of gray, its edges pixilated with
sharp vibration. What had Meghan said?

A grody spot.

What she'd seen had been less directed than this. Less
deliberate. A shout into the darkness, just to see if someone
answered. But when she'd crushed the probe, she'd inadvertently shouted right back at them, and now…*this*.

Her voice came close in his ear, close enough to
startle him out of his ward vision. Close and demanding; the faint scent of cocoa butter and sweet sunscreen
came along with it. "Well?"

"I see it," he said, but he didn't look at her. He looked
out over the property, the bright and innocent sky. He

saw it, all right—but he couldn't do anything about it. Not as he was. The false strength drained away; one knee abruptly went loose, popping out from beneath him.

In an instant, she closed the short remaining distance between them, her hand closing on his arm, strong and supportive. He caught himself, looked at her in surprise, knowing she'd forgotten—

The sizzle, the hum, the tight snap of connection, the ache, the want, want, want...

She cried out, jerking away to put quick distance between them. She looked down at herself in disbelief—at tight nipples so obvious through the T-shirt, at her trembling hands. She ran those hands down her torso—a strong, lean torso, the faint ripple of muscle beneath the material making her tense reaction all the more obvious—and then lifted her head to glare at him. "Stop it. Just *stop it.*"

He laughed; he held out his own hands. There, too, was the tremble of reaction. His button-fly jeans held back an erection of painful intensity; his legs held him up only because he couldn't, *wouldn't* allow himself to falter again before her. "What makes you think I can do anything about it?"

"You're the Sentinel here," she pointed out, crossing her arms over her chest and making no attempt to be casual about her need to cover herself. He doubted he'd see her in that shirt again.

Damned shame, really.

"That means only that I'm good at taking the jaguar," he informed her. "I have a modest skill with wards; I can see the occasional reflective aura or two. Whatever you did the other night, whatever you created between us...

that was *way* out of my league. There's nothing I can do about it. I don't know that there's anything *anyone* can do about it."

She glared at him. "Then there's obviously only one thing to do. You have to move. Away. *Far* away."

"What I have to do," he told her, forcing his voice into temperate understanding, "is deal with this new probe. It's not like the other. That one was looking around... this one is looking for trouble."

"Here?" She straightened, dropping her arms. "My people are in danger?"

He gave a short nod. "Probably. Hard to tell exactly what something like this is set to do until it does it."

"Then deal with it! You didn't like my way of doing things—*you* do it."

"Your way of doing things would be just fine at the moment," he told her, looking back into his mind's eye, finding the probe and its slow, slow process through the wards—wards that recognized it as the danger it was, and wouldn't let it pass so quietly as the first probe. "Except this particular grody spot would flare back on you and quite possibly burn you out."

She rubbed the arm that had been injured. "Burn me out," she repeated flatly.

He glanced at her, pulling himself from ward vision. "Yes," he said. "Might just be those skills your mother gave you that you think no one else notices. Might be your whole mind."

She merely stared, as though she didn't believe him. Or more likely, couldn't take it in. "Then fix it," she finally said. "Whatever it takes. *Fix it*."

"Funny you should put it that way." He took a step

toward her; she took an equal step back. "*Whatever it takes.* Because the problem is, those herbs of yours haven't left me alone yet. So I *can't* fix it. Not alone."

Her eyes flared wide a moment, but quickly narrowed down. He was coming to know that look—the distrust. The wariness. But when he took another step forward, she held her ground. *The strength.* "I'm sorry," he said. "I can't do it alone. I need your—" *Strength.*

A moment passed, during which she scrutinized his features with such intensity that he began to wonder just what he saw—what she *could* see. Finally, quietly, she said, "You're serious. If I want to keep this place safe…"

She let her words trail off, but he knew well enough what she meant, and he nodded. "Soon," he said. "There'll be a point at which I can't make this work even with your help."

She took a deep breath; she squared shoulders lean from work, feminine in line. Strongly drawn collarbones, graceful neck, that dark nut-brown hair spilling over her nape—he almost reached for her, almost ran his knuckles along those lines. But he caught himself, and—oblivious of his impulse—she nodded. "Okay. We fix it together."

Chapter 8

We fix it together.

As if it were that simple. Meghan shuddered, down deep inside where she hoped Dolan couldn't see it but pretty much expected he could. She'd known for days that her only chance to deal with this situation, to protect the ranch and her friends, was to keep her head. To avoid getting sucked up in the emotions that swirled around matters of her mother's death—or the emotions that swirled around Dolan.

If you could call them that. Emotions. Meghan herself was no longer sure what they were, these physical reactions, swelling up from within as though some force had crooked its finger and her body responded. It made her feel as though she were an outsider with no control over those responses, no say in their development. As if Dolan himself were irrelevant, as if she hadn't felt the

soul of him that night, and learned that all her precon-
ceived notions about him were wrong.

Except some part of her wondered if any of it would be
happening at all had not the seeds of it been there before
their blood had mingled with her herbs and incantations.

Not that it mattered. She had no intention of being
controlled by incantations or Sentinel ways. She had her
life—one they'd left her alone to manage in a mundane
world after her mother had died for one of their causes.
She had her chosen family. She'd do what she had to,
to protect them…but that didn't mean she'd hand herself
over to be a piece in some cosmic game.

Dolan still watched her. He'd given her thoughts time
to cycle around…and now she saw the flash of impatience in his eyes that said they'd run out of time. "What
you do," he said, "is find the thing, just the way you did
before you came running in here. Don't worry about
taking me to it…I'll be there. It's your strength I need,
not the know-how."

"Just leave me enough to finish chores," she said, and
added enough of a direct look to tell him she was only
half kidding. *Don't drain me dry.* Not when she still had
to keep an eye on this place. And then she closed her eyes
and tipped her head back and took herself to the place
she'd last seen the new invader. She found it almost immediately, closer to the ranch than before—but Dolan,
she didn't even see coming. Stealthy, a presence padding
softly over these ethereal hunting grounds, he found her
with such quick, efficient silence that she felt only that
sudden snap of connection, the intense internal humming that took her even on this level.

She fought to stabilize herself; she thought she heard

him, in the physical world, hiss between clenched teeth.
And then he swept her up in such sudden strength that she
left the physical behind altogether. Strength and assurance
and intent…except it all tasted just a tiny bit like…

Me.

But abruptly there was no *me* in this place, no
Meghan and no *Dolan.* His experienced vision took her
wide, where the world consisted of smooth earth tones
and overlapping wards and a huge panoramic perception that offered no room for feet grounded against good
hard earth or the warm afternoon air in expanding lungs,
or the smell of sun-heated cedar and juniper, sharp and
cutting. Just muffled, enclosing earth tones and wards—
and there, over there, the evil of the thing that had
brought them here this way.

Dolan's control brought them closer, weaving effortlessly through wards that recognized Meghan and
allowed them passage—coming so close to the malevolent danger that Meghan voiced a wordless protest,
digging in nonphysical heels until he somehow gave her
a little yank. A reminder. *This is what we're here for. I
know what I'm doing.*

But Meghan didn't. She *didn't,* and it scared her, and
she struggled against him anyway—hard enough so his
concentration wavered and the danger *looked* at them
somehow, its prickly edges freezing as it stopped its
progress to assess this new, uncoordinated presence.

Trust, Meghan.

Had he really said that? Had he said it out loud to her,
to her insignificant body in the insignificant ranch house
in the insignificant world? Or had he just thought it…?

Or maybe it had been her, convincing herself.

Trust.

She thought of him that night, so vulnerable—but trusting her to do right by him, pulling back claws that had been meant to rip her arm off...giving himself up to her.

All right, then.

Almost immediately, the malevolence lost interest. Just as quickly, Dolan moved them in closer. While she fought with everything she had to keep from recoiling in horror, he *reached out* to it...he *tickled* it—a great, ephemeral cat, playing with its prey. The dark spot rippled in response, and, drifting alongside, Dolan reached out again. She couldn't have said how he was doing it, or considered attempting it herself. But she saw, then, that the ripple effect had changed the thing's course.

So gently it didn't even recognize their presence, Dolan manipulated the invader until it became completely disoriented—and when he slowly backed them away, the thing was headed out of the little sphere of web lines and shifting energies that was, in another world, a small ranch called Encontrados.

Suddenly exhausted, Meghan receded abruptly from this world with its new intensities and feelings and vision, plunging endlessly back through bottomless darkness—and finally slamming home into her body, staggered and dazed and taking some moments to realize she wasn't where she'd left herself.

She wasn't standing aside. She wasn't *separate*.

She was, in fact, standing behind Dolan—standing up against Dolan, with her cheek centered between his clean-cut shoulders and his scent tickling her nose and her arms around his waist, resting there as though they belonged, hands clasping her wrists and forearms

somehow already familiar with the hard lines of a
muscled torso. She stiffened and would have pulled
away, had his hands not landed on hers and firmly
trapped her there.

And then the second wave of sensation hit, the hum
of things crescendoing up to vibrate in her bones, drawing warmth along her spine, tightening the skin over her
entire body. She tensed; her hands clenched against him
even as his fingers tightened down on hers. Abruptly, he
released her; abruptly, he pivoted within her arms,
facing her with a fierce and hungry expression.

She had only an instant to realize it, and then suddenly they weren't two people, they were one being—
one being in a frenzy of kissing and clawing at clothes
and pressing up against each other, form molding into
form and melting into a quicksilver warmth, fingers
clutching at hair, lips bruising at each other until
Meghan's legs built up into a quiver, her body building
into something not yet explored. Her hands skimmed
down his back as one leg twined around both of his, the
entirety of her being urging *closer, oh, please, closer* as
he gasped into her mouth.

As unexpectedly as anything else, her single grounded leg gave way beneath her, bringing them both tumbling down onto the age-worn wood floor. One of his
hands cradled her head, saving it from impact; the other
lay flat against her stomach, fingers twitching. And
though his breath came fast and his pupils were black
and huge in those deepest of blue eyes, something in his
expression had caught a hint of sanity.

Meghan felt nothing of sanity in herself. Horrified at
what she'd done, what she'd become, she was simulta-

neously bereft to be separate of him again. At first she could only watch him come back to himself, stages of awareness seeping back into his face, around his eyes. And perhaps the same was happening to her, for in a moment, his hand big and warm on her stomach, she was able to say, *"What—"* and then *"What—?"* again.

Dolan gave his head a sharp shake. "I'm sorry," he said. "I didn't realize. I—"

"Still want you," she whispered, a completion of her own thoughts as well as his.

He deliberately drew back. Not far, not so far that she couldn't still feel the warmth of him, hovering over her, but just far enough to finalize the moment. "Damn, *yes*." He made sure she supported herself on her elbows, released her head and her stomach, and drew a hand across his face.

"But it wasn't *my* decision," she realized out loud. "It wasn't yours, either. It was…"

"Whatever you created three nights ago," he agreed.

She felt her own scowl; she scooted back a little, putting enough space between them so she could sit and stand and brush herself off. "I make my own decisions when it comes to this."

He stood beside her, just that suddenly—fluid movement, a reminder of what he could be when he had his strength. His expression had gone rueful, but he nodded. "As do I."

But he caught her eye again, and stepped close without breaking his gaze; when she looked up, she was startled to realize how closely they hovered over another kiss. But he didn't dip his head down; she didn't stretch up. He said, "As it happens, I've made that decision. I'm just waiting for yours." He touched her bruised lips, the gentlest of caresses—one that sent her bones to singing all over again, pulling up such a response that she knew it was more than just the herbs and blood and unwitting connection she'd created, she *knew*...

Then he stepped aside so she could leave.

Chapter 9

Dolan stared at the ceiling, his preternatural night vision turning it into a swirl of textured paint that no pure human could see. *What the hell did I do that for?*

He'd moved aside—and she'd walked out. Squared her shoulders, set her jaw and walked out of the room. He hadn't seen her since. Oh, he'd *heard* her—outside, finishing chores and bidding her friends good-night after they'd tossed out evening hay to the various creatures of Encontrados. And he'd heard her come back inside, moving quietly through the darkened house until the faintest glow of light from the hall told him she'd turned on her bedroom light. Brushed her teeth...rustled through a change of clothes...

The light had gone out, and now Dolan stared at the ceiling, his body awash with so many aches he couldn't even separate them from one another—aside from that which came through loud and clear. The *want*. The *want* so strong he could barely stop himself from rolling out of this small bed and easing down the hall to Meghan's bedroom. The overwhelming awareness of her presence...

What little thinking he'd been doing, stopped.

He clenched his jaw; he breathed through his nose and out his mouth. He reminded himself that he was a Sentinel; that he had training and strength and thirteen years of field experience. He reminded himself why he was there...what was at stake. That the Core no doubt still lurked—that they no doubt already realized this latest probe had failed.

Meghan. He took another deep breath, let it go. Had there been no potential between them other than the incantation washing through their bodies, it would have been enough. Had he not wanted her from the moment he'd confronted her at the round pen, all spark and anger and defiance, wrapped around Sentinel skills so sweet and untried that even then they'd called to him, it would have been enough.

But he *had* wanted her. *Had* been drawn to her. Had found himself lingering around the ranch longer than reason or common sense or his mission allowed. And when the Core had taken him down...

She'd been the one he called.

And even uninitiated, she'd heard him.

Not, he thought, because her skills ran so deep, not without initiation.

But because she'd been listening.

Just as he listened now—for any sound of her, for any indication she was still awake, that she hadn't been able to shake off what had happened between them.

Get a grip. Big, bad Sentinel, obsessed with his physical reaction to a woman. Consumed by it. He snorted softly, rolling out of bed after all and ignoring the tiny voice protesting that it wasn't just physical—wasn't just chemistry and wasn't just incantations.

He didn't bother with his shoes. For the sake of propriety, he did pull on his pants, recently washed and stiff. He listened in the hallway just long enough to make sure he hadn't disturbed Meghan, and he padded down the hall to the kitchen, having already learned to open the door just so far and slip through if he wanted to avoid the most startling of creaks.

He stood on the porch, breathing in the crisp smells of junipers and cedars, the bitter taste of willow, the damp, cold night air holding down the scents of the sky island. He shivered, wishing he'd brought his jacket… and then realized he had no intention of staying in this thin human skin.

For the first time in days, the jaguar called clearly to him. And there, on the porch of the old ranch house, he reached for what had been waiting within, blanketed in herbs and illness. Impatient, eager…ready to run. Ready to hunt.

Ready to escape what hunted him.

A futile effort, and he knew it. But he lost himself to the change anyway, a flash of internal light that sizzled off the post-and-rail of the porch edge, reflected off the counters in the kitchen and faded away around the form of the jaguar, darker than the night itself.

He stalked off the porch, through the yard…and down into the wild desert highlands.

Chapter 10

Meghan dreamed not of Dolan or of their intense encounter, or even of the Atrum Core stalking this ranch.

Meghan dreamed of her mother.

Her mother laughing, her mother's wildflower scent, her mother's enfolding arms, the spare and satisfying hug of a woman as wiry as Meghan herself.

She woke feeling comforted and somehow serene… and she couldn't understand it in the least. She felt as though it was meant to be a message, and she hadn't the faintest idea what it meant. She stared up at the ceiling she couldn't even see in this darkness, and finally settled on gratitude.

If she'd ever needed a hug from her mother, it was now, confronted by this unexpected part of her mother's legacy, confronted by the Atrum Core and tangled up somehow with a shape-shifting Sentinel who asked everything of himself—and, it seemed, everything of her.

She reached out to him, an action quickly grown to habit, just to touch his presence, which was as much as she could do…and could do it at all only because of that impossible hum persisting between them.

If only she'd had some inkling of those unintended side effects when she'd laid the incantation on the herbs, or when she'd laid the herbs along his gums—or when she'd failed to duck his lightning-swift paw.

Right. Because then she'd surely have turned and walked away, leaving him to die.

Dammit. This *had* been her choice. Her choice to listen for him in the night; her choice to go to him when he called out in his pain and warning. Her choice to break out her mother's enhanced, preserved herbs, and to add her own touch to them.

She hadn't known what she was getting into…but in hindsight, that was no bad thing. Cowardly, cowardly hindsight—not knowing had spared her the struggle of an informed decision, and she was glad of it.

Only then did she realize she hadn't found Dolan where she expected—that he wasn't asleep in the guest room, succumbed to the exhaustion of the day and their hard work near the end of it. She sat up in bed, and the chill night air hit her bare shoulders. Sleeveless tank above, girly boxers below—snug, comfortable indulgences from Victoria's Secret. Not exactly sexy, no matter how it looked on the models with their chests thrust out.

But Meghan's life hadn't required *sexy*. Hard work, practicality and persistence…a love of life. But sexy?

The men around here were hard, age-bitten cowboys or adolescent boys.

No wonder Dolan's presence had hit her so hard.

Meghan cast her vision wider, hunting him as her mother, taking the coyote, had once hunted mice.

Except her mother had let the mice go. Meghan wasn't sure she'd have that choice with Dolan.

And there he was. Downhill from the ranch, stationary. She swung her legs over the side of the bed, groping for the hoodie sweatshirt she'd left over the wrought-iron footboard, then hesitating when she realized he felt…different. Bigger. More powerful.

Understanding hit her like a blow. *He took the jaguar.*

He was improving not only daily, but practically by the hour, and he'd found the jaguar again just as she'd so casually assured him that he would. The implication of it—that he had little reason to stay here any longer, that he was no longer virtually chained to this ranch, to her guest room—that he could leave at any moment—had her across the house to the pile of shoes by the back door, stuffing her feet into sneakers even as she pulled the hoodie on, running out into the yard where the cold air hit her bare legs and jolted her to a stop.

But only for a moment. Only long enough to orient herself. To accept that the man himself had touched her, and not just enhanced herbs and a shared near-death experience. To give in to instinct and drive and *want,* and run down into the scrubby tangle of foliage and rugged terrain.

To run for Dolan.

He'd stalked the hills, moving around in darkness when he would have preferred twilight. He stretched his muscles; he leaped from outcrop to outcrop, testing himself. He felt strength returning by the moment. If he was smart, he'd leave this place here and now and return to his mission.

Except it was about more than that now. This ranch had come to the attention of the Core...and for the first time in his bitter rogue's life, Dolan felt the impulse to let something come between himself and his primary goal. To think about more than that narrow mission focus. He'd continue to look for the manuscript, but he also had to make sure these people were safe. Until the Sentinel team finally arrived, he had to stay close to Encontrados. For if the Core was circling this ranch, Meghan was surely their ultimate target. She was the one who'd slapped their first probe down...the one who'd drawn attention.

He easily found the best vantage point in the area, outcrops jutting over the hill so profoundly as to create hollow, protected places beneath. He rubbed his face against the stone and then leaped lightly to the top, stretched out with his tail idly tapping the accumulation of leaves and debris over hard rock. Not Sentinel, not Dolan...just the jaguar, mind emptied of everything but the terrain around and below him.

But thoughts of Meghan constantly tickled his mind; he found the lack of her a bane, one that waxed within him until the landscape no longer had his attention and he lifted his lips, tipping his whiskers in a silent snarl. His tail gave one violent lash before he forced himself to stillness. He would have cursed what she had wrought between them, but he no longer had the heart. He could no longer wish she'd never come to him that night—not now, not having felt her lips and her body.

And there went his tail again, slapping rock. Not cool. He glared at it as though it were a separate entity, offering it its own silent snarl of warning. Big, tough Sentinel, tail out of control.

Maybe it was his own self-indulgent recrimination that allowed her to get so close before he noticed. Quiet as she was for a woman who took no other shape than her own, he heard her slipping down a steep section of land off to the side; he smelled the honest scent of her. And when he looked for it, he felt her presence within, marked by the increasing unrest of his bones. Of his tail, when it came to that. He stood, hesitating at the edge of his rocky platform, and found her making her way down the hill, clearly familiar with the dark terrain even with her limited human vision, and just as clearly looking for him. Scenting him, in her own way.

Limited light or no, he had no trouble seeing her. Bare ankles above sneakers, bare legs below skimpy night shorts, the gleam of toned skin, the shape of lean muscle. A hooded sweatshirt covered her arms and shoulders; the bare scoop of skin above her nightshirt's neckline caught and held his gaze. Her hair, on its own for once, was deliciously mussed. As he watched, she descended slightly below his level, hesitated and lifted her face to the stars. Listening.

Listening for *him*.

And she must have heard him. She turned on the spot, looking into a darkness he knew she couldn't penetrate—and yet looking straight at him. Moving more slowly than she had been—no longer uncertain of her path, but uncertain of her welcome. She headed back up the hill, stopping just below the base of the rocks that made up his overhang. Her sweatshirt had slipped, baring her shoulders. She opened her mouth, but if she'd had words to say, she evidently couldn't find them.

Dolan hung on to their silent tableau for a selfish moment, eyes narrowed, nostrils flaring, heavy jaguar head stretching slightly into the breeze, drinking in the scent of her. Drinking in, too, the rising power of what lay between them, letting it swell within him instead of fighting it, letting it rumble through his body until it verged on intoxication. It pounded in his veins, grew warm around his heart, shivered down his spine.

Below him, Meghan drew her sweatshirt together with one hand and shoved her hair back with the other, poised for flight and determined to pretend she wasn't. Suddenly vulnerable, and yet unable to keep from tipping her face up to the stars again, from leaning toward him ever so slightly.

It was his undoing.

He leaped from the rock, never minding the distance to the ground, invoking the shift along the way—riding the flash and crackle of the change and landing human. A good, square landing, crouched to absorb the tremendous energy of it all. Stronger, again, than any human would be. Stronger, finally.

And damned ready to face this thing between them.

"Meghan," he said, and his voice came out as more of a growl than he'd intended. At this distance, no longer clothed in the black, rippling pelt of the jaguar, he was perfectly visible to her.

She still blinked from the night-shattering light of

shift on the fly, of his sudden appearance—but she hadn't flinched before, and she didn't now. She took a single step forward, stopped.

Dolan—riding the pounding demands in his body, the ache of being so close and yet not touching her—gave up on breathing for that moment. Until she lifted her face slightly, leaning into what lay between them. She took a deep breath; she let it out on a single, quiet, "Yes."

He hesitated an instant longer—just long enough to be sure of what she'd said.

Yes, this was her making a decision. *Yes,* she was here to be with him. *Yes,* she'd felt the incantation, but she was her own woman, responding to her own desires.

And that was all he could give it before breaking—three long strides downhill, barefoot on stone and stick and gritty soil. She ran up to meet him, no wavering as they came together. He lifted her right off the ground and she wrapped her legs around him, tight and close, only the flimsy material of her shorts and his jeans between the heat of them—it felt like no barrier at all and completely intolerable interference all at the same time.

He ran his hands under her bottom—toned muscle clenching to stay close as he took her back uphill, kissing the hell out of her on the way. Her arms wrapped around his neck, keeping her where she could find his ear, a quick bite and nibble. That's when his legs nearly gave way; she laughed low in his ear and he surged against her and nearly lost his footing then, too. And again when she dropped her head back to reveal the graceful lines of her neck, and he buried his mouth against her skin, finding the sweet salt of it.

She cried out, a gasp of surprised pleasure, and that

did it. Finally he went down, balancing them as his knees found dirt and his toes dug against rock, and he leaned forward to delve into that sweet notch between her collarbones. She gave him that, falling backward, vulnerable and exposed and dipping back into his grip. Her back curved against his arm; her breasts waited for attention.

But her legs kept her close and tight; she moved against him and caught them both *just so* and she gasped and he growled, and his tongue left only a brief and longing path along her collarbone before she groped frantically at his pants, entirely supported in his arms— and getting absolutely nowhere, not with these Sentinel-tailored button-fly jeans. Nowhere, that is, except taking him close to the edge of his control, so close that he snatched her back up to him.

She flung her arms around his neck and took to nibbling his ear again, and he managed the jeans himself, reaching around beneath her—movements jerky with need, breath panting and catching and sometimes just plain forgetting to happen. And then, hands still free, he found her—warm and moist, no underwear beneath the skimpy shorts he easily pulled to the side; he touched her, cupping her—wringing a cry from her. Ready and waiting and poised to receive him, and still he hesitated—and she knew what he needed. "Yes," she repeated, her voice a needy whisper in the ear she teased, a warmth on the neck she tended. "Yes, dammit!"

And so he plunged into her, and the deep rumbling hum inside him burst into two and grew a fine alto counterpart, filling him so completely that his movements jerked to a stop—filling her so completely that she clutched him with arms and legs and inner muscles, both of them overwhelmed by sensation, and he knew, he *knew* what she felt, that sweet fire gathered along her nerves and joyful tears in her eyes and that they both tightened toward an inward crescendo of sensation without even moving, just by *being* and touching and—

He groaned, heartfelt and beyond all restraint, and she gasped at the mutual pleasure reverberating between them, starting its climb while they quivered and held on to each other and then quite suddenly neither of them could stand it any longer—they moved, and they cried out together, and again and again and—

The world came to an end, a loud and tangled and bursting end, pinwheeling through them both, back and forth and back again, until it finally eased off into echoes of itself and Dolan found himself sitting on his heels and Meghan sitting on *him,* still joined tightly but no longer clinging and clutching and demanding. Just breathing, the both of them, panting against each other. Her hair moved and fell, tickling him; eventually he stirred himself to gently move it away.

But where he stayed relaxed, Meghan grew tense; where he reveled in satisfied completeness—perfectly happy to follow his instincts and desires to this moment, to wait until late to sort out the unexpected tenderness he felt, the expected reluctance to separate from her in any way—Meghan grew distant without even moving. Her forehead still rested against his shoulder as she said, "What's…what *is* that?"

And unlike the moment at the homestead where their touch had ignited something between them and her reaction had been accusation and annoyance, this time he heard a thread of fear. He felt it in her as she lifted her head, pushing back far enough to look him in the eye—or as close as she could get in this darkness—while he could see her perfectly—and see that same thread of fear on her face, strong eyebrows raised, eyes widened, pupils huge. She searched his face in the darkness, but even in daylight he had no answers—

Ah. Unless he did at that. Unless he, fool, had underestimated the effect of Sentinel initiation. Sentinel blood with blood, releasing any hidden potential...

With a young Dolan, it had made little difference. Dolan's jaguar had roared upon him full strength in early adolescence, and initiation hadn't done anything to change that. But for a woman never encouraged to use her skill in the first place...a woman who hadn't pushed her boundaries, even if she'd never take another shape...

Dolan winced.

She must have felt it in him. Maybe in the flicker of tension through his arms, maybe because it suddenly seemed evident that they'd never again be able to hide anything from each other. She stiff-armed away from him, slipping through his grasp and finding her own feet—and as much as he wanted to close his arms around her and keep her here, still close, still *together,* he let her go.

She didn't bother to straighten her clothing; the sleep boxers rode crooked and her sweatshirt had slipped off her shoulders entirely, but she didn't care or notice. This he knew; this he didn't have to guess.

It did create an odd inward echo at that.

Her voice, when it came, was low and strained. "What *is* this?" Her stare was direct; he began to wonder just what she could see after all. *"What is this?"*

He hesitated, and then he stood, tucking himself away and then resisting the urge to gently and—there it was again—*tenderly* replace her sweatshirt over her shoulders against the chill of the night. And then he just plain hesitated, so suddenly aware that he'd made a mistake. Possibly a big mistake. By not being certain… by not pursuing it…by not bringing himself to deal with it earlier, when he'd been so focused on dealing with the manuscript…

"Don't even try to tell me you don't know what I'm talking about."

"No," he said, more abruptly than he'd intended. "I think…" He closed his eyes, resigned himself. "I mentioned this earlier. Sort of. Almost." He'd alluded to it, that's all. And she hadn't been interested, and he'd accepted that. His attention had been elsewhere, too.

Her fear was still there…but anger came on strong. "Then you not only know what it is…you *knew it would happen.*"

Oh, fuck. He was in trouble. Real trouble.

Chapter 11

Meghan stumbled on her swift way home, catching herself only because she'd fallen uphill and there really wasn't far to go. She slapped away Dolan's hand and he withdrew it. Had to give him credit, he knew when he wasn't wanted. *I don't* want *to give him credit.* Here she was, body still throbbing from their encounter—their *lovemaking*—and she didn't want him touching her, she didn't want him *close* enough to touch her.

Lovemaking. Meghan's few casual trysts in the past had been more about groping her way through the loss of virginity, about wanting to care about someone but discovering that she really didn't…about wanting a relationship in her life and learning it didn't work that way. And this time…

This time it had been very much different.

Even if one of them had apparently been expecting the aftermath.

This.

This, with the world blooming before her in an odd black-and-white view, a silver cast over all. With her normal sense of the world and its creatures—the same one that allowed her to crash through rattlesnake territory in sneakers even when the cold hadn't made the snakes sluggish—blown all out of proportion, reeling through her mind with such invasive force as to hinder, not help, her progress through the juniper and cedar woods.

And so she stumbled again, and this time Dolan did snag her arm—and this time she lashed out at him, not caring that she fell on her ass against the steep ground. "How *could* you!" she snarled at him, even more frustrated when she utterly failed to connect; he evaded her easily. "All this time, you knew…you probably *wanted* this, so you could *use* me—" And she kicked out at the ground in the fury of the thought, scattering gritty dirt in his direction.

His denial whiplashed back to her on a level she wished she'd never experienced. Stupid people, those who wanted to be so close as to read their lovers' minds. Stupid, *stupid* people!

"I didn't," he said, and she felt his chagrin, too. "I should have… Look, I knew you probably hadn't been initiated, but I wasn't thinking about it. It's not why I'm *here*."

"Initiated," she said bitterly. "Is that what it's called? Turning my head inside out? Making my body into some rutting—"

"No!" he snapped, and she felt his true anger, too.

"That's not what that was. You *know* that's not what we did. There was *choice*—"

"Not about this!" she snapped back. "I shouldn't have trusted you."

She hadn't expected her bitter words to sink in—to *hurt*. For his voice to turn raw. "No, dammit!" He closed in on her, ignoring her fisted hands. "That's not how it was. That's not *who I am*." He pushed in closer, way too close, his cheek briefly bumping hers; she leaned back into the steepness of the ground as he put an arm on either side of her. Bitter juniper scents clung around them, mixing with the scuffed-up dirt, strong in the higher humidity of the night. "That's not how it was," he whispered into her lips, low words with the same impact as a shout.

They breathed there for a moment, sensations swirling around them—surging and breaking against her until she didn't know if she wanted to ravage him or run from him or simply curl into a ball and put her hands against her ears to shut it all out. Abruptly overwhelmed, she twisted away—still beneath him, but no longer facing him. Half curled into that tempting fetal ball.

He dropped to the ground behind her, propped on one elbow—and nearly upright at that, on this odd patch of ground of theirs. His hand came to rest on her shoulder, then moved to stroke back her hair. "No wonder you can't keep it in that ponytail of yours," he said. "Too damned fine…" And she realized then that he comforted himself as much as her, soothing his fingers in the silk of her hair. When he spoke again, his resulting calm rested against her, softening her edges. "Don't tell me you haven't noticed," he said.

"When I have a goal, it fills my head. But not this time. Not since I met you. To have been unable to walk away…"

"Since when?" He'd walked away after they met, and now he'd been itching to walk away for days.

He sounded surprised. "Since I spoke to you at the round pen."

"You *left*," she pointed out.

His low laugh tickled her ear. She found herself relaxing against him. A stick poked her leg; before she could think to do it, he brushed it away, and then returned his attention to her hair—running it through his fingers, letting it fall against her neck…stroking it back over her ear. "I went somewhere else," he admitted. "But I never really *left*. Or do you really think I just randomly reached out to you after the Atrum Core got me?"

She said nothing. She let the words rest against her along with his calm.

"I knew you probably hadn't been initiated. It just wasn't…" His hand stopped moving her hair. "Relevant," he said finally.

She blinked into what should have been darkness and no longer was. "And *initiation?*"

"Hell," he muttered under his breath, startling her. His brief peacefulness evaporated. "I just realized… Carter…if they find out…"

They're going to find out. She could read that belief, clear as anything. *"Tell me."*

"They must have assumed there wasn't much potential going untapped. But now—*sonofabitch.*"

He would have shoved off to his feet out of the pure need to move, but she twisted around and caught his arm. *"Dolan."* And she wasn't about to let go. Not until she understood.

"Initiation," he said, all but vibrating with the need to move—to shift and snarl off some frustration and concern. "It's not that complicated. Anyone with Sentinel blood—whether you take the shift or not—has two levels of potential. One before you're initiated by another Sentinel, and one after."

"Initiated. That's a dull Sentinel term for *mind-blowing sex,* or what?"

He flashed a quick grin at her—unexpected, given his mood, and it struck a place deep within her, the part that still hummed with his presence inside her. "Not necessarily. At sixteen, that's what I *thought* it was, but it turns out I was wrong. The thing is, some of us have all our skills right there on the surface; the initiation doesn't make a lot of difference. And some of us run deep. That would be you. And because brevis regional assumed you didn't have enough of the blood to have that power lurking, they dismissed you. Cut you loose."

"Cut their losses," Meghan said bitterly, not quite ready to address the changes within herself. To ask him about them…or even ask for help with them. As if she could just pretend nothing had changed at all, and maybe it would go away. "It's just as well. They'd have gotten nothing from me. They still won't."

"When they take you in young," Dolan said dryly, "there's not much choice. You're one of them, and they don't easily let go of their own. Their secrecy depends on keeping us all trained and leashed and following their cabalistic little rules."

"Well, they're not getting me now." Meghan let her

hand slide from his arm, and straightened herself out to head up the hill. "They blew it when they blew it."

Dolan took her hand, helped her find her footing and then released her to cut diagonally across the slope to the faint game trail. "I suspect your mother had something to do with that. She obscured you, somehow. No doubt it's in these wards somewhere. Your mother and her wards..." He shook his head.

It was Meghan's turn to grin. "No one outtricked my mother. She had this special little smile..." She trailed off, because it had been a long time since she even thought of that smile and yet there it suddenly was, evoking the same happiness it had given her as a child.

Good God, in rejecting the Sentinels, had she somehow hidden her mother away, too? Had she lost what she might have had of that energetic, loving woman?

It didn't bear thinking about.

Right now, what bore thought was the shower she would take when she reached home. She automatically reached for Dolan's hand even as it dropped toward hers, and allowed him to pull her up over a rough spot. Allowed him, hell—some part of her reveled in his strength. Her mother had been like that, too—stronger than she looked. Stronger than she possibly could have been, in her wiry way.

But Dolan faltered, looking up toward the ranch— not so far now. And Meghan felt it an instant later— *heard* it, inside herself. A silent, wounded cry of pain—a cry for help. Wards shattered, land attacked—and beyond the edge of their very steep horizon, an ugly yellow-orange glow. It had the same *feel* as the grody spot Meghan had discovered not so very long ago—only this afternoon, as surreal as that seemed. The same malevolent intent.

"The ranch," she breathed. *Jenny. Anica.*

Dolan dropped her hand, lunged a few steps uphill and hesitated, looking back at her.

"Go!" she cried at him. *"Go help them!"*

And he did. The shift sent crackling blue sheet lightning into the darkness and then he raced swiftly, silently away.

For the first time since her mother's death, Meghan wished that she, too, could take the coyote. But that much hadn't changed. Her vision, her perceptions and possibly other things she hadn't found yet—but not that. There was no coyote lurking in Meghan.

So, being merely human, she ran. She clawed her way uphill, her breath coming sharp and rasping by the time she hit the gentler slope just behind the house and ran a diagonal up to the ranch flat itself. And there she stood, gaping, trying to orient herself—to turn what she saw into pieces that made sense. To turn what she heard into something coherent.

A woman shouting, sheep bleating, a woman's scream, an animal's cries overlaid in surreally inhuman tones. Flames burning the air, a dust devil of fire whirling through the yard, sparks shooting out from everything it touched—dirt and stone and pipe corral and the sudden whoosh *of a small outbuilding bursting entirely into flame. A horse bellowed in outrage; the pounding, solid hoofbeats of a warhorse charging into the yard where it—*

She suddenly did it, put it all together and saw Dolan skirting the edges of it all, dark and low, saw Luka loose and charging straight at the whirling dust devil turned to flame, ears plastered back and head snaking low, furious stallion herding behavior from a horse long-gelded but never entirely convinced of it.

It galvanized her into action. "Luka!" she screamed, and charged out into the yard herself, angling to put herself between the horse and the flame devil—as if she could do a thing to stop either of them. *"Luka, no—!"* And she projected it at him with all her newfound inner strangeness and strength until his stride faltered. He shook his head in fury, eyes rolling—and then gave in to the compulsion, whirling to kick out at the flame devil just before he would have reached it. Meghan had a sudden image of those sturdy white legs bursting into flame like so much shredded paper, and with a wordless cry, she *projected* something of herself between them.

Luca's back feet hit *nothingness* with the sound of distant thunder; he raced away, head lifted with that sideways threat that meant he would come around for another try, and then suddenly Dolan was there at Meghan's side, human as human got, breathing reassurance in her ear. "Good," he said. "This is your land. It's reaching for you, do you feel it? It'll give you what you need. Keep the ward up…keep it up and *push* it. I'm right here. I'll show you—"

Meghan realized then that she stood with her eyes tightly closed and her hands fisted at her sides, the reality crashing in on her. It all started to fall apart. Her whimper of dismay came unexpected, edged with panic.

"I'm here." His hands landed on her shoulder. *Follow me.*

His touch in her mind was as familiar and intimate

as his touch on her body. He dropped her into ward vision where she could see what she'd so instinctively done, and he reached out toward the curving shield of bright lines—unable to actually touch it, but showing her how—and then taking her mind's *hands* and guiding her. *She* could touch; she could draw on the unfathomable well of power that suddenly opened beneath her, shocking her, plunging her into it over her head until he showed her that, too, deftly slowing that source to a trickle, power that she could sip—could very well *see*— as it flowed around instead of through him. He used only the strength from within himself, and when she looked from her odd, split point of view, the strain of it showed at the corners of his mouth, the set of his brow.

She grew the wards; she tangled the bright threads into solidity. As Luka charged around again, swerving in for another kick, she frantically spread the ward all the way around the flame devil, encasing it. She just as frantically fed it power, tempering the wards as Luka dealt it two swift kicks and blasted away—and then Meghan staggered in surprise as the flame devil stuttered away from those kicks, damaged by the blows from one noble old white horse and dragging at her as it did.

Feel that? Dolan asked her, pouncing on the moment. *Now use that same feeling to* push. *Push it right out of your boundaries.*

She didn't ask why—she didn't have to. She just as suddenly knew; the knowledge leaked right over from Dolan. Outside her ranch wards, outside her claimed land, the flame devil would dissipate; the Core wouldn't waste energy on a failure. Tentatively at first, then more assertively, she pushed at the thing; she herded it and badgered it, as her inner eye showed her the way off the property…off Encontrados land. Dolan stood behind her and held firm when she faltered, reminding her to accept more of the land's offerings when she needed them.

And then came the moment when she gave one final shove and the land surged in a wave of good riddance and the flame devil fizzled into a sudden shower of sparks and nothingness.

When Meghan opened her eyes, she found her legs had folded out from beneath her. She sprawled on the ground, with Dolan right behind her and holding her upright. He drew her back, pressing a long kiss to her temple, leaving his mouth there as he murmured, "Damned good job for a Sentinel reject."

She might have fainted then, her body awash with unfamiliar exhaustion, her personal resources stretched and drained. She might have…except now her eyes were open.

Now she could see what the flame devil had wrought on Encontrados.

Chapter 12

Dolan's feet throbbed. He hadn't planned on taking back his human form when he'd left the house without his boots—or of walking any distance in the decidedly untamed juniper woods. For only an instant as he came out of ward view—wrapping his arms around Meghan's shoulders so they overlapped across her chest in a decidedly familiar and even intimate embrace—his feet grabbed his attention.

And then the rest of reality rushed in. The cries of pain in the background—that was Jenny; he'd seen her trampled by panicked livestock. Even sheep could break bones if they hit just right. Those same sheep crashed through the underbrush in the distance; Anica, who'd gone after them, probably no longer heard them at all. Another sheep cried out, sounding eerily like a child. On the other side of the yard, horses called into the night, seeking reassurance—seeking Luka, perhaps. They crashed carelessly around their stall runs; only luck would save them from injury.

Meghan stirred in his arms; her hair tickled his nose, along with the scent of Meghan herself. Recently loved, recently propped against the astringent soil, more recently yet in the singeing presence of a flame devil. He took a deep breath of her—a luxury, that— and as he let it out, she said, "Luka. Where's Luka?"

He had a vague impression of the horse from ward view, chivvying the flame devil, charging and kicking out as it moved along—herding it. Right on into the night. "Out there. Safe, last time I saw him."

"He'll find his way home, then," she said, but her voice was all worry and no confidence. Then she stiffened, the rest of the world finally coming into focus for her—her fear for that world striking home in her heart and spilling over into Dolan. "That's Jenny," she said, her voice rising. She pulled away from him, pushing herself to her feet. Each movement looked to be an effort, but he felt her reach out for the same strength he'd just shown her, sip at it and then straighten easily as she hunted the source of Jenny's cry.

Oh, the Sentinels had made a mistake with this one, all right.

He got to his feet right behind her, keeping his voice low—not breaking her focus. She was going to need it. "I'll get your herbs," he said. "I think you'll need them. And I think, Meghan…after this night, they have to know the whole truth."

"Won't that piss off your precious Sentinels?" She all

but spat the words at him, and he couldn't help but laugh. Short and hard, the amusement of it dark.

"Yes," he said. "It probably will. Go find Jenny—the sheep knocked her down, I don't think it'll be serious—but she saw me, and she saw the flame devil."

"She's terrified," Meghan murmured, her anger draining away.

"Yes. Go. I'll be right there." As soon as he found her herbs. And as soon as he put on his damned boots. He had a feeling that the jaguar would be out again tonight, but in the meantime it served no one if he heroically shredded his feet by running straight into the aftermath of the attack.

He ran to the house, treading lightly on hard ground scattered with stones. He barged into her bedroom as though he'd always been welcome there, knowing exactly where she kept her mother's things; he left the storage bin open on her bed, tucked the herbs under his arm and scooped up his boots, not hesitating to jam them on his feet, sans socks, when he reached the porch.

And then he could truly run, heading straight for Meghan and Jenny, orienting everything else as he moved. The sheep were farther away; Anica was returning without them, her scent strong on the breeze and filled with profound fear. And Meghan...her distress reached him on deeper levels.

When he reached her, he saw why; he smelled what he'd been trying to ignore beneath the charred wood and hot metal singeing his nostrils. At least one of the sheep had been caught up by the flame devil; it lay in a stiffened, charred mass. And it was still alive.

Meghan turned on him, even though she couldn't possibly have heard him over the sound of Jenny weeping and the sheep's weak bleating. "This wouldn't have happened if I hadn't gone after you! If I hadn't left them!"

He bit back his snort of response, forced himself to crouch quietly in the darkness, bitter smoke wreathing around them all. Holding out the wooden herb box, he said quietly, "It damned well would have. And we would have been caught up in the middle of it, instead of being in the position to deal with it."

Jenny twisted around to stare at him with puffy eyes, not quite able to target his gaze directly in the darkness. "You know what this was?" she asked, and her voice fast grew accusing. "You knew this might happen?"

"No," Dolan said, fighting the instant guilt, the voice inside that said he *should* have known, had he been thinking clearly. Two probes…the Atrum Core clearly hadn't been about to just go away. He'd drawn them here…he'd let them find Meghan. Now they were trying to flush him out…and to take care of an unknown threat while they were at it.

Meghan.

He said to Jenny, "I'm sorry. I had no idea they'd—"

And even that was too much, for Meghan hadn't explained about the Core. But Jenny looked away from him, blinking hard; her hand groped for Meghan's. "You tried to warn us."

"I didn't know," Meghan said, and her voice sounded as though she'd been inhaling smoke all evening long, as if the flame devil had scorched her throat. "I never would have let you stay."

The sheep made a strangled noise, and both women stiffened. Dolan cursed under his breath; Meghan said, "We need the rifle—"

"It's in the closet," Jenny said, sounding strangled as well. Not so far away, Anica called to them all, very nearly returned from her futile attempt to gather their scattered charges. "The shells are—"

But Dolan made an impatient noise and stood, moving off to the brittlebush that had somehow escaped the flames. Far enough away, he thought, so Jenny wouldn't seize up from fear on the spot. And there he changed, stretching into the strobe of blue light, into the form and its power. Physical power, this time—just what he needed. Meghan's angry exclamation, Jenny's little shriek... they barely registered as he stalked to the sheep and broke its neck with one swift mercy blow. And then he loped off into the small point of land that followed the base of the hill looming above them, knowing his scent alone would effectively turn the strayed sheep back home. He left Meghan to explain, to try to apply her herbs and talk her way out of the position he'd just put her in.

If she could.

Better to know now if she couldn't.

Meghan's cry of protest died in her throat. She didn't have to see or hear Dolan to know he'd left; she could *feel* it. Damn him for that—for the leaving, for the fact that she so easily followed his presence now. For taking the jaguar right in front of Jenny before he'd left.

He'd be back; she could feel that, too. His intent. She could even feel his understanding of her reaction.

Well, the hell with that. She had to deal with what was here. With Jenny, whose hand now trembled in hers, and with Anica's arrival—for the canny woman took one look at the two of them and demanded, "What happened?" And then she gave a small bark of laughter, ran her fingers through hair already sticking out in wild directions, and said, "I mean, what *else* happened?"

Meghan said, "Sit down. And give me a moment here. I'm too tired to do this and talk at the same time." Firm enough to preempt Anica's insistence…if only for now.

Anica sat as Meghan went to work on Jenny's ankle, applying a compress of the enhanced herbs and then feeling her unfamiliar way for a trickle of the earth's power to seal it all in place and put a fast start to the healing. Only a little…and cautiously. For all she knew, she could kill Jenny by misusing the power.

Of course I could. Such powers could kill or heal at the whim of the ones who wielded it, and now she had that power.

Dolan had changed her life forever, *initiating* her.

Anica craned her neck to look at the sheep enclosure. "Wasn't there one left behind—?"

"It's dead," Meghan said shortly.

"Dolan killed it," Jenny said distantly. "He turned into a jaguar and then he killed it."

Anica's laugh came short and hard. "Right. First some sort of weird ball lightning, and then Dolan turns into a big cat. I don't think so."

The words left Meghan's mouth unexpectedly, briskly. "I *warned* you." She closed the herb box with a *snick* of the latch, her movements jerky. *"I tried—"*

"Whoa," Anica said, and Meghan's new night vision showed her perfectly that her friend's eyes had narrowed. "You *warned* us? You knew it could come to this? That conversation by the barn was a pathetic attempt to warn us about *this?*"

"No." Suddenly miserable, so glad her friends couldn't see her as well as she could see them, Meghan nonetheless shook her head. "I had no idea. I didn't know they could...or that they *would*."

Anica suddenly sounded just a little bit dangerous herself. "Maybe you'd better start at the beginning. If you can find it."

Meghan knew exactly where the beginning was. She just didn't know how to say it. What the hell was Dolan thinking, forcing her hand like this?

Forcing you to face who you are.

"My mother," she said, but that didn't work so she stopped and tried again. "There are people..." And that didn't work, either. Where to start, indeed? With the Core, and their hunt for an ancient manuscript and the powers it would give them? With the Sentinels, just as ancient and secret and so impossible to even imagine?

He's back.

Why ever Dolan had left, he was back. Behind her, crouched in the greening brittlebush and creosote, and still the jaguar.

Meghan didn't have to turn around to know it. Or to know his intent an instant before it became obvious. He'd started this, and now he'd help her finish it. He flowed out from the darkness, dappled black on black, and Meghan knew the instant that Anica spotted him, the instant Jenny stiffened in fear.

Dolan didn't make her wait long. Ready for it this time, she narrowed her eyes against the flickering, blue-heat lightning of his change, trying to see past it to the nature of the change itself, and failing. And when Dolan stood before her, she said coolly, "Making decisions for others again, I see. Couldn't just let me sort this out, could you?"

"We don't have time for it." He looked at Anica. "The remaining sheep aren't far from here—they're in that little clearing against the hill."

She looked him up and down, then did it again. And then, eyes narrowing, blurted, "Where the hell do your clothes come from?"

Meghan laughed. Not a lot of humor there, but... enough. She'd once demanded the same thing of her mother. But while her mother had explained about organic materials and the changes the original Vigilia had made to themselves, Dolan barely acknowledged the question. "All part of the package," he said, and reached out to pull Jenny to her feet. "How's your ankle?"

She snatched her hand back from his. "Don't even try to pretend we're going to have a normal conversation!" she cried—and then stopped to consider. "It's... better. It's not normal, but...it's *better*."

Dolan gave her space, putting out a hand to Meghan in turn. Meghan glared at it, undecided, and he inclined his head slightly. "Go ahead, then." *You tell them.*

Still in her head, then. Fine. Then he knew she was tired of being pushed around. By him, by the Core, by circumstances. "My mother," she said bluntly, standing on her own so he offered his hand to Anica instead, "was a coyote."

"Oh, hell," Anica muttered. But she took Dolan's hand and came to her feet beside Meghan.

"There are others like her. Like Dolan. They're called the Sentinels, and they take the form of...coyotes. Jaguars. Other big cats, other carnivores..."

"Sometimes herd animals," Dolan said. "But not often."

"Yeah," said Anica, still muttering. "Because it wouldn't be sexy to turn into a cow."

Dolan coughed and turned away, but Meghan easily saw the glint of amusement in his eye.

"Are they the ones who did this?" Jenny demanded, indicating the ranch with a swooping gesture. "Your Sentinels?"

That turned him serious fast enough. "We don't wield those kinds of powers," he said. "We build wards; we shape existing power to influence natural processes. Some of us shepherd the earth's power while we're at it."

"Healing," she murmured, and looked down at her ankle—and then over at Meghan. "And you. Do you... all this time, have you been a..." She couldn't seem to bring herself to say it.

"No," Meghan said sharply. "I knew of the Sentinels through my mother. But she died for them, and they *let* her." She glanced at Dolan as his gaze went hooded, and without thinking about it, she privately added, *Not your brother. They let him die, too. I know that now.*

His eyes widened briefly; he looked away, his jaw clenched. Caught up in his own grief from that day. And—she felt it from him—gratitude.

"And if the Sentinels didn't do *this*—" Anica copied Jenny's wide gesture "—then who did? Someone sure as hell *wields those kinds of powers*."

"There's always a bad guy," Meghan said, darkly bitter. "The same people who killed my mother. They're called the Atrum Core. They want something that my mother was hiding."

"The lost Ark of the Covenant." Anica looked at Dolan. "But you're no Indiana Jones."

Meghan felt his quick flicker of annoyance. She could have told him that her friend was only protecting herself; that she hid her fear with sharpness. But Meghan thought he might just deserve to be on the receiving end of that sharpness. Too arrogant, by far...just like the Sentinels, whether he liked it or not. Too used to playing games with other people's lives.

He gave her a startled look; guilt spiked through her. She hadn't meant for him to perceive that from her. But...she gave the thoughts another look and discovered she stood behind them.

Jenny looked as though she might just faint. "Just how long has this been going on? Just how many of you are there...?"

"Not so many that we can spare any of us," Dolan told her. "We've been fighting them ever since two brothers of different fathers in Rome-occupied Britain squared off against each other. Over two thousand years."

"One of the brothers had a druidic father," Meghan said, her words coming from the stories her mother had told her, suddenly more real than they'd ever seemed. "The other had a Roman father. And the Druid's son could take the form of a fierce wild boar...."

"But the Roman's son had only the limited amulet-based powers he learned to steal from others." Dolan nodded. "In the end, the Druid swore to protect the world from his Roman brother—to hold vigil. Vigilia, they were called—but in recent times we've just translated it to Sentinel."

"And the Atrum Core?" Anica asked. Her sharpness

was fading; she looked smaller than she had. Finally overwhelmed beyond what any attitude could cover.

"We named them," he admitted. "Over the years. We didn't expect them to like it, but they took it for their own."

"Dark core," Meghan said. "Fits them. I wonder if they see the irony."

"What irony?" But Jenny's question came warily...fully aware now that the answers might not be reassuring.

Meghan could well understand that. "The Roman claimed to gather power only to keep the Druid in line. Even human, the man was stronger and quicker than everyone else. And although no one had yet developed ward craft, he could perceive the potential energies. The Roman saw that as a threat...but in the end, it was his own craft that evolved to threaten innocents."

Anica snorted. "I can't believe they'd want you to tell us any of this. Your Sentinels. Or even the Atrum Core." She said those words with distaste, the same way she might pick up a dead mouse. However shaken she'd been, she was already bouncing back. Tough, that Anica. Meghan felt a prickle of pride for her friend—and one of guilt. Maybe she should have said something sooner after all.

Dolan looked away, off into the hills. "If they'd kept their timetable, it wouldn't have come to this." But she felt his stab of guilt join hers, and she prodded it—and suddenly she knew. He wasn't supposed to have come. He'd done it anyway, counting on the team's imminent arrival. And he'd stirred up the unexpected...and now their backup was delayed.

Now they were on their own.

He gave her a quick, startled look—she knew he'd felt her presence, her invasiveness. And though suddenly she didn't feel quite as welcome—as if he'd tried to close doors against her—she knew she could stay there, so close as to have been joined, if she wanted.

But she'd seen enough. Enough to back away, emotionally dizzy—still throbbing with the awareness of him and the recent touch of his hand, and yet…so many reasons for fury. For resentment.

If you choose to look at it that way.

She wasn't the only one who knew how to intrude, it seemed.

But Dolan turned back to Anica. "The Sentinels are fairly regulated…we have a brevis regional structure, plenty of red tape and hoops to jump through. But the regional Core septs are family-run; their *drozhars*—princes—have more freedom…and more power. The local *drozhar* is a man named Fabron Gausto." He stopped, his jaw working on emotion. "Let's just say I'm acquainted with him. And the only way we're going to get through this is if we work together…not if we're wasting energy just figuring it out."

Jenny turned on him with unprecedented bitterness. Jenny, who so keenly felt the loss of any animal, along with their fears and pains. "If you weren't here, there'd be nothing to *get through*. Luka wouldn't be gone, the sheep wouldn't be gone, half this ranch wouldn't be scorched and burned—"

A flare of matching resentment took Meghan, resonating in her. Her nostrils flared at the acrid scent of charred flesh and wood; her hands tingled from the herbs she'd applied to Jenny's ankle.

And Dolan took a deep breath, looking directly at Meghan. His voice sounded rough…exhausted. "Yeah," he said. "Maybe you're right."

Jenny startled; she hadn't expected agreement. Meghan took her arm, just as startled—and unaccountably moved. Unaccountably *proud*. The resentment faded away. And she realized out loud, "Once the Core moved into this area looking for the manuscript, they would have found me. They'd have come for us anyway. Maybe not this night, maybe not this way…" She looked to Dolan, a dare of a glance—no platitudes, no patronizing reassurance.

He didn't give them. He said, "Probably so." But he didn't meet her gaze, even knowing she could see clearly in the darkness now. He looked off to the mountain slope rising behind the ranch and he said, "The thing is, now they know I'm still alive. And the Core's local *drozhar*—" He stopped, glanced back at Meghan and shrugged. "He's not going to let that stand. They'll be back."

Chapter 13

They rounded up the sheep, housing them in two horse stalls. Dolan dragged the dead animal away, far into the woods, and left it for the coyotes and vultures. In the background he heard Meghan calling for Luka until her voice broke, and when he returned he convinced the women that Jenny and Anica should stay at the ranch house—the only fully warded structure left on the property. They brought in Jenny's dog, who distrusted the smell of them all—not just the smoke, but the biting, bitter smell of the flame devil itself.

Anica took the couch, Jenny the guest bed…and Dolan pulled off his boots and jeans in Meghan's room, scrubbed his face, hands and arms in her bathroom and eased into the bed beside her sleeping form. Tonight, in here, they were safe. The rest of the ranch…not so much.

But if Meghan had guessed, she hadn't protested…

she might well have picked up from him the terrible danger of manipulating wards when exhausted to this extent. And the Core would need time to recover from the night's work as well. Whoever had created amulets for the probes and flame devil—the remnants of which would be just inside the boundaries somewhere—that person would need rest, too.

Come the following days, they'd repair and reinforce the wards as they repaired the ranch. And Dolan would call brevis regional and pry that team away from Tucson, whatever it took. And then somewhere in there, they'd find the manuscript.

He couldn't allow himself even a moment's doubt.

Meghan lay on her side, sheets slipping away from the strong, refined line of her shoulder, smoothed into the dip of her waist, tightened over the curve of her hip. He rested his hand there, tucking himself up against her; the tight muscles of her bottom spooned in against him, caressing him. The hum of her proximity, the warmth of her body, the trust in her murmur as she recognized his presence, turned into him slightly, and fell back into deep sleep…more than enough to arouse him. But not fiercely; not as it had been before. Comfortable and satisfying and enough just to be what it was—an exhausted man holding his lover through what remained of the night.

Dolan woke to weight settling on his legs, shifting up to his hips, offering a sweet swell of pleasure. Not quite awake enough for understanding, he nonetheless did what any sane man would do—he pushed into it, a groan rumbling from his throat and then a gasp as the pleasure pulled at him, tight and demanding.

Meghan. Daylight and morning and Meghan, helping herself.

She sat on him, her hands traveling the planes of his torso, her own sensations reverberating along his very receptive nerves. Clean and ginger-mint spicy, her skin still damp on his, her body still unexplored. He opened his eyes to find her watching him, still clothed in the clinging tank sleep shirt, but minus any bottoms whatsoever. A sharp jolt of heat wrung a gasp from him, loud and unrestrained.

She leaned over him. "Shh. Hear them?"

He did now. Bumping around the kitchen—cabinets opening and closing, the screen door opening with what was meant to be quiet, someone's footsteps on the porch. Jenny and Anica—and still Meghan moved, so he clenched his teeth on another groan and lifted his hips, trembling as she trembled. Through those clenched teeth, he managed, "Are you sure?" *Sure about this?* He'd felt her turmoil clearly enough the evening before, her fast-shifting emotions. And no wonder, given the events of the past few days. His sudden presence in her life…the sudden precipitation of their entwined nature.

She gave a short laugh. He felt it through her body, even though she hadn't taken him in yet; air slipped through his teeth in a hiss of *want.* She was ready enough, all heat and softness; she tortured them both with her gentle movement even as she finally answered his question. "No," she said. "Yes." *I hate you, I love you, I want you gone, I can't live without you.* "I don't even know you!"

His fingers clutched the sheets. "You do," he said. *No one has* this *without knowing.*

"Maybe I do," she murmured, and raised herself, hovering over taking him in. Hovering...

The sheet tore beneath his fingers.

Meghan gave a short, breathless laugh and eased down over him. He arched up to meet her, his head tipping back, his neck tight and straining. He faintly heard the screen door close, the sound of running footsteps; Jenny's call to her dog. The house was theirs.

Meghan whispered, "Go for it."

And he did.

"Still certain?" he asked of her as he emerged from her bathroom—an obvious modernization in this old house, full of saltillo tile and southwestern mosaics. Towel over his shoulder, jeans not yet buttoned all the way up—he got a start when she turned from her jewelry box, still fastening the back of a tiny onyx earring, to let her gaze linger on his body. Dressed in work jeans with a flat narrow belt still hanging open and another tank top—this one with Encontrados printed across the front—she watched him with an expression that in no way matched her practical appearance. He felt himself grow hard, and he growled, "There's only one place things will go if you give me that look."

Her surprise echoed gently through the both of them; she hadn't realized the hunger lingering in her eyes. She picked up the second earring, closing the top drawer of the scarred old chest of drawers with her elbow. "Certain?" she said, a stall in response to his question, though it seemed like forever since he'd asked it. She just as quickly realized she'd never fool him, and sighed. "I guess I'm not certain of a thing, except that we need to protect this ranch. No—" she shook her head "—that's not true. I know I can't stay away from you. I know that even standing here in the same room stirs up all kinds of things in me—and *that*—" she looked pointedly at his groin "—is the least of it."

He mimed a blow to his heart. "You wound me."

She grinned. "Okay. Maybe not the *least* of it. There's a thing here between us. I get that. I just haven't figured out exactly what it is or what it'll be. But I do know we have this ranch to protect, and that manuscript to find—and that means figuring out the rest of it later. They're okay out there, aren't they?"

Her sudden change of subject threw him for a moment—but he could never truly be confused over meaning where Meghan was concerned. Not any longer. "The Core prefers to attack at night. Doesn't mean we shouldn't be watching, but the risks are lower…and I'm betting there are animals to be fed."

"I'm betting they've already been fed," Meghan murmured. "That reminds me…we had the farrier on the calendar today. I've got to cancel that…and Chris was going to come out and work with Jenny to settle the new gelding. I don't want him anywhere near here—or the two who were coming to help shift hay—"

"Warn them off."

She wrinkled her nose at him. "Drama," she said. "Right from the start, drama. Showing up at the round pen with your dire warnings, taking the jaguar right there in front of me when you left…the world's a stage, huh?" But when he merely looked at her, entirely un-used to being called on such things, she grinned and said, "Never mind. I'll just phone them and reschedule. I think it'll raise fewer questions, don't you?"

"Right," he muttered, still off balance.

And she seemed to damned well know it. She leaned against the chest of drawers and crossed her arms. "Speaking of the Core," she said, "Last night, I got the distinct impression that there's more at stake than the manuscript. In fact, it sounded a whole lot like there might be a grudge thing going on with you and the local Core's prince."

Dolan frowned, the edge of his thumb passing idly over the faded scar on his side—not one she'd seemed to notice, and he caught himself, letting that hand rest low on his hip. Confrontational. More his style. "He finds me annoying."

"You might have said something. I've got a couple of traded memories, and sometimes I hear you pretty clearly in my head, and sometimes I just get little hints. Your mind isn't an open book or anything."

Thank God for that. "Would it have changed anything?" He lowered his voice, nearly hitting gravel…hiding defensiveness. He wasn't used to that, either.

She shrugged. "That's not the point."

"Coffee," he said desperately. If she'd flung the words at him, he'd have known his role—the same role he'd had since his brother died. The defiant one. The rogue. Dark and dangerous. But this civil conversation left him no easy knee jerks, no easy patterns into which he could fall.

"Sex would be better," she said, heading out to the kitchen. "But I don't want to wear you out. Big day ahead. Fixing the ranch, fixing the wards…"

Sex would be better. Holy damn cow. She'd done that on purpose.

And to good effect.

Newly warned not to underestimate this woman, Dolan rescued the shirt he'd washed in the shower and flapped out the wrinkles, hanging it to dry in her open window. He reached for the phone by her bedside, but only until he heard her voice in the kitchen—a matter-of-fact message-leaving voice. *The farrier.* The smell of brewing coffee hit his nose as she made another call, this one to Chris. He'd thought her tone casual enough, but the kid somehow caught whiff of trouble; she had to convince him not to come out and make sure everything was okay.

The moment he heard her finish the call, he picked up the phone. No better way to reestablish his balance, his dark and dangerous rogue attitude, than to have a sweet conversation with brevis regional.

"Carter," he said, barely giving the man time to answer the phone. "Where the hell is that team?"

Carter came back at him just as quickly. "Is this where I remind you that you went in early? That the consul didn't want you out there at all?"

"Two days early," Dolan said, falling into a near growl—and finding the familiar role to be a relief even as his ire rose. "We're long past the consul's timeline, and you know it. I don't give a damn if you've got the whole team there—send them on! Your latecomer will only be two hours away once he finally gets there."

"She," Carter said absently. Dolan heard the *tickety-tick* of a keyboard, knew Carter was checking up on the missing team member. "You're not the only one with

FREE BOOKS OFFER

To get you started, we'll send you
2 FREE books and a FREE gift

- -

There's no catch, everything is **FREE**

Accepting your 2 **FREE** books and **FREE** mystery gift
places you under no obligation to buy anything.

Be part of the Mills & Boon® Book Club™ and receive your favourite
Series books up to 2 months before they are in the shops and delivered
straight to your door. Plus, enjoy a wide range of **EXCLUSIVE** benefits!

- Best new women's fiction – delivered right to
  your door with FREE P&P
- Avoid disappointment – get your books up to
  2 months before they are in the shops
- No contract – no obligation to buy

2 **FREE** books
and a
FREE gift

We hope that after receiving your free books you'll
want to remain a member. But the choice is yours.
So why not give us a go? You'll be glad you did!

Visit **millsandboon.co.uk** to stay up to date
with offers and to sign-up for our newsletter

I0CIA

Mrs/Miss/Ms/Mr   Initials

BLOCK CAPITALS PLEASE

Surname _____

Address _____

_____

Postcode

Email _____

MILLS & BOON®

The Mills & Boon® Book Club™ – Here's how it works:

Accepting your free books places you under no obligation to buy anything. You may keep the books and gift and return the despatch note marked "cancel". If we do not hear from you, about a month later we'll send you 3 brand new books including two 2-in-1 titles priced at £4.99* and a single title priced at £3.19*. That is the complete price – there is no extra charge for post and packaging. You may cancel at any time, otherwise we will send you 5 stories a month which you may purchase or return to us – the choice is yours.

*Terms and prices subject to change without notice.

MILLS & BOON
Book Club

FREE BOOK OFFER
FREEPOST NAT 10298
RICHMOND
TW9 1BR

NO STAMP
NECESSARY
IF POSTED IN
THE U.K. OR N.I.

things going on. She's in the middle of something else. It's wrapping up—"

"Forget her! Didn't anyone at brevis feel what happened out here last night? The Core took this to civilians, Carter."

His response was dry enough. "We felt it. I have the reports to prove it." The rustle of said pages reached Dolan through the phone line. "No doubt they were coming after you. As far as we can tell, Gausto has his little contingent hunkered down in Sonoita. I'm not so sure last night wasn't a ploy to drive you to the manuscript."

"Yeah?" Dolan's voice slid down to a true growl. "Then it's working. Finding that thing is exactly what I intend to do. As soon as possible."

"To lead them straight to it?" Carter asked coldly. "No need to ask how you are, I see. Classic Treviño."

"Classic consul," Dolan shot back at him. "Leaving a Treviño hanging out in the field alone."

Carter didn't respond directly. He noted, "The consul had good reason to believe you were back on your feet. As it happens, we also caught a surge in ward view from that area. I don't suppose I need to tell you what it was—or that we can't leave someone of that power out in the cold."

Dolan paced the room—strong, angry strides that took him from one side to the other with brutal efficiency. "You stay away from her, dammit. She wants nothing to do with brevis!"

"That's not an option," Carter told him. "The team will be there soon, Dolan. Try to keep things quiet until then."

"For the consul's convenience?" Dolan laughed, short and hard. "Tell him to—"

Carter interrupted, his voice gone just as hard. "Don't go there," he warned. "No one here is in a mood to humor you."

"Then come out and stop me," Dolan said, and hung up.

"Coffee!" Meghan called into the back end of the house, putting the carafe back onto its heating plate as she snagged her brimming mug. Hot and black and as strong as possible—but not so strong that she wanted to face Dolan at the moment. Not after a phone call that went as badly as what she'd just heard.

Or not heard, really. But the waves of anger coming from Dolan were loud enough. She didn't fear him, but that didn't mean he couldn't use a little space. She left the house, letting the screen door squeak and slam so there'd be no mistake about it, and she hitched one hip up to sit on the porch rail and survey the damage from the night before.

She hadn't realized that hard caliche ground could scorch. Or that the flame devil had come quite so close to the house. And even from here, the sheep shed was a complete loss. She caught a flicker of movement, found Jenny's dog trotting along the pipe corral runs adjacent to the barn, and soon enough caught sight of Jenny and Anica in one of the runs, discussing the horse between them. Jenny moved with a limp, but not a big one. Anica glanced over to the house and Meghan lifted her hand in a wave, but Anica's nod of response was perfunctory, even at this distance.

Anica would be more angered by the fact that Meghan had been keeping secrets than the details of those secrets; she'd hold on to that anger. *Something I should have kept in mind this past week.*

A whole week since Dolan had come into her life. From their first encounter to this morning's most recent, much more intimate encounter…it felt as though it had been a lifetime.

She knew for certain that her life would never be the same. Even now she felt the trickle of his anger, the faint pain of abused feet…even his thankfulness for the coffee he was pouring. And even now, she felt the latent presence of the power newly available to her. The earth's power, available at a volume she'd never even considered…*right here, right now.* If she reached for it.

And she was tempted…but she also instinctively felt the wrongness of such a thing, to reach for power for which she had no purpose.

She stretched again. The last twenty-four hours had used her hard, even though she'd considered herself strong with her active ranch lifestyle. And Dolan…he was still recovering from his near-death experience, as much as he seemed to take himself for granted at this point.

She closed her eyes, tipping her head back ever so slightly to listen more closely to him—to see if he was as well as he pretended to be. The feel of him instantly broadened, giving her glimpses of his lingering pain, of muscles that still sometimes unexpectedly failed him. And there was something else, too—something new, a strange tingle in the periphery of her perception. Not alarming…not particularly meaningful at all. She lingered there a moment, and then moved away from it. One more new thing in her life that didn't quite yet make sense.

Like Dolan himself. Meghan wasn't sure yet whether

she regretted what had happened—the fierce lovemaking, the strength of what had happened so suddenly between them.

She did know there was no walking away.

Dolan emerged from the kitchen, wearing a damp shirt not yet buttoned, his feet clad where he might otherwise have gone barefoot. She knew why. She said, "Things okay?"

A scowl lingered behind his eyes, in the set of his jaw. "Just delays," he said. He took a sip of the coffee, looked at her as though he might say something else and then didn't. "How about out here?"

"I need to go check on them." She nodded at the barn. Her two friends had removed the horse from the run-out and now walked it out, studying its movement. Even from here, Meghan could see the limp. "After that, can we get started on repairing the wards? I want this place safe from those people."

He caught her gaze, held it. "Repairing the wards won't necessarily do that. They want that manuscript, and they know your mother is the last to have seen it."

"Because you led them here." She flattened the words, trying to squeeze away any blame. It didn't work.

"Probably," he said, just as flatly. "But I'm not sure brevis is secure any longer, and neither is the adjutant— that's one reason I didn't wait for the team. Besides, they always suspected your mother had last possession of the book. She and Jared would still be alive if that weren't true."

Meghan lifted her chin. "My mother was the best at warding and hiding. The Sentinels never should have wasted her as they did. Only a coyote, you know."

"She wasn't *only* anything," he said shortly. "She laid enough trails to convince everyone that she'd passed the manuscript off to some unsuspecting mule. Both the Sentinels and the Core gave up on this area long ago."

"Then what changed?" *Why come back again now?*

"Time," he told her. "Our techniques. We've refined them." He took another sip of the coffee, obviously appreciative. Meghan enjoyed watching him enjoy it, enjoyed the play of the breeze in his open shirt and the glimpses of skin it showed her. Scars, too, in this bright daylight—smooth, tight scars, well healed but significant enough to have hurt like hell. Thin, precise lines that didn't make any sense to her.

She might well have asked had he not stiffened, his attention leaving the conversation to center on the woods past the charred sheep pen, the little spit of flatland that curved around the rising mountain. That was warning enough; that he set his coffee on the porch rail was even more so. Meghan put her own mug aside, sliding off the porch rail to her feet.

But Dolan relaxed slightly before Meghan had even heard what got his attention, and when he turned to her it was with a grin. It startled her, that grin—genuine, carefree and for the moment, injecting lightheartedness into what had become a persistently grim situation. It was then she heard the cadence of hoofbeats.

Luka.

She barely caught her mug as it slipped on the porch rail, and then quickly set it at her feet, heading for the steps as Luka cantered into view through the woods, shying wildly at the charred sheep pen and kicking out at it on the way past. Right into the yard, as Jenny's dog caught sight and came charging up, barking a scolding at the wrongness of a loose horse.

And what would you have done with a flame devil?

Died, that's what.

But the quick grim thought didn't keep her from grinning like a fool at Luka's return, not even though his entire body spoke of his alarm—tense muscles, neck flung high, nose tipped to the sky, eyes rolling and ears canted back. His sleek grayed coat was marred with stains and one scrape along his shoulder, hair peeled away and skin raw, and never had Meghan understood more than at that moment: this was a creature bred for war. His hooves thundered against the ground, and at that moment she believed what Luka had always believed—that whatever stood in front of him, be it fence or house or mountain, it would damned well get out of his way.

But Dolan saw it, too, and lost his grin; he moved to step in front of her, not knowing—how *could* he know?—and Meghan reacted both out loud and silently, *No!* and "No!" making a double hit against Dolan, slowing him enough so she could push him back onto the porch. And although Dolan, too, was also clearly the sort who believed men and mountains would move before him, he allowed it—and she followed up quickly. "Not now. He killed a man, once. He was being beaten, but it's part of him now." Once sure he had heard her, she looked over to Luka—frozen in place, trembling, waiting for something to send him off or calm him down. Asking for her help, with the courage it took to overcome the stench of death and the flame devil and his wild night just to stand there at all.

Hands low but a little open, obvious enough so they wouldn't startle him if she reached out, she stepped off the porch.

"What're you—" But Dolan watched the horse, too, and stopped himself—both his words and his attempt to stop her—as Luka's head raised even higher, his front feet coming off the ground in warning. He hovered there a moment, instinctively imitating the levade he'd never been taught—until Dolan stepped back. "I damned well hope you know what you're doing." Hard words...but there was worry behind them.

"I damned well do," Meghan said between her teeth, a soothing singsong tone. "Luka," she said, crooning the name and ignoring the concern that beat against her back. "Brave boy. You're safe now."

Convince me, he seemed to say—to plead for it, in fact. Meghan made it okay in the only way she knew how...by making it perfectly normal. By walking right up to him and putting her hand on his shoulder— stroking it until he suddenly bobbed his head down, until his ears flicked at her once before pricking forward toward Dolan. For Luka, there was only one thing that truly made things right...and she gave him that, too, grabbing his mane and swinging up to his back—a little bit of jump, a little bit of twist, a lot of trusting that her legs would wrap around more than air.

He lifted up to meet her, another half rear, and came down poised to run.

"God, Meghan, what if he—"

"Then I'm gonna get dumped on my ass," she said, stroking Luka's neck. "Won't be the first time, will it, Luka? And then you'll come back and ask me what the hell I'm doing on the ground when I so clearly belong on your back."

"He killed a man," Dolan repeated, lifting a brow at her, waiting for confirmation.

She nodded, keeping her eye on the board-stiff muscles of Luka's neck beneath the veil of his mane. They were the key, those muscles; they told her Luka's mood exactly. "The man deserved it, of course. But that still makes Luka a killer…it took a lot to earn his trust. Or did you think our work here was all fluff and light? In come the cute animals, and Anica fixes them. Not like me, big clumsy wannabe with herbs, but subtly."

Dolan snorted—though he kept it low for Luka's sake. "There's nothing subtle about that woman."

"And there's Jenny—always knows just what's behind their behaviors. Half the time their history's wrong, so she never pays attention to it. Never needs to. By the time the public sees our rehabs, between the two of them, no one ever knows how bad it ever was. They never really understand what we start with."

"That's their mistake." Dolan had taken on the cadence of her words—the calm, for Luka. "As it happens, I think your work here might be more important than even you know." And though his concern lingered, it came with something else—something new. Pride. Right there between them, a warm breeze across the yard, caressing her. Lifting her, and somehow filling her.

And Luka's neck abruptly relaxed, his ears pricking into that emotional breeze. He lowered his head, arching his neck coyly as he stretched toward Dolan, lips twitching in invitation. He couldn't quite reach, so he took a step, and then another, and stuck his head in over the porch rail so Dolan couldn't help but lift a hand to rest just behind Luka's ears, gently massaging his poll.

"Well, huh," Meghan said. "That's one miracle down. Should we go work on the wards?"

Chapter 14

Before they tackled the wounded wards, Meghan hesitated by the barn to speak with her friends. An awkward moment, and one that clearly made her miserable. They weren't ready, yet, to let go of their hurt and confusion.

"Give them time," Dolan told her, as hypocritical as he could possibly be.... If anyone knew that time didn't always heal, he did. But he kept such feelings away from her, pressed his hand to the small of her back in a consoling gesture and took them out to walk the ward lines.

She turned out to be her mother's daughter, oh, hell, yes. Once he took her to ward view again, her sure touch made quick work of things. She had little finesse—how could she?—but it was there. It was waiting. And meanwhile he showed her how to smooth the damaged spots, and how to weave the wards anew as they walked the ranch in two different worlds.

"It's much easier this way," she admitted to him once, although she still struggled with knowing when to reach for outside power—still had a tendency to use herself up. "Looking at it all from here."

He couldn't hide his surprise. "No one does this work *outside* of ward view."

Her expression closed, both inwardly and outwardly. "Only those of us who were deemed too insignificant to teach."

"Their mistake." *But—*

She dropped out of ward view to put her hands on her hips and stare at him in demand. "This is all hard enough without knowing you're *not saying* things."

Yeah. So much for his ability to keep things from her. "They might try to rectify that situation."

Her laugh was bitter. "Screw them. I have a life, and I made it without their help. They aren't getting a piece of me."

"Later. Don't let it distract you."

She gave him an annoyed glance, but returned to the matter at hand—the worst of the damage from the night before, where a gaping, wounded hole tore through all the layers of the old wards Margery Lawrence had once laid around this ranch. From the outside, it was invisible—just another spot along the hillside, very near to the trail where Luka had not so long ago brought Dolan home. On the inside...

Meghan eyed it with trepidation. "I don't think I can... Look, I know I have to learn this stuff, but maybe you should start this one. Let me follow your lead."

He wanted to urge her to try…but he saw, then, that she was tired. And he brought to mind her headlong rush into the darkness to reach him at the old homestead, and her willingness to find him again in the woods below the house, and her courage in the face of Luka's wild ire.

This was not a woman who backed lightly away from challenges.

So he stepped in. He drew from the earth and he started the tracing, easily visualizing the pattern in his mind, the perfect tangle of symmetrical lines, the particular reflection of the earth's needs in this particular spot—

And suddenly he was on his back, coughing in big whooping gasps with darkness sparkling in every layer of vision he had, and Meghan kneeling by his side. Not that he could see her, but her hands were demanding on his shoulders, on his chest, cupping the sides of his face. Small but sturdy, completely capable hands. *"Dolan,"* she said, pushing his hair out of his eyes, touching his neck. "Dolan, *dammit*—"

"I'm here," he said, a strangled-sounding response; he coughed on it. "Hell, there goes my air of mysterious infallibility."

She released a gust of air and sat back on her heels. "Dammit," she said again, but without much in the way of vehemence. In fact, she sounded tired and small.

He struggled up to his elbows. "Your land isn't interested in my attention," he said, still coughing on words. "It's woken up right along with you…and it's damned opinionated at that."

He expected her to make a face, or turn away from him, or create a derisive noise. Instead—

"Okay," she said, and damned if he didn't think she was on the edge of tears.

"Hey—" Alarm drove him fully upright, fast enough so he almost knocked heads with her. "You weren't—"

"Hurt?" She shook her head—but her eyes were suspiciously bright. "I just…this is all happening so fast. All these things, suddenly in my life. *You.* How can I feel this way about you after a week? What just happened to me inside when the land knocked you down…how does anyone deal with that?" She gestured helplessly between them, and let her words trail away.

He didn't need them. He knew exactly what she meant. He leaned in toward her—that sharp chin, hair kept in check only by the cap she wore, the scent of sunblock tickling his nose. It was a moment before the words came. "Just let it happen," he said. "Don't worry about what it might be. Live in the now."

Her eyes narrowed in challenge. "Is that what you do?"

Yes. He didn't say it out loud; he didn't need to. She would have read it in his face if she hadn't felt it.

"Convenient," she said. "No real commitment to anything, just follow your nose."

The words brought a crush of pain at the base of his throat—pain he hadn't expected. "You've seen enough of my life to know better," he growled. He had commitment above and beyond…had given his life to his work.

Playing nice along the way wasn't necessary.

Meghan rubbed her closed eyes, focusing on the gritty feel of the painted porch post between her shoulder blades—quite possibly the only thing holding her up at all. *But the wards are set.* Her people were protected…as protected as anything in this world today. Dolan, looking as wiped as Meghan felt, had wolfed down a sandwich for dinner and gone to walk the land one more time, staying out of Anica's way.

No. Out of my *way.*

Didn't matter. She could still feel him. She knew exactly where he was, stalking the land black and sleek, indulging in the jaguar. Too damned fast, she'd gotten used to that feeling.

Odd, though, that it didn't quite coincide with the tingling sensation that now constantly nudged for her attention.

She heard footsteps—knew it was Anica simply because there was no accompanying patter of dog feet. "Hey," she said wearily.

"You've been busy," Anica observed. "I'm not sure doing what. But then again, I'm not sure I want to know."

"I'm not sure you want to know, either." Meghan opened her eyes as Anica sat on the porch step.

"I'm not even sure *you* know." Words that could have been hurtful, but for Anica's carefully neutral tone. Unusual, for her.

Meghan laughed…no humor at all. "Yeah," she said. "There's that. Just doing my best."

Anica propped her chin in her hand. "Never was much of one for woo-woo stuff."

"Oh, *right*." Meghan snorted. "So tell me, how's it look in the barn? How are they?"

Anica's brows drew together—not quite following that train of thought, but going along with it. "Three of them are emotional train wrecks, the rest are dealing. Sophie's the worst, but I think we all expected that. Old

Joe's hock is completely blown up, but I think hosing and light walking will deal with it. Young Joe probably should have had stitches last night, but it's too late at this point. We'll just see how it goes. The new horse added some abrasions, but took the chaos remarkably well— Jenny thinks he was still shut down from what he's been through. Buttercup's off in the trot. Hard to pin down, the way shoulder and front foot mimic each other, but I'm pretty sure it's shoulder."

"Uh-huh," Meghan said. She looked longingly at the steps beside Anica, but knew if she sat, she'd never get up again. "No X-rays, no vet and between the two of you, you've assessed a barn full of horses in a single day."

Anica stiffened. "Hey, if you want to get a vet out here to double-check—"

Meghan couldn't keep the *weary* out of her laugh. "No, of course I don't. That's the point. Dolan made it earlier today, too. None of us were ever quite *the usual,* were we? And now he's here, and it's in our faces. We can't pretend anymore."

Anica's offense turned to annoyance; she pursed full lips. "*You* can't," she said. "I happen to know that Jenny and I base our conclusions on observation. Observation of minutia based on experience, but observation all the same."

"Encontrados," Meghan murmured. *Found.* She'd chosen that name; her mother and the family before her hadn't bothered to baptize the place at all. The Lawrence ranch, that's what it had been. She thought she'd named it for the animals here…now she wondered if something deep inside her hadn't actually named it for the people.

"So let me get this straight." Anica abruptly stood, facing her. "We're a happy little functioning rescue organization. Normal as normal comes. Then your friend Dolan arrives, and you go racing off into the night—"

"I heard him call for help," Meghan interrupted. "He was dying."

"But you saved him with the same herbs you used on Jenny last night."

"Not the *same*…"

Anica might know vet care, but she had no interest in herbs, and shrugged off the distinction. "And now suddenly you two are joined at the hip—and it's obvious that's not even a metaphor, just in case you were wondering—and we've got wards and magical woo-woo and treasure quests."

Meghan shrugged. She wasn't going to play word games with Anica. "Close enough. Call it my inheritance." Not one she had any choice about taking, either. Not anymore. Not since she'd made that first decision to find Dolan in the dark.

"So this is the way it's going to be now? We never get our *normal* back? Or are you going to wrap this problem up and then Dolan goes away? Because I can tell you that for certain—we won't ever have *normal* as long as that man is around."

Meghan sucked in a deep breath, making a tiny, hurt little noise.

Of course Anica was right. *Dolan* and *normal everyday life* were polar opposites. After years of assiduously building her own family, she'd suddenly put them in a situation where they couldn't continue. Not as they had been.

"I don't know," she told Anica, which was only as honest as she could be. She couldn't stand the thought of losing her made family—of the realization that she might create circumstances under which they couldn't continue. And yet Dolan had become crucial to her on a whole different level. Even as she continued to discover him, she already knew the heart of him. The rebel not for rebellion's sake, but because he, too, had devoted himself to a cause.

She wondered again about the fine scarring on his flanks. But not for long, because Anica straightened her back, looked Meghan straight in the eye and said, "That's what I thought."

And then she walked away.

Dolan came back late, the jaguar free to come and go with Jenny's dog closed up in the casita. After the previous night, when the dog had survived only because he happened to be inside, Dolan wouldn't be surprised if he waited a long time for another chance at nightly guard duty.

Outside the house, Dolan resisted the urge to use the entire porch post as one big stretching and scratching post and shifted back to the human, shaking a bit of rabbit fluff from one hand and making the decision to wash up well before Meghan saw him.

But Meghan, it turned out, was asleep. She'd been crying—her cheeks were tear-washed, her eyes puffy— and his sudden rush of concern took him unawares. It mingled with his instant desire for her—and to his own surprise, concern won the day.

Somehow, before this moment, he'd been able to close his eyes to the impact of his arrival here. He'd taken greedily from what it had created—their connection, her power, the incredible pleasure he found in her body…his ability to offer the same to her. But he'd been willfully blind to what it cost her.

Until now. Now, when he stood beside the bed, looking down on her where she curled up against the cold spring night, putting her face where it could catch the breeze from the cracked-open window anyway. Tentatively, already full of the hum of her presence, he made himself a little more open—a little more vulnerable. Emotions drifted his way—sorrow and loss, and the bittersweet understanding that the important things in her life now hung in the balance. Response to him, even in her sleep. Fear that she couldn't do what was needed…that she'd fail both her purpose and his.

And there, layered over it all, her attraction for him wove through it all, laced with independently acquired regard. With true affection. With the very first tendrils of what could only be deeply rooted love.

He took a deep, sharp breath and stepped back from the bed.

And he watched her for a very long time.

Chapter 15

Meghan woke in the early morning and found herself oddly at peace.

The events of the past week were still impossible to absorb, and the events of the coming week were still impossible to predict, but she couldn't do anything to change those things. And the Sentinels and the Core had been at odds for thousands of years; she sure couldn't change that, either. Her friends—her made family—had trouble with who she'd turned out to be, and what she'd brought into their lives…and they'd either come to accept those things, or they wouldn't. Her ranch had taken damage—

And that was the one thing she could do something about. *Had* done something about, building wards with Dolan, learning how to trace patterns in ward view, learning how to siphon power from the land that had so obviously and surprisingly claimed her.

As if it had been waiting. All this time, waiting.

She opened her eyes, already aware that the day, barely dawned, would be overcast and oppressive. The quality of light leaking in through the blinds told her that much, as did the extra ache in a body driven to extremes these past days. And the land told her that.

She found Dolan still asleep, leaning against the wall. His knees had been propped up before him at some point, but now they slumped sideways and he didn't look particularly comfortable. His arms crossed loosely over his torso, twitching in sleep. She opened her mouth to say, "What are you doing there? Why aren't you in the bed? Or *a* bed?" and then, after a moment when no words came out, closed it again.

She needed this morning to herself. Even if it meant her mind was still filled with him, that her body felt bereft of him…wanted just to *touch* him. Just to be a little closer.

Not today.

But she had to amend that thought. *Well, not at the moment.*

Because it could be a long day before it was over.

She slipped out of bed and down to the laundry room at the back of the house, where folded laundry hadn't yet been put away. She changed there, jeans and a snug T-shirt under a flannel shirt, far too aware that Dolan's keen hearing would make it difficult to avoid waking him. A scrub of a warm washcloth over her face at the laundry tub, and she snuck into the hall bathroom long enough to grab a hair band. She'd use the barn facilities for other things.

Because today, she wanted to be on the land by

herself. Today the ranch would be back in full swing—several midweek volunteers would be in to move hay bales, spread manure and schlep grain bags, and the farrier had a handful of therapeutic trims on the schedule. They'd all be surprised to find the sheep in the extra horse runs…but upon Meghan's tentative suggestion that they refer to the charred remains of the old lean-to and corral as a gas weed whacker accident, Jenny nodded vigorously and Anica said, "Hell, yes!"

And now that the wards were up, here on the ranch was the safest place for any of them. At least, here at the main yard. Warded and double-warded… Dolan had admitted that something might well get through, but not without causing such a fuss as to reverberate through ward view and plain old worldview both. "They won't do it," he said. "Never mind how the Sentinels would come down on them for risking exposure to both groups—the Core itself would close in on Gausto with a lot less mercy than the Sentinels might be inclined to show."

So they were safe. And now Meghan needed time to absorb it all—time without Dolan humming against her nerves or the regular bustle of a working ranch to distract her. And she wanted to inspect the rest of the land as she could. Practice some light warding, see if there were other signs of the Core…see if Gausto's people were really working at a distance out of Sonoita, or if they might be closer.

Meghan grabbed a bagel, smeared a sloppy knifeful of cream cheese over it and took a swig of orange juice directly from the bottle on the way out, sliding sideways through the barely open screen door to avoid the squeal of its hinges. And she thought she'd gotten away with it, too—slinking out on Dolan, beating Jenny out to the barn—until Jenny's quiet voice said, "What now?"

The bagel almost squirted from her fingers; she juggled it an instant, then clamped down again and turned to find Jenny on the porch rocker, curled up inside an old winter jacket that had been on the ranch as long as Meghan had. Her grandfather's, maybe even a remnant of her disappearing father…everyone used it. *All in the family.* "What're you doing there?"

"Couldn't sleep. Just got to thinking." Jenny looked out over the ranch buildings. "I like it here, Meghan."

"That's… I mean, good." Smooth, that was Meghan in the morning. Real smooth. "Look, I'm…I'm sorry about all this. I didn't think there was any reason to tell you all about my mother—or that you'd have any reason to believe me if I did. The Sentinels and their battle with the Core…they were never a part of my life, until they took my mother away. And then they were gone again. It was just…everything to lose, nothing to gain. No point."

"You could have told us about Dolan when he came."

"I chased him off," Meghan said, but guilt settled heavily in her stomach. It didn't mix well with bagel and cream cheese. "And then things happened so fast…."

"You know," Jenny said, tucking the jacket sleeves over her hands for warmth, "I never fit in anywhere until I came here. I felt things no one else felt, and if I reacted to them I was rude or offensive or crazy. I never felt that way here."

"I hope not."

Jenny shrugged. "Now maybe I understand better why." She looked off in the direction of the sheep pen. "I guess this is the price we pay for that, those of us who find their way to Encontrados." She pushed her sleep-mussed strawberry-red hair away from her face, clumsy with her hand still inside the jacket sleeve, and looked directly at Meghan—a startling departure from her normal quiet demeanor. "It's going to take Anica longer. I'm not sure she'll get there."

"Neither am I," Meghan said, but a tremendous weight lifted from her heart nonetheless. Not taking the guilt with it…there'd always be guilt. But if this little family could get past it… "I'm going out," she said. "You'll be okay here? With Dolan?"

Jenny snorted. "He's hiding from Anica. And we'll be fine. There's plenty to do—those horses need follow-up care, and there's a ranch to run. It's not all that long till Games Day."

"It's *never* all that long till Games Day," Meghan said wryly. Their bane and boon, the biggest donation draw of the year. Horseback rides for the kids, treasure hunts in the barn, demo rides by the staff, a petting zoo…every animal's story told in simple, blunt terms and tacked up beside their stalls—too high for the children to read, low enough so the adults couldn't miss them. Took the whole year to prepare for it, done right. "Hold down the fort, okay? I want to make sure everything's okay out there."

Jenny said, "Yeah. I'd like to know that, please." Striking pale green eyes grew suddenly harder. "And if it isn't, you tell Dolan that he and his Sentinels better fix it."

But Meghan had no such intentions.

Here, out on her own and on the land, Meghan intended to fix things herself.

Practice.

She needed it; she wanted it. She had no idea what Dolan would do after this crisis ended; he seemed the kind of hard man who was perfectly capable of walking away from an inconvenient herb-and-power-christened relation—

No, she wouldn't even call it a relationship. Just an intense interlude. And she wasn't sure but that was okay by her, too. She'd have the memories and she'd have her life. *Yeah, that's convincing.* She was well beyond that point and she knew it.

She needed to be ready, either way. This land was hers; it always had been. And yet…now even more so. It, too, seemed to have awakened to her since the event Dolan had so matter-of-factly called *initiation*.

He'd known what he was doing.

He should have *told* her, let her make the choice….

Except her inner, sensible voice reminded her that he hadn't expected any significant change—that not everyone experienced it. That Dolan himself hadn't— he'd grown into most of his power already.

She thought of his pride in her—how clearly she'd felt it when she'd handled Luka. She closed her eyes, crouching on the flat above the ranch with Luka's reins in one hand, and remembered the feel of Dolan's body beneath her—the reverberation of pleasure between them, his willingness to abandon himself to her. His un-hesitating charge into the fray when the flame devil attacked, his strong presence at her back when she went after it. Emotions chased through her, strong and hot; even now she chafed at their separation, whether she wanted to or not.

She dug her fingers into the hard, pale alkaline soil, felt the grit of it like harsh reality. *More* than just an intense interlude. More than just an incantation-forced connection.

A round pen in the hot morning sun, a haze of evil on the horizon that no one else saw. Deep, dark blue eyes, a gaze fastened on hers with such intensity, such outright demand—

She'd felt it then. That moment. Days before her unwitting concoction of herbs and blood and life had sealed something between them.

And then there he was, an ever-present awareness on the periphery of her thoughts—growing a little louder, a little more insistent. Reaching out to check on her.

These past few days had taught her how little it would take to reach back to him, to turn bare awareness into true communication. But she checked that impulse. She stood, dusted her hands off on her jeans and turned to Luka. She kept Dolan closed out, she mounted up and she rode on—alone, inside and out.

Because she had to know that she could.

Chapter 16

At first startled that he couldn't reach Meghan, Dolan soon found himself grinning. He could sense her; he knew she was safe. And she'd chosen a good time, a natural time to reassert herself. He found himself wearing a little grin of pride—that she could keep him out, that she would think to try.

It had been nothing more than reflex, the reaching out. If she wanted her privacy right now, she could have it.

Besides, Anica had spotted him early in the day and silently pointed at the remains of the sheep shelter, handing him a pair of heirloom overalls that lived in the barn—probably had done so for generations.

Overalls. Surely not.

But a glance down at his own clothes had convinced him. They were all he had; they were the only clothes that would shift with him. Jenny donated an oversized flannel shirt and he slipped the overalls on over his pants, stripping off his shirt right there on the porch.

Jenny gave his side a pointed look. "Meghan know about those?"

He looked down, his arms already poking through the sleeves of his borrowed shirt. Fine, nearly invisible scars, parallel and thin and sheening just enough to see them in the sun. He and Meghan had shared many moments of their lives the night she'd saved his, but he didn't remember this being part of it.

Tiberon Gausto, Core drozhar, *wielding a sharp blade and a sharper smile.*

"I don't know," he told Jenny, dropping his voice into the cold tone that intimidated even the brash and the bold.

Jenny looked straight at him—neither brash nor bold, and not intimidated. Beyond it, perhaps, with the changes he'd brought into her life. "Don't play games with us," she said simply, and left.

It was Dolan who blinked. Dolan who wondered if in his pursuit of the big picture, he'd somehow become that callous...and if his ability to live in the moment hadn't robbed him of another sort of big picture.

Dolan who knew it was probably true.

He set himself to the task of tearing down what remained of the lean-to and corral, setting aside usable wood and dragging the rest into the woods, arranging a deadfall that would delight the birds as it aged. He missed Meghan; his body missed Meghan, too, preternaturally aware of her distance and her absence. But reaching out to her accomplished nothing...only confirmed her determination to spend the day on her own.

How damned fast he'd gotten used to that connection. *Too* fast.

He worked it off, sucking down water and sweating into the dry heat, salt building up on his skin and damp hair falling across his forehead. He marveled at how well he felt...knew he owed that to Meghan, too.

Somehow he had to get her people through this mess without further trouble. The ranch activity had gone on around him today, the new arrivals ignoring his efforts—no doubt directed by Anica to leave him be, if only for their own good. A hay delivery, a young man named Chris working with Jenny, the farrier with his distinctive truck cap...they filled the background of his thoughts with their noises and their scents and their locations.

He was so immersed in the day, in the not-reaching for Meghan, that brevis took him completely by surprise, pinging a *monitio* with startling assertiveness, loud and invasive. He jerked upright, dropping the corral rail he'd just wrenched free, muscles stiffening down his spine. A warning, the *monitio*—probably straight from Carter, with whatever backup he needed to send so strongly. No words, no specifics—the *monitio* wasn't meant for those. Just a warning.

Only the Core inspired such effort. The Core on the move, detected by brevis—with no one but Dolan to receive and act on it.

Dolan left the rail where it had landed and eased aside, backing toward the cover of the woods, personal wards reinforced. By the time he reached the scrubby woods, he'd dropped the overall straps off his shoulders and pulled off the borrowed shirt. By the time he'd taken full cover, he was ready to step out of the overalls.

Another step beyond that and he was jaguar, pacing this back perimeter of the ranch, scenting air…hunting from afar.

And then he knew. Moments before they strolled into the ranch yard, so terribly out of place with their designer suits and slicked-back hair and kohl-lined eyes, their vehicle just out of sight to make for this more dramatic entrance, he knew they were coming.

And he knew who they were.

Meghan! He expected nothing, got nothing, tried it again anyway. *He'd* been the one to tell her it was safe, to give her the room to experiment with her personal boundaries. *Meghan, let me in!*

For the wards were only designed to stop incantations and Core chantings. Physical trespassers might feel unwelcome and uncomfortable, but the Core was well used to that.

Especially their current *drozhar,* Fabron Gausto. Younger brother, *surviving* brother, to Tiberon.

A man with a grudge.

Dolan's flank twitched in memory.

Meghan, beware…

I can do it.

She could keep Dolan out, keep herself in. And that meant everything.

It meant she could decide what she wanted to do, and not simply be swept along in it. She could allow their connection and everything that came with it…

Or not.

And also it meant she could finally, clearly perceive

that the constant, nagging tug of awareness had nothing to do with Dolan at all.

She sat atop Luka high on the rugged terrain of the sky mountain, here where the snowmelt still trickled down in streams and the air felt noticeably crisp—just as Encontrados itself sat cool in the hills compared to the lower desert. Here, she was on national forest lands, riding narrow trails better meant for muleys and big horn sheep; the ranch land lay below her. The ranch itself had become a point of awareness…one so familiar she thought perhaps she'd always felt it and just never known. Down below and off to the west, it overlapped with the beguiling, enticing *want* that was Dolan.

And then, to the east, not nearly as far away…the *come to me, come to me* she'd been feeling since she and Dolan had made love in the wild night. The quiet siren call she had erroneously attributed to Dolan himself, but now suspected came from the old homestead.

Time to find out. She turned back down the hill. Luka mouthed the bit as he realized they were not, in fact, headed home, and then stretched his neck into the long rein she offered him, balancing his way down the slope with crouching quarters, controlled slippage and precise placement of his feet. Meghan moved with him, staying out of his way more than anything else…letting her thoughts stay in that place where she could feel what the land said to her.

Soon enough they hit the nearly flat feeder trail, the one running around the slope. She nudged Luka into a ground-eating trot, posting in perfect, unthinking rhythm. It wasn't so very long before she drew him to a stop in the old clearing—and for the first time, she slipped into ward view to see it with new eyes. Luka shifted beneath her and perked his ears in the direction of the stream, taking first one illicit step and then, when she didn't stop him, another.

Meghan sat on him in wonderment, watching ward lines slip past, watching them shift aside and then glide right over Luka's head, his neck, her own shoulders—caressing and welcoming, not warning. *Home,* they said to her. *Home, home, home.* She thought she heard her mother's voice; she thought she felt her mother's hand on her hair, brushing aside the inevitable strands escaped from her ponytail and hat. Luka eased through a stand of ponderosas to the nearly vertical stream sheening down through a minor earth crack, and found a slight dip from which he could drink his fill. There, Meghan dropped lightly out of the saddle, mixing worldview and ward view and reaching out to stroke one of the old lines, hunting her mother's touch again.

Welcome, welcome, welcome, the ward whispered in her mind. *Finally, finally, finally.*

And then there was that tug, now back behind her, squarely in the homestead they'd passed, *Find me, find me, find me...*

She tugged Luka away from the water, her hands familiar on the lead rope looped around his neck. She loosened its knot, made sure the rope was still securely clipped to his bridle-halter headgear and tied him off to a tree—all in a trancelike state, the whispers of the wards in her mind, the prodigal daughter called back to home...

An instant of regret intruded, that Dolan was not here to see this, to share it with her. But only an instant, because this was *her* past, not a Sentinel moment. This was *her* legacy, a secluded gift from her mother, just waiting for her skills to grow enough to perceive it. For the moment, Meghan ignored the implications—that her mother had known how deep Meghan's skills would run when initiated. That she'd even expected the initiation to happen…which meant she hadn't expected the Sentinels to cut Meghan off so completely.

She could regret that she hadn't found the truth of this place sooner. She couldn't regret her isolation from the Sentinels. Not from what she knew, or from what Dolan's memories had taught her.

She stood in the center of the old homestead yard and lifted her face to the sun, letting the sensations wash over her…soaking them in. For once she felt no pull from Dolan at all; the homestead overflowed her senses, blocking out everything from outside.

And then, slowly, the overwhelming nature of it subsided, the layered whispers retreating; Meghan again felt the tug that had brought her here. She closed her eyes, shifting entirely to ward view, and turned a slow circle, surprised at how easy it was to recognize the structures by their warding. There was the old homestead itself, with an odd dead space in the fireplace area, the house wards somewhat tattered by Dolan's original intrusion. A fine spiderweb of wards crisscrossed the roof, holding it together long past the time the old tiles should have cracked and fallen away. Off to the side, a gentle dome of protection hazed out the shape of the lean-to that had once been there. And set away from it all was a little house warded from black widows.

Meghan frowned, looking closer. A small anomaly flickered in and out of view, skidding away if she looked too closely. She had to ease up on it, soften her approach…almost let it come to her, waiting for the land to welcome her in that one final way. And then she could see it—a casual assortment of lines in a small package, looking careless but set with too much strength to be any such thing.

Slowly, Meghan approached the object. Only as an afterthought did she drop out of ward view—how natural it felt there already!—leaving only a faint overlay of the wards over her normal vision. The little house turned into a leaning shack of an outhouse, the door crooked but mostly closed—still latched, out of someone's long habit, long ago.

She put a hand on the door, hoped very hard that the black widows had indeed been kept away and tugged. It didn't come easily, at least not until she got it halfway open—at which point the top hinge broke and left the door canted permanently aside. Meghan winced. "Sorry," she said to no one in particular.

Inside, she found the classic one-seater, cracked and splintery. As a luxury, the sturdiest of the walls held a little shelf, and the shelf held a thick old catalog—

No. Surely not.

Meghan took a step back, switched into ward view, confirmed what she'd seen a moment earlier. All the times she'd been up here, all the times she'd idly studied the protections her mother had laid over this place, and she'd never been able to perceive what she did now…the subtlety of protections on this catalog. The steel silk strength of the wards involved.

Dolan hadn't seen it, either. Dolan had gone straight to the fireplace—to Margery's decoy.

Meghan looked again at the catalog. Old, yellowed, but otherwise fairly well preserved. A goodly number of the pages were torn in half, already used for the purpose of old catalogs everywhere, once upon a time. "Mama, you *didn't*."

But she already knew the answer to that. She already knew that Margery Lawrence damned well *had*.

That the *Liber Nex*, indestructible manuscript of power coveted by the Atrum Core and desperately sought by the Sentinels, sat in this old abandoned outhouse...disguised as toilet paper.

For some reason, Meghan thought of her mother's smile. Of the wicked glint often hiding behind it. Until now, she'd associated that glint with other memories of her mother—like when the hardware store owner thought he could sell a woman substandard wood without notice, and Margery let him load every piece of it before "discovering" she'd left her wallet at home. Or the pious preacher's wife who'd dropped by in ostensible friendliness to pass judgment on their single-parent home, and left with the bemused intent to call back for advice about certain personal matters. Or the—

All of them. Any of them. Meghan understood now that her mother knew how to play the game in both large and small scale. That her courage had been bigger than Meghan ever suspected. Her eyes stung with the unshed tears of it, the pride...the new recognition of what she'd lost.

But only for a moment—because then the fear hit.

She was looking at the *Liber Nex*.

It was the book her mother had died for; the book Dolan's brother had died for. The book that Dolan himself had nearly died for. What the hell did she think she was going to do with it? She couldn't even bring herself to touch it.

Leave it here. Turn around and ride away. Let Dolan know where it was…let Dolan handle it. What did Meghan know about games on this scale? She was happy enough with her own corner of the world, always had been. With her made family, her life's work. Dolan was the hero, the Sentinel…the one with the strength to deal with such things.

She took a step backward. She planted her heel, ready to pivot away.

And she hesitated.

What if in finding the thing, she'd inadvertently exposed it? At the least, given the Atrum Core a place to start looking?

She turned back to the outhouse, to the door that wouldn't ever go back in place just right—that would clearly look disturbed. She took a step toward it, and another, and by then she felt the book itself—the pure quagmire darkness of it, the tendrils of its hate, oozing out in response to scrutiny. An unfathomable and bottom-less swamp of evil, straining to touch her…staining the inner wards and making it instantly clear that the crys-talline steel of those wards was there to protect the world from the book as much as the book from the world.

And still she moved closer, until she stood on the threshold and could lean inside and reach for it—never intending to touch it, not even sure why—

Because it wants me to. She snatched her hand back, clutching it tight to herself. Revulsion touched her; she swallowed hard against nausea.

And yet again, the book spoke to her.

No. The *wards* spoke to her. The wards recognized her just as the land had recognized her. They knew her mother's daughter. *Finally, finally, finally,* they said, and then a wistful directive: *hide me, hide me.*

But Meghan knew what was really behind the subliminal impression they pressed upon her. *Hide me better than this. Or destroy me.*

Or you, too, could die trying.

Chapter 17

Dolan lurked at the edge of the woods, flattened to the ground in sinuous, contained fury. To involve civilians this way…to expose both the Core and the Sentinels…

Fabron Gausto, prince of the local Core sect, must be out of his mind. His people must be out of their minds to allow it…and in the monarchy-like structure of the Core, where court intrigue and power plays were a constant grumbling in the background, it would be astonishing if they allowed it for long.

Unless Gausto came back with the book. If he accomplished that, no one would challenge him. And if the book's powers were his to wield, anyone who challenged him would quickly die anyway.

Dolan gave a silent snarl, whiskers tilting back, ears flattened. By coming here, Gausto had raised the stakes beyond measure. He no longer dared back down. That

meant there was no telling how far he'd go, how many
more lines he'd cross. The trio had been spotted now. Not
because of Jenny's dog, who wisely slunk around the
edges of the yard, perceiving the taint of the inexplicable
on these men. No, Dolan was willing to bet that Jenny
had felt their arrival—that she'd alerted Anica, who now
came out to greet them. Her manner was friendly enough,
but Dolan saw the tension in her back, heard the hard note
in her voice. She might have no idea who these men
were, but she knew enough to want them gone.

"Can I help you?" she asked, and it really meant
please leave this place.

"We want Dolan Treviño," Gausto's sidekick said, not
even trying for pleasant. He and the other man were pure
muscle and more…. To be by Gausto's side, they were
whip-smart, accomplished with amulet and wet work both.

Anica shook her head. "He's not one of our volunteers," she said, admirably evasive. "Meghan might
know who you mean. If you leave a number, I'll have
her call you."

Gausto said, "Meghan Lawrence," drawing the words
out as if he were trying them on for size—and his tight
smile said he liked the feel of them.

Anica took a step back, and even from his hiding
place, Dolan could see her giving him the wary eye.
Good for her. "I'm sorry," she said. "We're a working
ranch, and this is a heavily scheduled afternoon. If you
leave your number, I'll have Meghan—"

The sidekick gave no warning. He snatched Anica's
upper arm in a movement so fast it blurred even to
Dolan's eyes; he frowned, tail twitching, ears still flat,
snarl still silent. The Core members were as human as

anything else. Such preternatural speed was not theirs to command. Not normally. Not when it was the very physical dominance of the Sentinels that inspired the Core's attempts to dominate them. "Treviño," the man said, his voice a malignant warning. Dolan dug his claws into earth, holding himself there by dint of will—it would do none of them any good if he flung himself into the hands of the Atrum Core, leaving Meghan unprotected. Leaving this ranch and its people unprotected beyond the moment.

"Asshole," Anica snapped. "Let go of me. You think someone's not dialing 911 right now?"

The man backhanded her—oh so casual, and yet with the force to send her spinning away and down. The other sidekick looked around the yard, raising his voice to carry. "Treviño!"

And Dolan flexed his claws, holding himself. *Not yet. It hasn't come to that.* Not with the Sentinel team delayed who knew how damned long, leaving Meghan on her own without Dolan. *Not yet.* He had to wait… wait until there was nothing else for it….

With typically abysmal timing, a deep ping rang in his head—a query from brevis regional, a wordless *what's happening?* He sent them his strongest possible message, in terms they couldn't misinterpret. *Fuck you,* he snarled back at Carter, snug and happy in Tucson, withholding the help they needed. The words might not make it through…the meaning behind them would. Dolan's fury that he had been hung out to dry, that civilians had been left exposed. *Carter, damn you,* do *something about this.*

It had to be Carter. The old man hadn't emerged from

his cave for such day-to-day matters as this for nearly a year now. Had become so ineffective that someone beneath him had leaked *Liber Nex* intel to the Core in the first place.

Anica climbed back to her feet—and kept her distance. She visibly fought and lost the impulse to look around—looking for *him*. Hiding in the brush...*and how is that different from brevis?*

No. Not yet. Not quite yet—

"Hey!" A male voice, offended and protective and a little hot. Dolan winced, sinking down against the earth. Damn, damn, damn. The farrier jogged out of the barn with long, heavy hoof nippers held like a weapon; Jenny ran out after him, one arm outstretched as if to stop him, but not nearly fast enough to do it. "Whatever welcome you had is gone, fellas."

Not so close—! Dolan rose a few inches, restrained himself. Reached for Meghan...found her unapproachable—no longer closing him out, but simply so full there was no room for him. *What the hell?* Another impulse tore at him—to go find her. She was all that mattered. She could still find the book. She could still weave this land back together. No one but Meghan...

And she had no warning. Not yet.

"We've called the sheriff's office," the farrier said, standing uneasily between Anica and the men. "You'd best leave before they get here."

But they ignored him. They didn't so much as glance at him. They brushed past him to the center of the yard as Anica, fear on her face, slowly backed toward the barn, not daring to take her eyes from them. She saw something in them that the farrier hadn't or couldn't—

and she cried out in warning as he stalked up to the trio, reaching out—

One of the sidekicks turned, spoke a word, thrust out his hand. Nothing more than that.

The farrier crumpled. Dolan felt it clear and sharp and piercing as the man died. No fuss, no muss. Dead.

What the hell? The wards should have stopped any object of power—and these men had no power of their own, no way to draw on this earth. Just as the Core shouldn't have been able to find him at the old home-stead....

Jenny cried out and ran from the barn—Anica inter-cepted her, dragging her back to shelter. And this time when Carter pinged him in a more demanding, more personalized repetition of the first call, Dolan dropped the attitude, he dropped the waiting curse and he sent back the purest, strongest impression of alarm he could muster. The purest cry for help.

For if the Core could kill with a touch, this was suddenly about so much more than Dolan or Meghan or this ranch. This was the Core gone amok—changing thousands of years of clandestine push-and-shove into outright war.

Dead, while I hide in the woods....

And then the man who'd killed the farrier faltered. A look of surprise crossed his face as he went to his knees; he said, *"Drozhar—"* and quite neatly pitched onto his face.

Gausto did not appear to take notice. He stopped in the center of the yard, surveying it.

But Dolan took close notice. Only two of them now. He had personal wards; they could not find him. They couldn't know for certain he was here. They might look, but they would tire…they would drop their guard. Only two of them. He could end this right here and now—

"Dolan Treviño," Gausto said, a stage voice for the benefit of everyone else on the ranch—a ranch come to a standstill, with someone's soft sobbing in the background and a hushed, urgent exchange in the barn doorway, Anica and Jenny holding back a young man whose face twisted with grief and anger.

Gausto lifted one fisted hand and opened it—a tiny vial, almost invisible except for the wink of it in the sun. "Dolan Treviño, murderer! The time has come to pay for your crimes." He closed his fingers back around the vial and admitted, much more conversationally, "Of course, it is a convenient thing, indeed, that we can also follow your trail to the *Liber Nex.*"

Not yet, you can't. And not ever, if Dolan could get there first.

But that meant walking away from these people under siege to finish the job for which he'd come. For the first time, he wasn't sure he could do that.

Gausto gave the vial a little toss. "Do you think I'm out here talking to myself?" He handed the vial over to his remaining sidekick, who took it with a certain distinct, stolid reluctance. The man murmured a few words, just enough to shift his lips; his hand tightened around the vial.

Dolan grunted with the sudden pain across his flank. Remembered pain, come alive again. Black, dappled jaguar skin twitched in response, involuntary and unwanted.

Tiberon Gausto, sharp scalpel smeared with blood. Looming. Smug. Certain of his control and his victory.

Just a little sooner than he should have been.

Except now Dolan wondered if he'd been a little too certain of his own escape. It had been years—his capture while in search of revenge, his revenge while captured. His apparent escape.

All the trouble he'd caused between then and now, and they'd been biding their time?

Or maybe they just now had the tools to deal with him.

Gausto nodded at the man, who muttered more words yet—and Dolan snarled silently at the tug of them, at the renewed pain. Gausto looked into the brush woods, his gaze unerringly accurate. "Come out," he said. "I can find you wherever you go. If you leave, you sacrifice these people for nothing."

No. Not even with the *Liber Nex* at stake, with Meghan at stake.

Dolan padded out into the bright sunshine of the day, just as he was—sleek and dark and deadly. Anica and Jenny already knew…and now the others would understand, too. They'd know to stay out of this battle, that it was far beyond their influence. That they could only die, as the farrier had died.

And the jaguar would remind Gausto that walking out into the open was far from giving up.

"Very showy," Gausto said. "Now be respectful, and dress yourself for polite company."

Dolan offered nothing but a silent snarl, bright whiskers tipping back. He circled Gausto, lowering himself into a slink to make his intentions clear. *Stalking his prey.* He smelled bright blood and didn't understand it, ignored it.

Gausto nodded at his companion. The man's reluctance broke through to the surface, coming out in wary eyes, the infinitesimal shake of his head. Abruptly, Dolan understood: the Core's unexpected new abilities came with a price. With one man dead, this man, feeling *something,* was unwilling to risk more.

Except that Gausto smiled tightly and said, "Do it. Bring him out."

Big and brawny, muscled by exercise and drugs both, the man nonetheless had to steady his trembling hand with the other, clasping his wrist as his knuckles whitened. He went gray around the lips and Dolan, stalking them both, at first felt nothing.

And then the pain ripped down his side, striking deep with remembered pain as well injury anew. He snarled again, no longer soundless, as his back leg collapsed beneath him, losing strength with the shock of—

Again. And again. And *Meghan, dammit, let me in, let me warn you,* and Dolan suddenly twisted right out of the jaguar and back to his human self—still graceful in movement, still powerful in intent, straightening to stand against the pain while the hot sun beat against hot blood, sheening down his bare torso to obscure the deep stripes of opened scars beneath. From the barn came exclamations in a teen's breaking voice; a horse called out.

Gausto's sidekick wavered, staggering slightly. Gausto took the vial from him, prying it brusquely from his hand; Dolan found himself still on the prowl, still circling the men—and found his gaze drawn to the vial. He slipped into ward view and saw...

Nothing. Nothing around the vial, nothing lingering around the man. No wonder they'd come right through the wards with this new power, flinging death around

Encontrados. There'd been nothing to detect, nothing to stop. And no wonder they'd found him at the old homestead. This was no ordinary object of power, no predictable storage vessel. This was—

"Your blood," Gausto said.

Dolan flicked his gaze up to Gausto's, as if he could find answers there. Power drawn from blood? It was a myth left undisturbed, condemned as too heinous even for the Core's power-driven goals.

A myth.

But his flank ran red, old wounds burning with more than just the slice of skin.

"We found some intriguing new toys while looking for the *Liber Nex,*" Gausto said. His sidekick stepped back, a muscleman trying for the unaccustomed—to be as unobtrusive as possible. To fade so thoroughly that Gausto wouldn't think to thrust that vial back into his hand. "Pretty little things, indeed."

Dolan gave the man on the ground a pointed look. "Those *things* obviously come with a price."

"His own clumsiness." Gausto shrugged. "He lacked control. And, as you've seen, it's so much easier when one has a sample of the intended victim's blood."

Dolan would have snarled, if he'd had the right body. He almost did it anyway—nostrils flaring, a twitch of his cheek—but clenched his jaw around it and swallowed it down. *"Victim,"* he said, disdain for the blithe assumption. "Your brother made that same mistake."

Gausto's olive skin went ruddy, his slicked-back hair emphasizing the angry distortion of his features. "My brother didn't have *this.*" He clenched his fist a little tighter. "With *this,* you have no chance. And your blood is going to run thick, indeed, before the end of this day. We have questions we'd like answered. It's just a shame we seem to have missed the little Lawrence bitch, or we'd have answers already." He slanted a knowing look at Dolan. "*You* should have those answers by now, Treviño. It's not like you to go soft on a mission."

No. It's not. But the realization didn't bother him. "I'm good with that," he said, gave it another moment and nodded. "I'm damned good with that." For Meghan, it seemed right. *Was* right.

"Then you'll be content when you die," Gausto said dryly.

Dolan only growled. Blood power or not—

The sidekick cleared his throat. *"Drozhar."* Respectful but insistent, a man with something important to say. *News.* Dolan gave him a narrow-eyed look. The wards should have stopped any direct communication—and the Core had even fewer tools than the Sentinels when it came to distance contacts.

But when Gausto glanced aside, the man held up the BlackBerry he'd had tucked away. "They've found her. They're in position to acquire."

Gausto looked purely annoyed. "We have no further need of Treviño, then."

But the exchange told Dolan more than they'd ever intended. They had Meghan in their sights, but they didn't have her *yet.* And the annoyance…that meant Gausto's little trip to this ranch hadn't been sanctioned—that he couldn't finish this the way he'd prefer. It meant Gausto had come here on his own, flinging around forbidden power, revealing Core secrets. He'd been charged to find the *Liber Nex,* not to play revenge games while he was at it. Possibly he'd even been warned against such distractions.

For the Gausto family did like their games.

"Tell them to assess the best opportunity and take her," Gausto said—and then glanced at Dolan. "Tell them not to put so much as a scratch on her. That privilege will be mine."

Dolan stiffened. *"Son of a—"*

Gausto smiled. "I see that you understand. I hope you'll consider those to be worthy dying thoughts."

Meghan needed protection. The Sentinels—they needed to know about this new manipulation of power, that which they now faced in the field. And if the Core got their hands on the *Liber Nex*...

Screw dying. Dolan had things to do.

He dropped into hunter mode—changing nothing but attitude, barely shifting his stance—but Gausto saw it. His bodyguard sidekick saw it, hastily stuffing away the BlackBerry in search of his gun. But the forbidden workings had drained him, and he fumbled—

And by then Dolan was upon him, ripping the half-aimed semiautomatic out of his hand and using it to bash up under the man's chin. No finesse, just power and speed against an opponent who hadn't stood a chance of facing the jaguar within Dolan.

But as the man went down, Dolan followed. Agony doubled him over. Grit shifted beneath his hands, beneath his knees; his body clenched, banded in pain and fighting to breath. Only as his vision grayed did he finally gasp air into his burning lungs. Just that fast, a pointed boot in his ribs drove that precious air out in a grunt; he rolled away from the blow, grinding grit into the stigmata of old wounds. A looming shadow told him that Gausto had followed.

Damned well not gonna happen— Dolan barely made it to his feet, a low crouch from which he launched himself with a jaguar's wiry strength—straight into the arc of another kick, one he took in the junction of crossed wrists to flip Gausto over on his back. Dolan threw himself down on the man, jamming his forearm over Gausto's throat and fumbling inside that expensive suit coat for the baby semiautomatic lurking there. Finding it, Dolan flung the gun aside—far aside.

He sat back on his heels as Gausto scrabbled away, hunting the pistol—in no great danger of finding it, with Anica's hand already closing around it. He wiped dirt from his chest, winced as his hand crossed the open stripes of wounds and spat grit as he climbed to his feet. "We'll see who reaches her first," he said, and turned away.

He'd half expected it; it hit him no less hard for that. The blood power washed over him, wringing out a deep groan; the knee on his weak side buckled. But he caught himself, and he whirled around...glaring at Gausto's fisted hand, knowing the vial rested within. He said, "Two choices. I can come and get it, or you can let me walk away." He lowered his voice. "Do you think you can take me out before I reach you? Do you think you can do it without killing yourself?"

Gausto looked to his men—a quick, reflexive glance, his mouth open as if he might actually command a dead man to act, or an unconscious man to give up the rest of his life.

"You shouldn't have played with me," Dolan said. "You used them up."

He saw the reality of the situation reflected on Gausto's face—the gun in Anica's hands, one man dead, the other unconscious. But even then, defeat was no part of the man's posture.

Dolan knew why. He lifted his own gaze to Anica, meeting her gaze across the yard. "Let them go," he told her. He didn't even need to see Anica's surprise turn to stubbornness—and he didn't blame her. But they could do nothing with Core prisoners. "If you turn him over to the cops, the Core will come for everyone here."

Understanding wilted her. Only for an instant, and then her mouth tightened and her gaze narrowed. "All right, then. We'll stay here in the barn until they're gone. As long as they leave us be."

Dolan eyed Gausto, waiting for the acknowledgment that would free him to leave. The nod that meant Gausto accepted the terms, and would live up to the Core's own odd honor over standoff deals struck when it meant avoiding official notice. He spat again, discovered that somewhere along the way he had acquired a fat lip.

But the nod didn't come.

Dolan tilted his head, eyeing the sullen inflexibility of this man. "I'll do it," he said softly. "We'll both die. You know that."

Fury burned behind Gausto's dark expression. "Then I'll wait for the next time."

Dolan knew that fury…he felt it. His voice barely made it to a whisper. "Yeah. Next time."

And he took the jaguar and bounded away, dripping blood and ire in equal measure—already reaching for Meghan, calling out in spite of the her absence, her lack of response.

'Ware, Meghan! The Core is here.
Nothing.
He'd just have to find her in time.

Chapter 18

Meghan found herself mounted upon Luka, moving out at a pace brisk and snorty enough to suggest that if Luka had his way, they'd be moving along even faster. *Where—?*

For a moment she was mired in utter disorientation, not sure where they were or how they'd gotten here. How *she'd* gotten here. The pines surrounded her without context; she knew she was high above the ranch, but had no idea where. She'd been plunked onto a hillside on the back of her horse and—

Her fingers tightened around the reins, stopping Luka; she squeezed her eyes closed, searching for some distinct moment to pin to her *now,* to rebuild the past hours. And, without thinking, she reached out for an anchor. *Dolan.*

Her stomach turned cold and heavy. There was no

response from Dolan…there was no echo of her own thoughts. *Dolan, are you there?* But the words thudded dully within her own mind, going nowhere.

On impulse, she opened herself to ward view.

Nothing.

What the hell had happened?

Luka swung his head around, reaching back to nibble in question at her foot, equal parts impatience and concern. She patted him, opening her eyes to search the trail. All she needed was a familiar rock, a downed tree, an unusual twist in the trail…then she'd know where she was. It wasn't a matter of getting home—Luka would take her there without hesitation. It was a matter of knowing what had happened, these past hours.

Such things were no longer to be taken for granted. Whatever she'd been up to, she knew damned well it wasn't a simple trail ride in the high pines.

Her gaze fell upon a split pine; relief washed over her. As fast as that, the terrain fell into place, resolving into familiarity. She knew where she was; she knew what lay ahead—and what lay behind.

The old homestead.

Wards and buildings and the book, the book, the book—

She'd found it.

She'd found the book.

Fully initiated, barely trained but brimming with natural talent, she'd finally been prepared to hear its wards. But in finding it, she'd made a trail for others.

So she'd had to re-ward the thing.

For now, having touched it, she understood. She knew why Dolan had been so single-minded about his pursuit of this manuscript, and why her mother had been willing to sacrifice her life to hide it. The faint, lingering taste of its howling darkness still clung to her, washing through her in a wave of vertigo. She clutched the saddle while Luka shifted uneasily beneath her.

The *Liber Nex,* disguised as an outhouse accessory. And she'd left it there. There was no fixing the door, so she'd used the facilities, creating a reason for the disturbance. And then she'd wrapped her awareness around her mother's wards and painted her own over them, tapping the earth for unfettered, unfiltered power. She'd felt the difference in what she was doing, not understanding it until too late—until she'd given those wards something of herself, something that wrenched free from deep within, settling into the wards with a slight sizzle.

Power and swells of emotion and a startling shock of pain and—

And here she was. Finally coming back to herself in the wake of it—having tapped herself dry. For good?

The doubt came with sudden panic. Never to feel Dolan's presence again? Never to hear his silent words?

She must have clenched her body; Luka gave a startled grunt and lifted both front feet off the ground, valiantly trying to respond to a mishmash of conflicting signals. "Shh," she told him. "I'm sorry." And she let him move forward rather than compound his frustration. She knew where she was now. She knew where she'd been.

She wasn't at all sure where she was going.

After a moment, she worked up the nerve to try ward view again. Tentative, this time—no demand to it. All gentle and allowing.

She almost sobbed in relief when the faintest haze of it overlaid her normal vision. Maybe she'd just over-reached herself...stunned herself with the power she'd wielded. It's not as though she truly knew what she was doing. Maybe it would come back....

"Whoa," she said out loud, which Luka quite rightly ignored because her body language said *keep going*. "Listen to my brain, Luka. What am I even thinking? I've had a handful of days with my mother's Sentinel toys, and suddenly I can't live without them?" A handful of days with Dolan's fierce, pushy, intense presence, and suddenly she couldn't live without it?

From deep within came an unexpected answer, as fierce as anything Dolan had ever said to her. *No. I can't*.

She dropped the reins over Luka's crested neck, pulling up the hem of her shirt to wipe her face. Tears she hadn't expected, sweat she'd worked up while also working wards. "Okay, buddy," she said to him. "Let's get home, then."

Whether she used mundane words or regained her connection to Dolan, she had a lot to tell him. *Oh, by the way...found the book thingy. It's disguised as toilet paper. You want it?*

And then the Core would have no reason to dog her, and she could settle down to integrating her new aware-ness with her old life. And Dolan...

Just because she suddenly knew she couldn't live without his touch in her life didn't mean he felt the same. Or that he'd stay once he had the book.

"Sucks," she muttered to Luka, who shifted his weight back to handle the steep, rocky trail shunt before them, the one that would dump them back on a main trail. She gave him free rein as he snorted his opinion of such steepness, and they moved out into the open, a bare patch with pines above and gnarled cedars and junipers cropping up below. They balanced in tandem, Luka tucked together like a cat, Meghan leaning back over his quarters and swaying with his movement, never interfering with his efforts.

Until he flung his head up, stopping short to sit back on his haunches so hard, so steep, that Meghan's stirrups touched the ground. "You're fine," she told him, soothing him...not at all sure she'd convinced either him or herself. For Luka didn't spook at the trivial. He barely spooked at the significant. But now...

He was spooked. Ready to fling himself into stupidity.

With care, without pushing, she eased into ward view. *Yes.* Not yet normal, but stronger. But it showed her nothing. The wards in this area were nothing more than scattered lines of awareness, sensitive only to intruding energies. So she came out of it, patted Luka's neck and encouraged him to move forward.

Even as he responded, she tried one more time, reaching out to Dolan. Gently...not pushing it. A whisper, just looking for that connection.

Meghan.

She gasped with relief, barely able to take the emotions behind his single word of response. *Fear and exhaustion and pain...* She shot back a quick, hard query—felt it hit dead air, and forced herself to take a breath and go gently with it. *What's wrong?*

The Core, he said—and that was all for a long moment, until even more faintly he added, *Coming....*

The Core. Meghan lost the feel of him, washed away by her pulse of fear. *The Core is here.*

And Dolan was coming. But not with strength—with determination alone. She'd heard that much.

Luka's neck jerked up; his nose flipped against the reins. Still angled steeply down the rocky slope, he somehow lifted himself up—an impossible rear under an impossible situation. Meghan cried out in futile protest as the footing skittered out from beneath him; he fell backward and sideways, front legs flailing as the bulk of his body rolled onto Meghan's leg.

Flesh ground into rock with shocking clarity as Meghan grabbed mane. If she could stay with him…if she could stay on him…she could still get home, no matter her leg—

But Luka made no attempt to rise. No panicked scramble, no shuddering heave. He lay half on her, half off, his front legs propped against the hill and trembling hard.

Meghan! Dolan came stronger now, his fears more clear. She understood then that it had never been fear for himself; it had been fear for her. *Of this.*

"Luka," she crooned, and it came out dry and croaky. She swallowed, tried again—finding enough strength in jellied limbs to tap his side with her free leg, her complete focus on his neck and ears and the back of his head, reading his frozen uncertainty. "Come on, son. Let's go. Let's go home."

But Luka flung his head up and lurched, shifting over her trapped leg so she cried out even though it didn't hurt yet—didn't yet feel anything at all.

Hands closed around his reins beneath the bit, effectively capturing his head. And Meghan, her vision still filled with Luka's neck and head and the blur of shock, abruptly realized that they were not alone.

Meghan! Dolan's cry held an anguish she'd never heard before, reached out and captured her and drew her into his world for that instant—the burning pain of his flank, the smell of blood, the strain of powerful muscles never meant for endurance charging endlessly uphill. Coil and lunge, giant paws sinking into thin soil, skidding off bare rock, coil and lunge and—

Too late.

They knew it—as one, they knew it. *The book!* she told him, as hands reached for her. She showed it to him. She *shoved* it at him. She gave him her understanding of the stakes, of the absolute need to keep the manuscript from the Core. And she told him, *Go save it.*

Not me, she didn't add. She didn't have to.

And then she felt what it was like when his spirit wrenched, his heart torn—his utter denial to what had in truth already happened. Utter determination to stop it from completion. *Coming…I'm coming for you….* Coil and lunge, lungs burning, legs heavy, muscles twitching—

But she was already gone.

Chapter 19

Dolan angled upward, bypassing the switchback trails in favor of barging straight up the mountain—leaping over the unexpected earth cracks, twisting around jutting stone, ducking the sharp, jabbing lower limbs from the junipers. Already drained by ancient and forbidden blood workings, still bleeding, he charged upward, hearing her voice, closing on her, hearing her cry of shock and fear echo down along the slopes. *Hold them off, Meghan, just one more moment, just one more breath—*

But Meghan never had a chance. He hadn't warned her, hadn't expected the Core to break so many rules of conflict in one fell swoop, hadn't known they'd already embraced powers forbidden these long millennia—powers that would prepare them perfectly to capitalize on the *Liber Nex* if they stole it. No learning curve, no fumbling through the early process. If they acquired the manuscript, they'd come out running. And they'd already crossed the moral line that would free them to do it.

They'd come a long way from *protecting the world* from the preternaturally capable Sentinels.

Dolan hit the main trail, swerved to follow it. Easy running—but he stumbled anyway, flanks heaving. He barely heard the thunder of hooves coming his way, had only enough time to spot a blur of white and pounding hoof—he flattened himself against the trail as Luka rounded the corner at a panicked gallop, every bit as startled to find a huge black jaguar in his path as Dolan was to be there. Dolan snarled a warning; Luka flung himself into a mighty leap, landing in an awkward flurry of missteps and almost going down. He regained his feet and his purpose and charged onward—homeward.

Dolan pushed back into a heavy trot. He emerged into the open, found the trail skirting the base of a steep slope. Here, they'd grabbed her. *God, Meghan!* Here, their scent mingled strongly with hers. *I'm here for you, Meghan!*

He found the sign where Luka had gone down, great chunks of dirt and rock displaced on the trail, white horse hair and smudged blood on rock. He found the scent pools where the men had waited, felt the lingering taint of Core amulets. Plain old amulet-based incantations, mild enough to slip through the thin mountain wards. A glint of metal, a whiff of bitter herbs…he found it, jammed in among the stones where Luka had gone down.

And now, drifting in on the breeze, came the acrid scent of engine exhaust.

Meghan?

Silence. Dead, heavy silence.

But he hadn't expected otherwise. She'd barely been

able to reach him in the first place, her natural resources drained dry. She'd been hurt—he'd felt it happen. And yet still he'd hoped—

She could be passed out. She could be drugged. She could have an amulet hung around her neck, isolating her.

Give her time.

She had the strength to overcome any Core nullification amulet…if she could only regain her strength.

Dolan's legs quite abruptly went out from under him; he sprawled in the dust, panting heavily, half closing his eyes against the sun. Fatigue warred against the impulse to follow the ATVs against the knowledge that he had to let brevis know against…

The book.

She'd found it.

Dolan drifted away from the distractions of the outer world—the stripes of pain down his side, dull agony in abused limbs. Blood trembled on his whiskers; he licked it away, not sure of its source. With the tang of it on his tongue and in his nose, he focused on what she'd sent to him before she went silent.

The *Liber Nex*.

She'd found it. She understood. She'd protected it the best she could. And there, embedded in that information, was the heart of Meghan. The demand that he find the book, that he protect it, that he keep it from the Core. That he do so *before* trying to find her.

And then another memory pounced, just as clear and just as stabbing. *Tell them not to put a scratch on her,* Gausto had said, his intent obvious in his voice and words.

He'd take Meghan for his own. He'd do whatever he wanted with her…and to her.

And the Gausto boys had a bad habit of killing their pets.

Unless the pet kills you first. Dolan had done that, and now Meghan would pay for it. Meghan would be Gausto's revenge, completely apart from whatever happened with the *Liber Nex*.

Dolan opened his eyes, staring down the trail, absorbing the lingering scent. Two men on foot, Meghan in the air…the ATV already long out of reach, carrying her away.

Save Meghan.

Save the book.

Save—

Dolan snarled, a mournful and gut-wrenching sound. He dragged himself to his feet and headed up the hill to the old homestead.

Meghan woke in the back of a moving car, quite instantly aware that she'd fainted upon being lifted to a man's broad and muscle-bound shoulders, but just as instantly aware that she'd had help to stay out of it so long. Something burned between her breasts—it felt like a last-ditch flare of power, a lightbulb filament glowing extra bright before it burned out. Even before she opened her eyes, she groped for it, her hands closing around a metal disk just warm enough to be uncomfortable.

Bigger hands closed over hers, pulling them away.

"Ah, leave her," someone muttered. "If she's awake, it's burnt. They should have sent us with stronger 'lets for this one." The car shifted around a sharp turn and Meghan grabbed the leather seat to keep herself in place; she opened her eyes to find scenery zooming past the window of the small SUV. They'd made some effort to arrange her securely on the backseat, a belt awkwardly crossed her hips; her leg stuck straight out on the seat, the swelling straining her jeans. The leg itself felt oddly, throbbingly numb; she had no idea what damage she'd taken. Gingerly, she wiggled her toes inside her riding sneaker. The movement sent shooting pains up her shin, but the toes complied.

In the front, the passenger twisted to look back at her, bracing himself against the middle console. Both men had obviously seen the same stylist—tailored suits, slicked-back hair and the faintest hint of kohl around their eyes. Both had an earring; both had olive skin and craggy features. A matching set.

She met the gaze of the one who looked back at her, found it cold but curious. Not much point in asking questions, then. Besides, she understood the situation. The Core had her. They'd somehow decided she was worth the effort when the Sentinels had not, and they thought they could get something from her.

Hell of it was, they were right.

Liber Nex.

Meghan held the man's gaze, found the now-cold metal on her chest and the line of thin chain that kept it there. Deliberately, distinctly, she closed her hand around the amulet and yanked it from her neck; the chain snapped with the satisfying sound of broken links. With as much disdain as possible, she dropped it to the carpeted floor.

The man smirked. "You'll see," he said, and turned his back to her.

Not if I can help it. Not if Dolan *can help it.*

Bold thoughts for a kidnapped woman trapped in a

speeding car toward the bitterest enemies she'd only just discovered. But Meghan clung to those thoughts—those hopes. She clung to the memory of Dolan, knowing she'd told him to deal with the book first and knowing he'd do it—knowing he had to. But still...

She closed her eyes and thought of Dolan.

There was no more run in Dolan. His flank had stopped bleeding, but it burned with an unnatural ferocity; he suspected that Gausto's insidious magic had left more of mark than it first seemed. He trotted onward with heavy steps and finally staggered down into a walk just outside the homestead grounds.

Here. The book was here. It had been here all along. He'd walked right past it, lured to the chimney dead space just as Margery Lawrence had intended. No sign of the special warding within had leaked through the leaning, twisted walls of the outhouse. No hint of the deception had slipped through—not to him, not to the Sentinels, not to the Core. His whiskers tilted in brief, dark amusement. He'd have to make sure Gausto knew what he'd missed.

The outhouse door tipped open now, the interior lit by the merciless high desert sun. Dolan kept to the short noon shadows of the yard, brushing up beneath the pines, panting heavily from exertion and pain. He circled around the old building, hunting any signs of what Margery had left...any signs of what Meghan had done.

Damn. Like mother, like daughter.

But Meghan shouldn't have been *that* good. Not yet.

Still, when he peered inside the outhouse, just as happy to stay in the jaguar for now, he discovered the old catalog she'd pictured for him. Tattered at the edges, pages brittle and yellowed. It reflected nothing of her; nothing of Margery. Slipping into ward view showed him nothing more than the faint haze of a vaguely protected object.

Gingerly, he reached for it—one giant paw wielded with precision, claws neatly tucked away. He hovered on the point of touching it, ears flattening in spite of himself—and then he felt the first wash of Meghan's touch, and he opened himself to it, and—

—appalled understanding and terror and have to stop them *and help me do this thing—*

And suddenly the wards were open to him, recognizing him, revealing their inner works and their incredible strength, finesse bound in thick ethereal steel. The impact of it reeled him; the implications of it sent him staggering back. *Meghan, what did you do?*

He must have cried it out loud, for he heard her faint response, only the echo of a whisper over distance. *Dolan?*

Meghan! What were you thinking? Horror painted his inner landscape, splashing out to his thoughts.

Meghan's wordless shock of response made him realize his carelessness—and made him realize she hadn't known. Hadn't known her own strength, hadn't realized what desperation had driven her to do.

And it was his own fault. There was no way she should have been faced with this book alone, no way she should have been left to fend for herself with such raw but potent skills.

No, she said, much more strongly now. He could even tell she was in a vehicle; he could tell that her leg had been hurt but not broken, that she was otherwise unharmed. *You couldn't have known I'd find the thing. If I'd told you what I felt…* She hesitated, gave a mental shake of her head. *No. I didn't know, either. I kept thinking it was you, my awareness of you. Only when I got far enough away—*

Meghan— He sounded broken even to his own mind, and struggled to keep his thoughts orderly—to protect her from the despair of them. *I can't do anything with this book. No one can. What you've done here…it's the* aeternus contego. *You're the only one who can release it, and until you do…*

Tell me, she demanded. No longer dazed, though still terribly frightened—still completely aware she was in the hands of the Core, speeding away from safety. *There's something you're not—*

And then she said, a heartbroken little sound, *Oh.*

The jaguar growled, a tiny yowl of sound, knowing she'd gleaned from his thoughts what he'd been trying not to say: that her death would also release the final lock on the wards.

Don't let them find out, he told her fiercely. *Whatever they do, don't let them know! You give them everything about me, you tell them your mother's life story—but you keep those wards to yourself! Keep the book to yourself!*

Or they'll kill you and come for it.

If I— She stopped, tried again. He felt her sway with the movement of the vehicle, knew she was on a paved but sharply winding road. She never quite finished that thought, the implication of it hanging as she went on. *If that happened, then the Sentinels could take the book. Hide it again, the way they were supposed to have done before. Then this would be over.*

No, Dolan said fiercely. *It wouldn't. Then I would have to live with it. Then I would have to live without you.*

His words rang between them for a moment, fully imbued with longing and despair…and the awareness that what lay between them wasn't anything he could walk away from, not ever. And then Meghan laughed inside, and he could feel the smile on her lips. *Finally figured that out, did you?*

Apparently so. Years of looking past human connections, of keeping the Sentinel mission so large in his mind as to make room for nothing else, so large he had to run rogue half the time to fill both needs and expectations…

Yes, he told her.

Yeah, she said, still smiling. *Me, too.* And then, *Oh—!* and a jolt of startled fear, the bruising grip of a cruel hand on her arm and *Dolan—!*

And she was gone.

Dolan snarled; he tore claws into ground and shredded caliche, lost in fury and grief. It didn't last long…he'd been drained before he started. So he stilled—and then he froze, a jaguar about to begin the hunt, his gaze riveted on what he could see of the book from this vantage point.

What if first impressions had been wrong? What if he'd made assumptions? What if Meghan's inexperience had left them an out, a way to crack those wards after all?

The jaguar had taken him, stalking the little building as if it were live prey. Dolan forced himself to straighten, to sit on alert with his tail wrapped around his body. Thinking. Considering. And this time when he moved, it was with casual assurance. Back to the book. Back to not quite touching the book.

Time to tell me your secrets, book. Time to let me in.

* * *

Let me in.

Impressions of Meghan flowed to him—more easily this time, when he knew what to look for. All the things he'd sensed of her the moment they'd met—the strength, the determination, the intent to do right by those around her. The deep love of her life, her land, her chosen family...the deep bitter grief and scars from the circumstances of her mother's death.

He'd read her from the outside in that first meeting, just like anyone would. Damned if he hadn't fallen just a little bit in love right that very moment.

And he'd thought he could just walk away. He'd thought he could pretend he hadn't been touched by all those things. Even after they'd shared memories...shared thoughts...shared bodies. He'd thought he could go on with the rebel's life he'd chosen all those years ago.

Damn, Treviño, way to be wrong.

But feeling all those things, absorbing them and reveling in them...he had no time for that. He pushed his way through that emotional cloud, fully immersed in ward view. The tight, thick steel webbing of the protection around the *Liber Nex* gleamed back at him, pulsing softly in response to his presence.

Aeternus contego. The Sentinels forbade such wards outside of personal items—and few personal items were so precious as to inspire them. Unbreakable, unviolable...

Or maybe not. A ward placed by a woman who didn't truly know how, and read by a man who'd only seen it done once before...maybe they still had a chance to get around it. And if he could secure the *Liber Nex* and get it to safekeeping, then he'd be completely free to find Meghan.

His physical body forgotten, Dolan reached for one of the ward lines. Not a plump, pulsing artery, but a line that lay quiescent and unreactive. He traced it; he found the connections and the root *ligo,* and he pondered it. Wards could be manipulated and moved aside; they could be dissolved, line by line. But the single most effective way to perceive the exact nature of the ward was to read the root of it, the keystone knot where a single tug in the right direction would release it and a tug in the wrong direction would only tighten it down. Releasing this fine secondary ward out of order would gain him nothing...but he might be able to discern a sense of the whole from here.

He hovered in close, hunting subtle clues, listening for the ward's purpose and quiet humming. Ah...this was the illusion. This one had been laid years earlier, by Margery Lawrence—woven and tied by a woman with experience and finesse. It had little awareness of the outer wards, the thick, angry and desperate lines— they'd swollen in response to his presence, but weren't sophisticated enough to trigger when they hadn't been directly challenged. He hadn't tried to pick up the book; he hadn't even tried to touch it.

And he couldn't. Could he? Could he resolve this standoff simply by relocating the thing, hiding it again? An old, misplaced catalog...it would do, for now.

He could take the safe way, or he could test the book. Touch it. Take the chance that it was all just that easy after all.

A sudden frisson of impatience ran through his physical body, drawing him back to it—weighing him down with fatigue, a sudden awareness of gravity pulling down on him and the earth pushing up at him. The sun had moved, the shadows around him significantly changed...his body stiffened. He drew back slightly, sneezed a tidy feline sneeze, and licked his whiskers down, staring at the ragged catalog before him. *How long have they had her now?*

He could go back in and try to read the wards, but they were clumsy, reactive weavings, set with passion rather than skill; he could tell little other than what they were *meant* to do...not if they'd actually accomplished it.

Or he could—

How long? Gausto could be torturing her already. Mind and body, making the puny scores across Dolan's flank seem as nothing. *How long has it been?*

Or he could—

Dolan slapped his flexed claws down on the book, and the world exploded.

They'd slipped another amulet over Meghan's head as soon as they realized she was in communication, damn them—but they didn't bother to blindfold her as they approached their destination.

As if I'm too stupid to figure out what that means. No incentive to cooperate, that's what. She'd get out of this if Dolan got her out. If the Sentinels got her out.

Yeah, right. The Sentinels who had abandoned her to this fate in the first place. So, if Dolan got her out.

For all of that, they were careful with her. They eased her out of the car into the brilliant sunshine under a classically beautiful blue desert sky, and they did what they could to protect her leg as it bloomed to shrieking life. They each put an arm over their shoulders and stood, walking her inside with her feet dangling just above the ground—rushing her through the gravel parking area and onto the flagstone walkway.

As if she didn't already know where she was. As if there were so many ranch-run bed-and-breakfasts in the vicinity of this crossroads town and grasslands that she didn't already know *exactly* where she was. The Sonoita Double B, a pricy private resort…and from the looks of the empty parking spaces and the utter lack of activity, the Core had it to themselves. Megan gave the property a desperate once-over—hunting the manager, hunting *anyone* among the guest lodges, the neatly trimmed xeriscaping, the cactus garden…she glanced at the road, a quarter mile away and it might as well have been a thousand with her feet not even on the ground.

One of the men made a sound of amusement at her futile efforts. They walked her swiftly to the main lodge, adobe and sprawling, luxurious with shaded alcoves and airy ceilings.

But she didn't think they'd take her into luxury, and they didn't. Right down to the basement they went, a hard-dug area still littered with the furnishings of what had once been a wine cellar for generations of wealthy Spanish landowners. Now it held a big worktable, and a cot with the look of the unused about it. Handcuffs waited on the dull green army blanket; off to the side stood a tall tray of medical instruments, a stainless steel bucket with a giant metal syringe the size of a rolling pin, a bright blue tarp still in its plastic package.

Meghan shivered. Maybe the instruments of her impending mistreatment were something she should have expected; maybe any Sentinel would have. Torture was certainly all the rage these days. But she hadn't grown up Sentinel—hadn't been offered that life, hadn't wanted it.

The two men paid no heed to her revulsion and—okay, face it, downright terror—depositing her on the cot with her leg stretched out. It still filled her jeans, swollen to shocking proportions. But the sight gave her a surprising hope; she associated such swelling with high-impact surface bruising. Maybe there'd been no serious damage after all…maybe she could force it to work, if she could only get it loosened up a little—

She suddenly realized there was a third person in the room. The two men stepped back to make room for him, and he moved forward to regard her with enough interest that she suddenly felt inadequate.

"I think you have the wrong person," she said. "I'm not as important as all this."

"You'd be surprised," he murmured. Like the others, his dark hair had been slicked back; a single diamond earring winked in his lobe and his olive-hued skin had a ruddier look, his eyes were more obviously kohled. His expensive suit was wrinkled, hanging on to the remnants of a dust bath; he'd clearly taken a tumble. When she looked harder, she found bruising on his throat, and the crisp white collar wasn't quite as crisp or white as those of his men. And the look in his eyes…a harder, colder expression—a certain obsession, a certain resentment. And something else, too—a hint of fear. Fear of what, she couldn't imagine, but…

He realized her scrutiny and irritably waved one of the men forward. "Secure her. And cut off her pant leg. She wasn't to be injured, I told you that."

Right. Gotta have me in one piece before you take me apart.

"The horse fell on her, *Drozhar*," the driver said in apology, quickly stepping forward to pull a plastic restraint cuff off the tray and bind Meghan's hands, pulling her back on the cot and then stretching her arms overhead to secure them to the cot frame. "We have treated her most carefully since then."

As if she could possibly feel more vulnerable, her body arching with the awkwardness of this position, her breasts and stomach exposed and chill in the basement air, one leg deadweight and the other…the only free limb she had.

Until the man cuffed it to the side of the cot.

Damn them anyway. *Dolan, come and find me, oh, please find me…*. Resentment warred with terror; she twisted away, naked, naked, naked even though she wasn't, and muttered an unkindness at them.

The *drozhar* looked down at her without concern. "Do you know why you're here?"

That took her back. She couldn't help but twist again, wishing she'd worn some big oversized T-shirt this morning instead of a snug ribbed tank. Wishing she'd worn a more substantial bra, so her nipples—tightened by cold, by fear—weren't quite so obvious. She lowered her voice, trying to hide her uncertainty. "You think I know something. You're wasting your time. The Sentinels never thought I was important enough to do anything but ignore, and they had the right idea." Already her arms ached.

"You're here because of Dolan."

She didn't understand it, but the cold burn of his

gaze told her it was true. The *drozhar* gave a little laugh, just as cold as his gaze. "He didn't tell you, did he? I keep special tabs on him. He led me right to you." He raked her with his gaze, spreading his hand over her belly in an oddly possessive gesture that Meghan found more disconcerting than anything he'd done yet. She stopped breathing, shrinking inwardly from him; his gaze shifting sharply to hers in a way that told her he'd noticed. "I found you because of him. And I took you because of him. Because of what you mean to him, as much as for what you know."

"I—I'm not sure I understand." *And I'm not sure I want to.*

"At first I meant him to die knowing he had condemned you by association. But he escaped, and now he will live knowing your death—the manner of your death—rests directly on his shoulders."

Her thoughts whirled, her brain unable to comprehend such malice—horrified at that thought that this man might yet get his hands on the *Liber Nex.* "Why?" she blurted. "How can you possibly hate him that much?"

His lips thinned; his nostrils flared. Not a handsome man, in the extremity of emotion. "He did this. He came sniffing around, years after his brother's death. We caught him, of course...but my brother...*underestimated* him. Now my brother is dead—and now, until I kill Treviño, I'll make him wish he was dead."

"But...you—" and there Meghan stopped, for she couldn't bring herself to speak so casually of men killing one another. All these years since her mother's death, and she'd still thought of the ambush as a horrible thing, an isolated thing. But this man…this man flung death around with a terrifying casualness.

"You truly aren't of the Sentinels, I see. Treviño would understand…he knows where he crossed the line. His brother's death wasn't personal; it was war. A quiet war, but war nonetheless. When Treviño came after us, he made it personal. It shouldn't have come to this. But Treviño doesn't have a habit of acquiring weaknesses. This is not a chance I would have passed up even did you not have information I want."

He doesn't know about the book, Meghan reminded herself. He doesn't know. He just suspects I might have an idea….

"I'm surprised," the *drozhar* said gently, spreading his fingers over her belly, pressing down slightly in threat, "that he didn't tell you. How negligent of him, to put you in such danger without informing you. Treviño is nothing if not aware of my interest in him." With his free hand, he withdrew a small, leather-bound notebook from his inside jacket pocket, and caressed it with his thumb.

Meghan looked at the tray with its instruments; she looked at the little book, blinking at the fine miasma around it, a dried blood veil that made her look away again. The *Liber Nex,* it seemed, was only the next step in the Core's use of ugly, tainted powers. She wondered how Dolan could have failed to warn her, could have failed to understand the target she'd become; she understood, suddenly, some of the memory flickers she'd seen. But she took a deep breath, hunting strength to put behind her words. "He probably didn't think you were important enough."

Score. His eyes grew colder; he removed his hand from her stomach and she suddenly breathed more easily. "It serves me well enough that you are your mother's daughter. Before you die, you'll tell me what you know of her last days. All of it."

Instruments of torture beside her...a book of dark powers in the hands of a cold, cruel man with a point to prove.

She had no doubt he was right.

Chapter 20

Searing red internal explosion and well, Dolan, you really screwed up this time and Meghan needs help and the book...the book...

Dolan started to awareness at the touch on his shoulder, ready to attack, teeth already bared in a snarl.

A human snarl.

That jolted him...he didn't remember shifting back. And it gave the man beside him enough time to say, "Lie still, Treviño."

The book. He'd touched the book, desperate to find a way around the wards. *Stupid, stupid.* And now he lay sprawled some distance from the outhouse, his human self very much battered, blood dried along his side...

How long? How many hours had Meghan been in Fabron Gausto's hands? He tried to ask; it came out as a grunt. *Who the hell are you?* came as an afterthought, and was enough to pry open his eyes. They wouldn't focus, but he could nonetheless see several figures moving in the background, and one woman standing in stillness between him and the outhouse, her posture one of intense concentration and alert attention.

The Sentinel team. *Finally.* If they'd only been here a few hours earlier...

But they hadn't been. And now, if they knew the *Liber Nex* sat just a few yards away, they'd spend all their time trying to break the wards and none of it looking for Meghan.

Light, impersonal hands went over his limbs, his bare torso. "You're a damned hell of a mess, Treviño," said the one who'd roused him.

"Carter?" Or at least, that's what he meant to say. It came out a gravelly croak, laced with astonishment even so.

"That's right." No mistaking that dry tone. "We'll lay a healing on you, but it'll take time to kick in. Most important thing is to get those wounds cleansed. They're... I've not encountered anything like them. *Tainted.* That position looks as uncomfortable as hell. Ready to sit up?"

Given the twisted way he'd landed and then apparently stiffened into place, Dolan was more than ready. He hadn't expected to need help; he hadn't expected the patient strength in Carter's assistance. He discovered he wasn't far from an old hitching post and leaned against it, gladly taking the water Carter crouched to offer him.

He wanted to gulp it down; he knew better. He took a few slow swallows and finally had enough presence of mind to glare at the man. "Where the hell have you been? Do you have any idea—"

"Some," Carter interrupted. He regarded Dolan with serious pale green eyes, arms loose and relaxed over his knees, his expression grim for a face that usually absorbed its emotions. Sable hoarfrost hair spoke of his timber wolf nature; so did the way he moved as he uncoiled to look out over the homestead, his attention on the woman who still stood, alert, eyes closed…hunting. "We trailed you in from the ranch, once we got past that Anica woman. Messy there, very messy—Core sign everywhere, none of it making much sense. The wards…those are fresh, damned well done. We found the amulet on the trail…followed you here. You want to fill us in?"

Cut to the chase. "Meghan found the book. But they took her before she could show me." Well, that was truth enough, literally speaking. Carter took it in and swallowed it, his eyes closing as the implications of it hit home.

The Core had the only person who knew where the book was.

He turned to the woman as three other team members moved back into the yard. "Lyn," Carter said, and when she looked at him, a tip of his head was enough to call her over. "This is Lyn Maines. She's our tracker."

Not a big woman—tidy in form, tidy in her practical appearance. Dark hair tied back, wide jaw, pointed chin, and a distinct smudging of natural color on the outside edges of her eyes. Feline of some sort, he was certain.

And he was just as certain that this was the woman who'd held them up. It was worth an unfriendly glare of blame.

Carter wasn't slow to notice. "Lyn is the best," he said. "She was on trail in Europe. Circumstances, Treviño. She couldn't be in two places at once."

"Then you shouldn't have waited," Dolan growled. "You damned well should have come out here without her. If you had, then Meghan would have had protection. You'd have your hands on the book right now."

Carter regarded him for a long moment. "You may well be right. Things at brevis are...*complicated* right now. Not entirely secure. Your Meghan...may have paid the price."

Your Meghan. As obvious as that, was it?

Good. Then they'd know how far he'd go to find her. To save her.

Lyn Maines hesitated as she closed in on them, regarding Dolan with wary interest. "What *is* that?"

"I don't know," Carter admitted. "I was hoping you'd seen it before."

And Dolan suddenly knew. "Gausto. He had a vial of my blood."

Maines moved in closer, still wary; she closed her eyes and shivered visibly, but when she looked at him again, her deep brown eyes didn't flinch from whatever she saw. "Blood," she said. "Yes. And corruption. Very dark."

"They killed a man. With a *touch*." Dolan scrubbed a hand over his eyes, dropped it to look directly at Carter. "They're changing the rules, Carter. If Gausto has this blood stuff, then so do the others. Of course," he added, "the guy who did it promptly keeled over."

"*Sceleratus vis.*" A big, bearded, shaggy-haired bear of a man joined them.

"Ruger," Carter supplied for Dolan. "Our healer."

"Blood violence, blood force..." the man murmured. *Bear,* all right. He looked at Carter, dark bushy brows drawn together. "Ancient stuff, draws power from the blood of the ones doing the workings, or the ones being worked upon. Even the Core forbade it back then. I guess they couldn't bring themselves to throw out their crib notes."

Dolan noted dryly, "I got the impression that Gausto was overstepping himself. He'd planned to kill me with it, not let me go to spread the word that the Core has it."

A moment of silence passed between them, a stark, mutual awareness that the stakes had risen considerably. Then Carter cleared his throat and asked Ruger, "Can you clean it out?"

Ruger crouched beside Dolan, large and looming; Dolan couldn't help but tense—and then Carter offered the faintest of nods. *Reassurance?* Unexpected enough to get Dolan's attention. And then the big healer made a sound deep in his throat—annoyed—and asked, "What's behind it?"

"Years ago, Gausto's brother decided to play with me before he killed me," Dolan said shortly. It was enough; they all knew Tiberon Gausto had died at Dolan's hands. Pretty much everyone knew that bit of history. "They must think ahead... Gausto used my blood today, and these came back."

Ruger looked up at Carter. "I can clean it out," he said. "I can set a healing on it. But it'll take a while— it's through his whole system. That run we tracked up the mountain didn't help any."

Dolan set his chin, felt his anger go hot. Ruger held up a hand. "Whoa, whoa," he said. "Speaking objectively there. You didn't do anything I wouldn't have done." But he paused, stroked his short beard and admitted, "Well, no. I'm not exactly made for running. Doubt I would have made it halfway up here."

"How long?" Carter asked.

"Too long," Dolan answered for him, orienting himself on the shadows, realizing he'd lost at least an hour. "You need to find Meghan. She's the only one who can give us the *Liber Nex*." Also the strict truth. "And unless you get there soon, Gausto is going to figure that out first."

Ruger cleaned out his system, cleaned off his wound and left him with rations. The big man carried an essentials-stuffed pack in both of his forms, including those things he'd enhanced just as Meghan enhanced her herbs.

While Dolan contemplated protein bars and herbal glop tea, the team decided to split up. Carter and Ruger would return to the ranch, hoping for enough of a welcome to more thoroughly investigate the area, hoping the county coroner had not yet made it out there to remove the farrier's body. And then they'd pick up the team's vehicle and meet Lyn and her companion—the muscle of the crew, a man of streaky, rusty hair and golden-tinged skin who could only take a tiger—wherever Meghan's trail and the road crossed.

Likely the Core was lurking somewhere in Sonoita... but they couldn't assume it.

Dolan's job was to rest another hour or two, and then return to the ranch—to watch over it in the unlikely case the Core should return.

His *ostensible* job.

But it was make-work as much as anything else; he'd been more or less dismissed from the mission. Too

battered, too involved…blah, blah, blah. Dolan hardly
listened as Carter made his excuses; his mind was on
the book, on his intention to stay right here and watch
over it…to once again attempt the wards. With his
system tainted by the *sceleratus vis,* he hadn't had the
faintest chance of success the first time he'd approached
the thing. But if Meghan had unwittingly imbued the
wards with her connection to him, and with his system
cleaned thanks to Ruger…just maybe….

In the background, Lyn Maines circled the yard, her
head tipped in a listening posture—an ingrained gesture.
At one point she stopped, frowning…taking a step back,
a step to the side…trying to define what she'd discerned.
Damn, she knew her stuff…that book was as good as
invisible. Meghan's efforts had done nothing to interfere with the original camouflage.

He had the first hint of why the team had wanted her,
if not why they'd waited for her. If they'd been *here*…

Then the Core never would have come. Never would
have driven Meghan to the desperate measure of double-
warding the book—to the very desperate measure of unwittingly warding it with her life.

He found Carter staring at him, eyes ever so slightly
narrowed. "So you're good with that?" he said flatly.
"With staying here."

That grabbed Dolan's attention, as Ruger taped a
pricey surgical dressing over his side. He stared back
with offended ire. "Hell no, I'm not okay with staying
here! But there's no fucking way *not* to stay here
without holding up Meghan's rescue, is there?"

"Ah," Carter said. "There's the mouth that tells me
you're really with us. No, indeed, Treviño, there's no

fucking way not to stay here without holding us up. Get down to the farm when you can; we've got a satellite cell phone in the vehicle. We'll update you and decide how to proceed from there." No such things as phones or radios when a Sentinel was afoot…. They didn't survive shifting, even within prepared containers.

Besides, Dolan didn't need a phone to hear the unspoken. *We'll update you* was just polite-speak for the truth of things. They'd left him dangling out here on his own; they'd left Meghan dangling. And now that he was truly involved—now that he had personal stakes he'd never even imagined—they expected him to back down and play second-line support.

Something within his chest went hard and cold; he swallowed it down, trying to keep it from Carter—from Ruger, who raised an eyebrow and shared a meaningful glance with Carter.

In the background, Lyn Maines gestured to her partner—the bodyguard, the one who kept watch while she lost herself in the tracking—and headed down the path. Human, but Dolan doubted they'd stay that way long. Ruger had already scooped up his pack, preparing himself for the change. Carter looked down on Dolan, hands on hips, head cocked ever so slightly in what could be interpreted as a challenge. "Meghan is our first priority, Treviño."

Right. Because they thought she could give them the book. If they knew the thing sat fifty feet away…he could easily imagine them leaving her to die so the *aeternus* wards would release. Or going in to extract her but careless of her fate, knowing they'd have the book either way.

But the book was safe enough here, whether or not they knew about it. If Lyn Maines, tracker so extraordinaire as to hold up this entire mission, hadn't found it under her nose…then it was safe. And that made it Meghan's turn to be safe. To be their *first priority*.

"Not," Dolan said, catching and holding Carter's challenge, never mind that he still sat weakly against the old hitching post, side throbbing and body overused, "the same way she's my first priority."

He expected some sort of admonishment, some reminder of his duty. And instead Carter simply said, "I know," and turned away to take the wolf.

Fabron Gausto removed the second amulet from Meghan's neck. It wasn't quite the first thing he removed; first he had one of the men cut Meghan's jeans away from her leg. She initially thought it was some unexpected mercy—the tough jeans were cutting into her swollen limb—but soon enough she understood it was so he could examine the injury, pondering how it fit into his own plans.

But shortly after, he removed the amulet. And by then she had an understanding of the way he thought— that he wanted her to reach for Dolan; wanted Dolan to understand exactly what she was going through.

And so she didn't.

Shivering, having seen enough of her own leg to shudder at the blue-black blotching and spreading wash of purple, she relaxed her head back onto the hard cot. God, she felt naked. With that cold, flat black gaze looking at her, she felt more than naked.

Shark's eyes. That's what they were. No intense blue gaze here; no warm, laughing amber coyote eyes.

She closed her eyes, conjured up those coyote eyes. Conjured up the renewed closeness she'd felt to her mother since her initiation, her new awareness of the many facets of her mother's world. Enclosed in that warmth, she remembered Dolan—standing before her on that first day, her anger and her fear of him—and her hindsight awareness that along with history she'd been reacting to the very instant attraction between them, the virility she'd seen in his every move and the way her body answered to it.

He'd never thought beyond his own response, she understood that now. His life had not left him room for such things as a future. What a shock it must have been to recognize love.

She'd felt it, that shock—she clung to it now. She'd opened something between them that night at the homestead; they'd sealed it that night beneath the ranch. In the space of a week, they'd found each other, learned each other and loved each other.

Whatever happened here, she had that.

Because she *knew* what was going to happen here. She couldn't yet anticipate the agony of what Gausto would do to her, but she knew she wouldn't be good with it. She knew he'd play with her and torture her and get what he wanted, and then he'd kill her in the way that would most hurt Dolan.

Inevitable, that death. And yet it would also free her clumsy but irrevocable iron wards on the *Liber Nex*—she knew the truth of that from Dolan's dismay, from the internal cry of pain and denial he'd tried to hide from her.

So. Best she be the one to choose, instead of giving

that power to Fabron Gausto. Best to make that her gift to Dolan—to the world.

Her mother had done it. So could she.

Dolan rested for as long as it took to eat, until the sun declared it to be mid- to late afternoon. Already Ruger's help had made a difference; he ached, but only in the way he should after such a run. His side no longer bled. His Sentinel strength and healing had kicked in, no longer squelched by the taint of what now had a name. *Sceleratus vis.*

But he still couldn't do Meghan any good, not as he was. Let Lyn Maines find her while he recovered, and then he'd be there. As fast as it took, he'd be there.

And meanwhile—if Meghan wasn't rescued...wasn't killed...if they turned her, God forbid...then the Sentinels would need access to the book. They'd need to move it. Worst case, this old homestead would hold a Sentinel/Core showdown—shattering the area, shattering their illusions of secrecy. And then they'd be fighting not only each other, but the various governments who couldn't risk the existence of two such powerful groups. Or worse...who wanted to study them.

Life was suddenly already a lot more complex than it had been a week ago.

"Stop it." He said it out loud, realizing that his heart had snagged on Meghan's fate in a frisson of tightening fear. "I won't let that happen." And as long as Carter thought Meghan held the only key to the book, he wouldn't let it happen, either.

So Dolan took one last savage bite of the jerky Ruger had provided, chewing the tough substance with quick efficiency and washing it down with a foul infusion, a favorite of Sentinel healers. It hit his stomach with a pleasant warmth, spreading out into a tingling along his limbs, and he set the container aside to approach the outhouse.

Sitting cross-legged before it, he took a scant moment to appreciate Margery Lawrence again—her clever, wry humor, her skill. With no backup, no chance to plan ahead, she'd nonetheless hidden the book so efficiently that it had taken her daughter—initiated, attuned to this land, welcomed by the wards—to find it. Without Meghan, the book would as yet be sitting undiscovered in a crude abandoned toilet.

On the other hand, if the Sentinels had not set Meghan aside, they'd have had this book years ago. Meghan...trained early, initiated when the time was right...she'd have been looking for the book all along. She'd have known what to do when she found it. She wouldn't have panicked and tied her life to it.

You don't know that. The sudden thought startled him. If the Sentinels had taken Meghan in for training, she might well have not been here to learn this land. Or the Core would have reckoned her important in light of the brief activity here when she was a child, and gone after her much earlier.

So do what you do so damned well. Concentrate on what to do *now.* Not the past, not the future.

His heart slipped out one final, yearning *want,* and he stopped that, too. He closed his eyes and slipped into ward view, instantly oriented on the now-familiar lines protecting the book. The fine illusionary webbing beneath, the strong bold tangle of Meghan's death ward. *Aeternus.*

He'd never break it directly—and he might not recover if he tried. But when he'd been here before, it had responded to him. If in some way Meghan had made him part of this...if only enough to whisper around the edges...

He might have a chance. If he made himself part of what it was, instead of battering against it.

Problem was, Dolan was no Margery Lawrence; when it came to that, he wasn't even an untrained *Meghan* Lawrence. His strength lay in the wards, but more in tracing them than in manipulating them, just as reading and speaking a foreign language were two different skills.

He took a deep breath, settled himself. Gave a moment's attention to the outside world, taking in the scents and sounds of it...heard nothing of concern. Returned fully to the wards, closing in slowly...watching for the response he'd seen earlier, and very well aware that the entire construction might be sensitized by that earlier, ill-considered encroachment. A stupid decision, based on desperation. Stupid—and yet he fought the impulse to do it again, driven by need.

But he couldn't afford another wipeout. He had to be ready to spring into action when the team found Meghan.

So...another breath. Deeper, slower. He struggled his way back into the same frame of mind from which he'd always worked—detached passion, the determination to get it done without the emotional stakes. He eased closer...closer...

The big, fat lines of energy sat unapproachable. Unbreachable. Unresponsive.

Dolan backed off, fighting frustration, a surge of impatience that made him twitch and straighten, fighting himself. *Get a grip, Treviño. This is about more than Meghan.* And still, at the very thought of her name, his chest tightened so tightly he nearly cried out with it, wanting to leap up from this place and find her himself, to free her and hold her and to look at their future. Together.

He startled to attention at a flicker of change, looked directly...looked hard. Saw nothing.

No. It was there. Barely, but—

He'd been thinking about Meghan, that's what. He'd lost his detached nature and slipped into the pure emotion of the situation.

Meghan. He thought of the look on her face when he'd approached the corral, the annoyance, the narrow-eyed defiance he'd come to recognize as a sign of her own determination—the need to keep her made family safe, to keep Encontrados safe. Her reverence of beloved childhood memories of her mother, butting up against the reality of it—her mother hadn't been the only one to die that night. Another Sentinel had died, trying to keep her safe. And back to the essence of Meghan herself, the feel of her touch in ward view, the feel of her touch in life. The complex nature of her passions, once she'd accepted him into her life, into her body.

Meghan.

And the ward lines surged; they softened at the edges, growing hazy with a still-solid core.

Detached passion...there was nothing of it in his relationship with Meghan. And nothing about it that would serve his attempts to bypass the ward. To make himself part of it, he'd have to be in that place where he felt it all. The frisson of promise, the ecstasy of completion, the privilege of touching heart and soul and body.

Meghan. The wards softened to him…invited him. And though he was so full of what lived between them that he could only grope a fumbling, uncertain step at a time, he nonetheless took a deep breath and took that first step.

Big brave Sentinel, terrified by a little emotional truth.

And then real terror came rushing in to slap him hard—terror from without, from Meghan herself. Dolan reeled away from the wards and staggered hard under another swooping blow; his hands clenched into fists as—

Pain and terror and dread and—

A scream rent the air, silent in all but his head; Dolan swayed with the shock of it, with the impact of what she felt—

Meghan!

His shout came as reflex; she was beyond hearing.

Pain and terror and agony and—

She screamed again, catching Dolan up so tightly that he cried out in tandem, head thrown back and his voice raggedly echoing in the trees—and suddenly he was there, sharing not memories but the crystal clarity of life. Cool biting air in his nose, agony ripping through one leg and despair—*defeat*—ripping through his mind. He arched back against new pain, the slice of sharp, heavy metal into skin, gently and lovingly following the curve of a rib; he choked on the acrid taste of bile in his throat. A camp cot shifted beneath him even as someone crouched beside it—cold, flat kohl-rimmed eyes inspecting his own handiwork, mouth set in satisfaction with just a little quiver of excitement.

A flash of realization—of recognition—filled him. An opportunity seized, a decision made. Not his own, but so intertwined that he understood instantly and it didn't matter that he said, "No, oh, *no, Meghan, don't*—"

Pain and terror and dread and—

He twitched as she twisted her body away from the man, straining against the invisible bonds that held Meghan's wrists, not his. And he cried protest as she reversed herself, flinging her body toward the one who hurt her, wrenching every muscle to unbalance the narrow cot, to tip it over onto Fabron Gausto.

Sharp metal bit deep, deeper…she fell on the substantial knife, every bit of energy she had focused on that blade, on the strangely painless passage through her midriff and down into her body, down to the pulse of the massive vessel traveling down from her heart.

He felt that *wrongness*. Strength gushed away from him; he crumpled to his side, gasping for air that didn't seem to be enough. His breathing turned harsh, rapid…a vicarious last-ditch effort to live. For *her* to live.

Pain and terror and sudden peace and complete awareness and faint tendrils of love reaching out to wrap themselves around her—

And the ward abruptly faded away.

Chapter 21

Dolan still breathed. On a deep level, he didn't believe it; each breath came as a surprise.

Her death clung to him, spiraled around him...absorbed him.

Her death, her choice. She'd taken that power from Gausto, reclaimed it. A sacrifice in the face of the inevitable, to keep the book from the Core and return control of it to the Sentinels.

Dolan pushed himself off the ground, heedless of pale clinging dirt and pebbles. He scrubbed his face, wiping away tears and sweat, and he stared bleakly at the catalog in the outhouse. Margery's wards still cocooned it, the illusion and protection as fine as ever.

But no trace remained of Meghan's outer wards.

The *Liber Nex*. Power beyond imagining in that book. It would take so little to sweep through the finesse of Margery's wards and reach that illicit power. To reach *out* with that power, destroying Fabron Gausto and his sickened clan—those who had already crossed the line with their blood power.

Pulling his feet beneath him, Dolan took a few crouching steps toward the book—not quite ready to stand up yet, but unable to be still. To resist the lure of that power.

That revenge.

That's what it had always been about, wasn't it? The revenge? Revenge he'd once gotten with the death of Tiberon Gausto, and yet somehow it hadn't changed a thing. It hadn't changed a thing, and yet Dolan had soldiered on, pretending it was just always about doing the job in the first place. Pretending not to notice that the hollow spot inside hadn't gone away. And now... Meghan...

But revenge on a large scale...putting a stop to the Core once and for all...

Even through its illusion, the book called to him. He'd touched it once. He'd opened that connection between them and now it reached straight to him. Inching closer without even realizing, he responded to its reflection of his inner landscape—the anger and hatred and a grief so unbearable he couldn't yet even completely feel it. Just the shock of it, the waves of it lapping his soul, were already too much. Gausto needed to pay.

And with a startled blink, Dolan absorbed the book's knowledge of how to wipe out those who had taken Meghan, those who had participated in her death. *I can put a stop to this right now.* And the only regret that accompanied that thought was the regret that he couldn't reach out to the Core entire.

But if you can't, said some entirely practical voice within him, *then they'll come back down on the Sentinels with no holds barred.* The simmering underground conflict would be exposed to the world, just as if the Core had taken control of the book in the first place.

He slowly sank down to the ground, sitting back against his heels. The call of the book snapped away, leaving him bemused—caught up by the renewed clarity of the world around him. Stellar jays scolded him from high in the pines; the sharp scent of the pines warmed by the sun tickled his nose. The antiseptic Ruger had used lingered around him; the bandage itself, a transparent dressing that showed neat rows of butterfly bandages beneath, pulled at his skin.

Meghan had given of herself so the book wouldn't fall into the wrong hands.

Meghan had given of herself. Dolan closed his eyes, felt the sting of tears and the true honest grief, unfettered by fantasies of revenge.

He couldn't let the wrong hands be *his*.

Dolan left the book behind. He glared at it, he accepted one more time that he couldn't carry it as the jaguar, that to move it at all was only to draw attention to it…and he left it behind.

The sooner he reached the ranch and the phone there, the better. It didn't matter that he was still reeling with loss, could barely move for the crush of it. What mattered was making that loss count.

Make it count.

Ruger had intended for him to rest for several more hours, to let the healing make significant progress before he took the jaguar and lost the bandages by default. So much for that. Dolan stretched into the waiting jaguar with a relief he hadn't expected, testing strength and limb and finding Ruger's work solid. Not full, rippling strength...not the jaguar who oozed personal power and a certain confidence he not only wouldn't be stopped, but he *couldn't* be stopped.

But he'd take it.

He cut across the trails, heading overland and down the mountain to Encontrados. For the sake of those who had already been so badly shaken up, he took his human self outside the ranch yard and, wary for anything out of place, stalked into the yard on two feet instead of four.

Jenny's dog skittered across the yard in front of him, barking near to hysterical; he shied off into the shadows of the casita porch to bark from what he considered safety. By then Jenny had stuck her head out the door and Anica came out of the barn, running to him with such speed that she couldn't quite stop as she reached him. He caught her up and settled her back on her feet, earning a wary response...and a surprised one. She apparently hadn't expected the consideration—or the gentle strength behind it.

"What's going on?" she demanded. "What was that all about? We played nice, we told the coroner we thought Larry had had a heart attack, we sent everyone else home, we didn't call the cops when your *people* showed up. But now I damned well want answers! And where's Meg—" She stopped, gaze searching his face, even as Jenny approached.

But Jenny knew. Jenny, who read the horses so well, had no trouble with Dolan's grief and anger, simmering so close to the surface. "No," she whispered, stopping just out of reach. "What…what happened?" And to Dolan's utter astonishment, she then flung herself at him. He drew himself back, ready to fend her off—but she only threw her arms around his neck and wailed.

And by that, Anica knew. Her face paled; she bit her lip, hard, and looked away, mouth working anyway, tears spilling down her cheeks. Dolan surprised himself then, lifting an arm in invitation so then there were three of them.

Only for a moment. Then Anica drew Jenny away, patting her back in a soothing, mindless gesture while her own bright eyes pinned Dolan. "When Luka came back without her…" She stopped, took a breath and retreated into the anger that seemed to serve her as well as it did Dolan. "They came for her because of you, didn't they? That man this morning…he hated you. He *wanted* you. *You* brought them here. This is—" And she bit her lip again, heedless of the bright smear of blood she'd already created there.

Dolan opened his mouth to respond—and nothing came out. No words could make it past the tight band of pain in his chest and throat—pain that had somehow eased slightly when the three of them had been huddled together. *This* was what Meghan had been so desperate to protect. This was what he'd been missing for so many years he'd forgotten what it was like.

So he wasn't about to lie to them. He worked his jaw, hunting composure, and said, "Yes. I underestimated him. He came because of me. He found Meghan because of me. He took her on the trail, and I couldn't get there in time."

"So you just let them go?" Anica cried. It wasn't fair, the look on her face said she knew it wasn't fair, but she lashed out anyway. Hurting. He understood that.

"The man who was here…Gausto. He was using forbidden techniques…even the Core doesn't allow them. Or didn't. I'm not sure which it is right now—he's capable of defying the Core and thinking he'll get away way it." Dangerously close to babbling. He drew his thoughts back together. "I wasn't ready for that kind of power. He…"

"He hurt you," Jenny said, stepping back from Anica, her fair complexion splotched, her nose pinked.

Dolan hesitated, then nodded. "I tried—I *tried*—" And found he had to jerk himself away from them, unable to even say the words, and unable to face their grief and accusations, no matter how fair. *Make it count.* He stalked into the house and straight to the phone, dialing the number Carter had given him.

The phone barely rung before Carter barked a response. "What?"

"Meghan is dead." Dolan said it coldly, the only way to get the words out at all. Anica and Jenny entered the house, coming up to wait behind him—to listen. What the hell? They deserved to know whatever came of this call.

Carter muttered an expletive, moved the phone from his mouth just enough to tell the rest of the team before returning to demand, "You're sure?"

Dolan laughed, no humor whatsoever, and let it stand as an answer. "I want them. Have you got a location?"

Carter should have said, *It's not about what you want.* But he didn't. He hesitated, and he said, "Gausto tangled the trail. Lyn is just about through it." A rustle of material as he shifted; Dolan got the impression he was checking on Lyn's progress. "I don't think anyone else would have had a chance of getting through."

Right. Carter being careful to cover his ass now that they'd lost a civilian—and one of their own, at that, long abandoned. Dolan said, "I want in on it. I want to recover her."

"What makes you think—"

"You're still going to go after evidence of what Gausto is doing," Dolan interrupted. "You're probably going to play nice about Gausto, because you don't want to rock the cold war into a hot war." *As almost happened when Tiberon Gausto died at my teeth.* "But you're going in, and I want to be there."

"Treviño—" This time Carter cut himself off, obviously hunting words. Dolan already knew what they'd be—hedge words about Dolan's track record of working with a group, shuffle-footing over his less-than-optimal physical status. All true enough.

Dolan just didn't care.

Make it count.

"I found the book," he said, and left the threat unsaid. *I'll tell you where it is* after *I'm in on this raid.*

Carter said, "Son of a *bitch*—!"

"Where are you?"

"Son of a—"

Dolan exploded into a shout. *"Where?"*

Tense, taut silence followed, and then the murmur of commentary in the background. A gust of a breeze blew across the phone, followed by Carter's breath. "Just picked up Casa Arroyo." Barely a pause, and then he came back again, just as demanding as Dolan. "And Treviño, if you screw this up—"

Dolan laughed. "It's already screwed up, Carter. Didn't you notice? It was screwed up the moment you didn't back me up. The only unexpected thing is that I'm still alive to hold you to it." And he hung up.

"Dolan—" Anica started.

He didn't trust himself to turn around and he didn't let her finish. Hand still on the phone, closed around it with white-knuckle tension, he said, "I need a vehicle. And a shirt. That one I was wearing before."

"You want one of our cars?" Anica said flatly.

"And a shirt." He drew a deep breath, finally turned to face them. Jenny was still blotchy and pale, but she watched him with an avid interest, with some faint hope—unlike Anica's hard, lingering judgment. He told them, "I'm going to get her. And to stop them, as much as can be done."

Anica watched him for a moment, her face unreadable, her gaze flicking from his expression to his exposed wounds and then finally to Jenny…who gave the slightest of nods. Anica looked back to him, no less judgment in her eyes and maybe a little bit more of warning. "I hope you can drive a stick."

This can't be right.

Even the presence of that dim, confused thought wasn't right. The presence of *any* thought.

"Yes, yes." An impatient voice prodded her. "Not what you expected, is it?"

That self-satisfied comment brought the world back in a rush, and brought awareness along with it. Meghan's eyes flew open; she sat up. She sat up on the same damned cot in the same damned basement, with the same damned man sitting beside her, that same cruel expression on his face.

Along with something else. Smugness, definitely. But he seemed pale as well...and as though he sat because possibly he couldn't stand.

And then she realized she wasn't restrained any longer. She realized that her leg only throbbed lightly, and that the damp spot of blood on her snug tank top was cold. She stuck her finger through the hole the big knife had left in the ribbed material, stretched it out to discover no corresponding hole in her skin. She couldn't believe it; she drew the shirt up to expose the flat, toned abdomen beneath, finding nothing but faint, dried blood smears. Nothing where he'd cut her, nothing where she'd thrown herself on his knife.

"I could say you played into my hands," Gausto told her, crossing his ankle atop his knee and leaning back to regard her, "but the truth is, I had hoped to play longer. For Treviño's sake."

Dolan. Instantly, Meghan reached for him. *I'm here,* she wanted to tell him, and *what happened to the book?* and *are you all right?* And she remembered with crystal clarity those last moments, the entanglement between them, his horrified understanding of what she'd done...

"You're trying to reach him," Gausto guessed, head slightly tipped as he watched her. "You won't. I've taken that from you."

She couldn't quite comprehend it. She couldn't comprehend any of it. She looked down at herself again, and then to Gausto. *"I was dead."*

He nodded. "You were dead." He eyed her with respect, if with lingering annoyance. "I didn't think you'd have it in you. The Sentinels, after all, have had no chance to brainwash you."

"Imagine that," Meghan said. "Just little ol' me, making my own decisions." She smoothed her shirt, examining her uncovered leg. No longer grotesquely swollen, it still bore a rainbow of bruises…but none of the cuts Gausto had made when he'd first started in on her, wanting to see if she could feel such cuts beyond what the limb had already endured.

She could, of course.

"Unfortunately, the injury to your leg was too established to heal completely," Gausto said, but he said it without compassion—he said it with the annoyance of a man who has not accomplished perfection. "But the cuts…the internal bleeding and the blood loss itself…all are resolved."

She'd been dead. Now she wasn't. "What did you do?"

"Not much gratitude in your tone, my lady." He raised an eyebrow. "And you *are* mine, to bid as I wish. You can no longer contact your lover, you no longer have the least influence over your destiny."

"I can damned well walk out of here," Meghan said, lifting her stiff leg over the side of the cot and standing up, testing it—and walking for the exit with much more assertion than she felt, as if she had no worries that the leg might not hold her, that Gausto's men weren't on the other side of that arching doorway, waiting to stop her. But stiff as it was, the leg didn't buckle, and no one appeared to stop her, and a spark of hope dared to bloom—

"In fact," Gausto said, and sounded bored, "you can't. I bid you stay."

And she stopped. She didn't think about it, she didn't see it coming—she just stopped. Halfway to freedom and she stood, feet planted, swaying slightly, trying to understand.

"Why don't you sit back down?" Gausto said. "You don't seem to be fully recovered yet."

Without being the least bit sure if it was her own choice—or somehow *his*—Meghan returned to the cot. Slowly, careful of her leg, she sat at the edge of it, shifting backward slightly when it threatened to tip.

"Ah, yes, must secure that," Gausto said. "It's been inconvenient enough already."

Meghan found she could barely speak, that her words came out hoarse and thick. *"What did you do?"*

"What I'd meant to do all along. You died, I brought you back. I made you mine in the process. You'll do as I say…and won't do those things I forbid. We'll have a nice discussion about the situation with the *Liber Nex*—with the difference being that now, of course, you're too valuable to damage. You're the only one of your kind."

The only one of *what* kind?

But Meghan didn't ask it out loud. She didn't want to know. She looked at her hands; she turned them over and clenched them. She closed her eyes, awash with the knowledge that Dolan thought her dead—make that *still* dead—and that he still grieved for her, still blamed himself for it.

A man's murmur from the exit barely caught her attention—not at first. But as Gausto impatiently indicated the man should speak, the tone of the conversation brought her out of her internal floundering with the unimaginable.

"I'm telling you, the sept's prince has figured out we're using the *sceleratus vis*," the man said. "He wants to talk to you…his people aren't taking my excuses any longer." He lowered his voice. "If we can't put them off, and they come out here…one look at her…we've got to get rid of her!"

"No!" Gausto's controlled tones rose sharply; he spoke as if she wasn't even there. "She is my finest achievement…and once I prove what we can accomplish when we unfetter ourselves, the sept's people will forget their foolish restrictions and see only the success. If anyone knows where the *Liber Nex* is—if anyone holds so much as a clue—it is this woman. That we can use her to take down Treviño makes her all the more important."

Greatly daring, the man said, "I'm not sure Treviño matters to anyone but you. He's only one man."

"A man who constantly interferes with our efforts in this territory!"

Now Meghan opened her eyes, looking for confirmation that Gausto was as close to losing control as he sounded. She found him flushed, his eyes wild—and as if he felt her gaze, he visibly reined himself in. He said to his lackey, "Continue to stall them. Meghan and I are going to have a discussion, and then the only issue will be just how much strength we gain by providing the Core with that manuscript. Until then, you will do as your *drozhar* says."

The man shot a quick and skittering glance at Meghan, and as he nodded respectfully to Gausto and turned away, she realized belatedly that he'd been afraid of her.

She wasn't sure, but she thought she was afraid of herself, too.

Chapter 22

Carter glared out the window of the SUV as it rolled down, sleek performance on a sleek vehicle. "Where's the book?"

Dolan had no intention of answering that one. He looked down the road, where Lyn stood on the shoulder and appeared to be admiring the rugged ridges-and-grassland scenery half a mountain and a thousand feet below Encontrados—but the tension of her stance told him she was hard at work. "She just about got this?"

"She's got it," Carter said sourly. "She's just being thorough, as long as we had to wait for you. Tell me you left the information somewhere, in case you don't come back from this."

Dolan gave him a fierce grin. "Better make sure I come back from this."

Carter narrowed his eyes ever so slightly, putting the pale green irises in shadow. "Lyn will ride with you."

Dolan looked at him a long moment, processing this unexpected offering. For an offering it was—a guarantee, of sorts, that they wouldn't play games with him on the road, or try to delay or ditch him. None of which they had any reason to do...but he'd learned well not to trust his own people, lessons ground into granite pain this past day. *Things are complicated,* Carter had said, acknowledging the price Meghan had paid for Sentinel delays.

That the gesture was necessary in the first place...it said too much about brevis regional these past years.

So Dolan didn't demur, didn't play nice. He said, "We'll take lead, then."

Lyn Maines didn't seem the least surprised when he pulled the old Jeep Wrangler around the luxury SUV and crunched onto the narrow graveled shoulder beside her. She walked around to the passenger side and slid in, automatically hunting the seat belt.

"Doesn't have one," Dolan said. "Sorry about that. Best I could beg, borrow and nearly steal on short notice."

"Under the circumstances, I'm just glad it's fully enclosed." Lyn settled into the seat with precision—not quite dressed for rugged terrain, though he had no doubt she could take it well in her natural form. "Jaguar?" she confirmed, glancing his way as the SUV rolled up behind them, a less-than-subtle nag. "I take the ocelot."

Dolan grunted, uninterested in the small talk—especially when she spoke from behind a guarded mein. "What did Carter tell you? I'm an uncontrollable rogue? Can't be trusted?"

She braced an arm against the door as Dolan accelerated and moved up through the gears, not all of which took smoothly. "Almost the opposite. He said you could be trusted to do whatever it took to accomplish what you want done."

Dolan snorted. "True enough."

"He said you don't spend any time at brevis. That they're lucky to track you down if something comes up. That they can't count on you to be available."

He slanted a glance at her. She sat quietly, not the least disconcerted by their rough ride or the fact that for the moment, her fate was linked to the man she so dispassionately damned. "They might see it that way. I see it as getting things done."

She caught his sideways glance and held it a moment, direct and comfortable with it. "And do you? Get things done?"

"Yeah," he said. "I do. Unless I'm caught waiting for a team from brevis."

She didn't flinch. "That's my fault. I'm sorry it couldn't be avoided."

"Unless you're the one who decided you were the only option for this team, then I'd say it's probably Carter's fault." He bit down on the words, and this time she did flinch, ever so slightly. Ocelot. Sharp, quick grace. She probably used finesse, not power. But he couldn't be sorry for what he'd said. If it opened her eyes a little, maybe she'd be prepared for the day it happened to her.

Instead, after a hesitation in which she seemed to be mulling over words, she said, "Brevis let you down, Dolan...there's no arguing that. But if you spent enough time there to understand who you were working with... what's going on right now..."

"I'll send an e-mail sometime," Dolan growled. "Right now, we've got a body to recover."

"I know." She looked away, out the window. "Someone you loved."

That hurt too much to linger on, to even look at it straight-on. So he said, "Carter's glad enough to go, to hunt intel on Gausto's *sceleratus vis.*"

"Scary bad stuff, sounds like," she said, quite seriously. "Ruger's the only one of us who's even heard of it, and from what he says, everyone's treated it as long lost and good riddance."

He nodded, slowing as they approached a split in the road, then smoothly following her direction to head north toward Sonoita. "It's bad," he affirmed. "They got right through my personal wards. I should have been invisible to them, and impermeable to that attack—but I wasn't, and I'm pretty sure this damned *sceleratus vis* is the reason why. They would have killed me if—"

But he stopped, because he didn't want to talk about Meghan.

Make it count.

I will, Meghan. I will. Because Dolan didn't care about politics and balance and simmering cold war. He cared about stopping Gausto. Whatever it took.

They pulled up alongside the edge of the road, a mile from Sonoita and yet already out in the middle of nowhere, surrounded by juniper-studded dry grasslands with weather-beaten ridges rising starkly all around them. The property of interest stood out like a sore thumb—landscaped with elms and willows and cottonwoods in the area between the road and the B and B office, the long lane of the driveway full of cinder gravel and edged with worn split-rail fencing. Closer to the office was a patch or two of green, and a small riot of flowers provided a nod of color. Beyond was the housing—haphazardly placed minicottages and little adobe tourist homes. Rising beyond was a larger building—the original ranch house. Dolan eyed it.

"Yes," Lyn said, opening the door and giving him one glance back before she exited the Jeep. "That's where they are."

He wouldn't know for sure. Not without his connection to Meghan. He hadn't expected to get used to it so quickly. Or feel its loss so sharply.

He shoved the door open. They wouldn't go undetected for long—Gausto would have amulets seeded through this entire area—and that meant there was much to gain from decisive action. Carter seemed to know it; his own vehicle emptied rapidly, and he was already talking as Dolan approached. "Remember our goals here—we need evidence of the *sceleratus vis*—and if we're going to develop countermeasures, we need to find all the information we can. We will avoid encounters if possible." He looked at Dolan. "*All* of us."

Dolan said nothing.

"We'll move up to the buildings together—then Lyn and I will scout the area. We need to know the placement of their welcoming snares. We've got stun guns—" and Lyn's silent companion, the man who took the tiger, tossed one to Dolan "—and we'll secure the area as we go."

Stun guns. Standard Sentinel gear. Easy to tuck away, quiet, nonlethal…and if one had to be left behind after a change, it was a lot better than leaking handguns. All the same, if Dolan was going to get that close, he'd prefer to use claws. Hand to hand, the Sentinel nature prevailed.

He tucked the stun gun in his pocket, waited for Carter to finish his little spiel and moved out. He didn't crowd them; he hung to the back, ranging out to the side, moving with the fast, fluid efficiency of his nature. Let them think he was playing their game.

For now.

Make it count.

And he would. Because he was exactly what Carter had said. A man who would do what needed to be done.

Chapter 23

Noise filtered down to the cellar where Meghan waited. She'd been told to stay there. She'd been told not to hurt herself. She'd been told to eat and rest.

And Meghan obeyed.

She even realized, with remote surprise, how very little she thought about such complete obedience. There was no war within, no struggle to regain control. There was only a fleeting wistful awareness that she would choose to escape—and barring that, to pace and prowl, and barring that, to explore the corners of this cellar for anything useful.

Like the bare knife sitting over on that tray—still streaked with her blood, just as Gausto had left it—long blade curved to a wicked tip, beautiful in its workmanship. He'd traced designs across her flesh with that blade, reveling in its keen edge, in the lines of blood—in her fear and pain. He'd left it there as a reminder, she was certain. Of his power, and of the futility of her efforts.

She'd given everything, and it hadn't been enough.

Otherwise, it was just a cellar. An old barrel; old pallets leaning against the wall. An old wine rack, empty. And there, off to the side…a stout wooden work-table with arcane objects, notes and notebooks and vials and beakers. Gausto had made no attempt to hide its contents; he had no reason to. She was stuck on this cot, and could investigate no more closely.

Another thump from above—a scrape against the floor. She welcomed the distraction—something to which she could react. Gausto had not left directions on how she should respond to the noise of…was that a scuffle?

Dolan?

But she wasn't permitted to reach out.

A man cried out, made a gargling noise and fell—directly overhead. Meghan sat up on the cot, and rebellion stirred within. It didn't go anywhere, didn't translate to so much as a twitch of directed movement. But she felt it flutter, and she embraced it.

Hasty steps hit the basement; after only a week with Dolan, they sounded clumsy to Meghan's ears. She sat quietly as Gausto and his favorite lackey came down the second section of the switchbacked steps and reached the arched doorway, conversation in full swing.

"Are you sure—" the lackey asked, in the careful tone of a repeated query that he didn't quite finish.

Gausto turned on him, stopping in the doorway and driving the man back a step. "You may not question me!"

Brave Man. Submissive, but persistent. "I haven't

questioned the *sceleratus vis;* I haven't questioned the acquisition of the girl. But now we're under attack—"

"Then *listen.*" Gausto stabbed a finger at the man. "They're only here because they're scared. We've finally gained an undeniable advantage after all these years, and they know it. Once we learn the subtleties of the *sceleratus vis—*"

"But we haven't," the lackey said, determined and wary at the same time. "And I think we should withdraw so we'll have time to do that."

Gausto looked over his shoulder to Meghan. "I have what I need now. Did you pay no attention to what the probes revealed? This woman is a natural wards master—the daughter of the woman who hid the *Liber Nex.*" He glanced at his lackey to see that his words had hit home. "She is my weapon and my defense in one— and when we're through here, she'll take us to the book."

"*Drozhar—*"

The man would never get to finish a sentence, Meghan thought. Gausto strode away from him, to the middle of the cellar; he stabbed a gesture at the work-table there. Meghan's impulse—to rise, to get a better look—manifested in nothing more than a twitch. Still, she managed a wince at the large crash directly above.

By then Gausto was speaking again—shouting, careless with his spittle and his zealous gestures. "This is the beginning! All these centuries, the Core has struggled to free itself from oppression by the Sentinels. Thanks to what we've done here—to what I'll gain when I find the *Liber Nex*—we'll no longer worry about them, or about anyone else. We can accumulate power across the globe!"

Meghan hadn't planned it. Maybe if she had, if she'd thought about it, she wouldn't have been able to do it at all. But in the silence that followed Gausto's impassioned tirade, she found herself clapping. Slow, distinct— clap...clap...clap.

Gausto whirled on her. "Silence! Be still!"

Her hands fell back to her lap of their own volition— but had they not, she would have obeyed him regardless. His eyes were too wild, his face too out of control. Even the lackey moved back another step.

Moved back a step to where a dark, silent form dropped from above, leaping the stairwell to land crouched behind the man. *Dolan.* Human form but evocative of the jaguar, powerful and deadly. By the time the man reacted to Meghan's widened eyes, Dolan, still crouching, jabbed something into the back of his knee. The man spasmed and cried out and went down, limbs jerky and flailing; Dolan avoided him, immediately targeting Gausto.

Meghan held her breath. Still silenced, still quiet on the cot, she fought tangled fear and relief—and thrilled to be feeling such sharp emotions at all. Dolan, with his blue eyes gone black in this light, his face full of intent and focus, approached Gausto with deadly fury barely banked and clearly visible. "Gausto," he said, a growl, and struggled visibly for his next words. He held a stun gun, but it no longer seemed to be his weapon of choice; the fingers on his free hand flexed—putting out claws that were only phantom in this body. He showed no sign of noticing Meghan, obscured as she was behind the tray of instruments, unmoving and silent on all levels. He saw nothing but Gausto, so close—prey about to go down. "We thought you'd run."

Gausto had gone from overwrought to calm, a transformation so quick and complete—and unnatural—that Meghan feared him anew. He had to know he couldn't stand against Dolan; Dolan certainly did.

"I had no reason to run. Everything I need is right here."

"What a coincidence. Everything I *want* is right here." And yet still he didn't see her…and still Meghan couldn't speak, couldn't move as Dolan eased closer. "Really don't know what you were thinking, Gausto— your own people forbid what you've done here. They're not going to climb down our throats for stopping you."

"Do you think it's that simple?" Gausto smiled, blocking Meghan from Dolan's ready line of sight.

"I think you're going down. That's simple enough for me."

Meghan found his grim smile frightening, scary in the way of a man who has little to lose. But Gausto said nothing. He smiled a tight, victorious little smile and took a deliberate step to the side, taking the instrument tray with him—leaving Meghan completely exposed. Leaving her perfectly positioned to know just when Dolan—

There. He saw her. He finally saw her. And though she wanted to get up and fling herself at him, though she wanted to reach out for him…she sat. But not perfectly still. Not perfectly controlled. Her fingers clenched at the side of the cot; her lower lip trembled.

Dolan froze, his expression gone blank in the face of the impossible, his eyes widening—and then came the disbelief, the pain of the conflict within. She tried to lift her hand, to reassure him. *It's me,* she thought at him, but those thoughts stopped inside her own mind, dull sendings that went nowhere even though her whole body now trembled with the effort. *It's really me.*

Dolan turned on Gausto, the vulnerable pain hardening into fury. "Don't fuck with me," he snarled. "You *killed her.* She's *dead.*"

"In point of fact, she killed herself." Gausto gestured at her. "But as you can see, it didn't quite take. Meghan, you may tell him."

Something in her throat eased. But now that she had the chance, she didn't begin to know what to say. Only after several attempts did she manage words. "I'm sorry," she said. "I'm so sorry. I didn't know he could—"

She saw understanding wrench through him—a jerk of his shoulders, a twitch of his jaw, his eyes filled more with horror than hope. "What the goddamned hell—" But he didn't finish, because he knew. That showed in his eyes, too, gleaming with horror.

And Gausto gave Dolan the time to think it through, to fully realize what had happened, to realize that Meghan was clearly under his control, that they had no vestige of the connection that had grown so strong between them. He did no more than give his head a single shake when Dolan took a step toward her, half lifted his hand.

Dolan didn't fight it. He stepped back, closed his eyes; regained control. When he looked at Gausto again, the pain was still there…but well layered under the understanding of what still lay at stake here.

Gausto said, "Meghan, where is the *Liber Nex?*"

And Meghan's mouth opened and Meghan's lips and tongue said, "In the outhouse."

But while she glared at him at such a violation and

while he in turn offered Dolan an expression of much smugness, Dolan growled, "Nice try. Now ask her if I already knew its location, and if I had time to move it."

"Answer that," Gausto demanded, visibly shaken.

And Meghan gladly heard herself say, "Yes, he did."

Dolan shrugged. "Nothing left here to gain, *Drozhar.* We've secured this house and we'll find every last scrap of information about the *sceleratus vis*—can't you hear the search?" Meghan could. Drawers pulled out, furniture moved, suitcases upended… "And when we leave you here, tied and gagged, we'll make sure your people know just what you've been up to and where they can find you." He grinned at Gausto, a sudden and surprising grin…a fierce grin. "Unless you think you can take me?"

Meghan winced inside. *Oh, God, Dolan, maybe that wasn't such a great idea.*

Because she saw Gausto's face, the expression of a man backed into just the corner he'd wanted. And when he affected thoughtful surprise, she knew what was coming next. "Why, yes," he told Dolan. "Yes, I think we can."

We.

"In fact," Gausto said, "I've been waiting quite a long time for this."

"Wards, please, Meghan." Gausto said it casually, but he was quick enough to add, "For myself, if you would."

Dolan instantly understood. He'd had the suspicion earlier, and now he knew for sure. Gausto intended to use Meghan against the Sentinels, against Dolan himself. It didn't matter that Meghan's skills were raw and unversed; the Core's entire existence was based on borrowed energies. Gausto knew well enough how to channel whatever she could give him. Anything but the wards…those had to be Meghan's doing.

And she did. Hands tight around the edge of the cot, with only a flicker of reaction, she used the ability Dolan had so recently woken within her. She was pale, his Meghan, her hair completely escaped from her ponytail, her toned, slender body straight and tense. A single blotch of blood stained her snug ribbed tank top; her jeans were torn on one leg and completely missing on the other. Ill-used, wounded…she'd died rather than reveal the information she'd just so freely imparted.

And now she raised a swift protective warding around the man who'd killed her and then brought her back. It was as much demonstration as strategy, and Dolan forced away the ongoing snarl of fury within himself at the implications.

Gausto had complete control of her. And now he had Meghan's warding ability…if not her knowledge of its use. For Dolan could see it well enough—she'd raised wards on one level only, those meant to keep out probes and incantations and offenses perpetrated by the Core.

But Dolan was a physical creature. As a Sentinel in action, he was all power and muscle and quick, flickering movement. It must have shown in his eyes, in his internal switch to stalking mode.

"*Complete* wards, Meghan," Gausto said through his teeth, reaching into his pocket. Wards that, like the book's, would prevent Dolan from physically touching him—would repel him with damaging force. But nothing happened, and he snapped, "Meghan!"

Dolan wasn't about to take any chances—not with

the stink of blood magic everywhere, and not with
Gausto's hand dipping into his coat. Three long, swift
strides and his fingers closed over Gausto's arm, his stun
gun jammed up against the man's neck. "Stupid," he
said. "Ask her, why don't you, if she can do that? Ask
her what kind of power that takes, when you've left her
access to nothing."

Gausto's mouth twisted, a sneering defiance; his arm
tensed against Dolan's hold, still straining for his
pocket. "Whatever you do to me, she's still mine. Do
you think the Sentinels will suffer her to live?"

No. He didn't.

If Carter had had any clue that Gausto lurked in this
cool stone cellar, he'd have sent Dolan to search the tiny
third-floor rooms instead. For Gausto was the *drozhar*
to the local sept, inviolable...strictly hands-off.

Yeah. Whatever. Dolan abruptly yanked the man upward, tearing that fine suit, shoving Gausto back,
back—up against the wall, scattering the instrument
tray, kicking over a metal bucket of bloody water and a
giant livestock dosing syringe, crashing past a pair of
old wooden sawhorses dusty from lack of use. Gausto
scrabbled backward, trying to maintain his footing, his
eyes widening. The wall stopped them, cemented stone
as old as the house; Dolan slammed Gausto back against
it and for good measure did it again. "What happens,"
he said, teeth gritted, "if you die? What happens then,
Gausto? She'll be free, won't she?"

"They'll kill you," Gausto gasped, barely finding the air.

"Who? Your people? You're an embarrassment.
You've crossed lines no one wanted crossed. My people?
Whatever the price, I'll pay it." And he would have taken

the jaguar, right then and there, his prey already against the wall, the stun gun no longer adequate.

"Meghan!" Gausto shouted. "Complete wards! Whatever it takes! Do it!"

Dolan had time only for a grim little smile, a surge of hope at what Gausto had so unwittingly done—and then physical wards sprang to life, knocking him back to land hard. He rolled, he twisted—he came to his feet again.

From above, Carter's sharp demand filtered downstairs. "Treviño! What the hell is going on down there?"

He'd have to come down and find out for himself. Dolan had no time for response, tangled up in determination to free Meghan, tangled up in the faint awareness that she was back, that she'd done just as she'd been told and reached out for power—and through that connection with the earth, was now reaching out to others as well. That she had rediscovered something of herself and needed time—

I'll get you time.

Because Gausto couldn't realize what he'd done, not yet, and so Dolan flipped the stun gun back into a better hold and bared his teeth as Gausto's comical triumph gave way to disbelief, and he charged.

Whatever it takes. She'd obeyed without second thought, and now...now she existed in a flood of energy. She saw the astonishing dark bands that tied her to Gausto, ignored them for now. Drawing mercilessly on the earth's power, daring burnout, she flung up a quick physical ward—nothing as strong as what she'd done for the book, nothing that would hold out past an assault or two.

Dolan can tell that—surely Dolan can tell—

She reached out to him, too, brushing past a tumult of emotions so strong she didn't dare linger near. And while her mind raced, while she tried to think ahead and beyond, she found herself reaching across meaningless distance to her beloved made family, Jenny with her constrained nature and Anica with her unconstrained nature, to the brief taste of Luka and the gestalt of Encontrados as a whole. A startled whisper of response brushed back against her—of awareness she hadn't expected. Of hope and sudden determination. It fed her, awakening those parts of her that she thought had died with her and not come back.

She let it spread to Dolan, saw the look on his face—saw understanding and intent. Heard his grim, faint *I'll get you time.*

How—? But she cut herself short. Didn't matter how. She had to be ready—she had to be one step ahead of Gausto. When the wards went down he'd demand them back, demand better ones—

And she'd have them ready. She'd have them ready on her own terms.

A raw cry of pain jerked her back from ward view to the horror of physical reality. To her body, still sitting quietly on a cot—and to Dolan, latched on to Gausto so tightly the wards couldn't throw him away, crying out defiance of pain and power and jamming the stun gun against Gausto's side, taxing the wards.

Giving me time.

The flickering blue light of the jaguar sliced the air, hovering, invoked by surging powers and extreme effort. Gausto shouted nonsense, trapped against the wall but untouched, power playing all around him, and Dolan cried out again, fierce and agonized all at once, not backing off for an instant.

Until three men rushed into the cellar and yanked him away.

Even dazed, the wards stripping his bones from the inside out, Dolan understood. *Carter. The team.* They couldn't stop him from trying to rise from the wet floor, to slip the hands on his shoulders, his shirt, his arms, the arm looped around his waist. *Ruger.* He'd never break that hold. "You can't—you've got to let me—"

"Treviño!" Carter snapped. "Stand down! Stand down!"

He snapped his head back, hard—hit someone's face, no doubt—but in spite of the muffled cry, the hold on him only tightened. And in his struggle he caught a glimpse of Gausto, coming forward off the wall ruffled and flushed, his temper eroded, the wards diminished but holding steady around him. And he held up his clenched fist and by God, Dolan knew what was coming next and yet he couldn't have imagined. A flash of heat rushed through his body; fiery pain slapped him and he arched up in surprise, another cry ripped from a throat going raw. Blood filled his mouth, trickled from his nose and the hands stopped holding him back and instead held him down, Carter in the dim background shouting his name and Ruger rumbling, "What the fu—" and then it stopped, because Gausto, panting audibly, hadn't yet drawn on the power Meghan could offer, but had used his own energy instead.

As Dolan sagged back, the Sentinels eased him down to the hard concrete floor and Ruger was immediately upon him, hands checking him, healer's senses intruding. Dolan rolled to his side and spat blood, ignoring the spatter from his nose and already clawing his way back to his knees.

"Holy crap," muttered the man whose name he'd never learned, the tiger. From behind them, from the doorway, Lyn Maines skidded to a stop with a horrified noise, and Carter motioned her back, crouching beside Dolan with a hand on his shoulder. And when Dolan lifted his head, his eyes were filmed with red, sticky bloodied tears—but he saw Gausto's intent well enough.

"Meghan, attend me!" Gausto barely glanced her way, all of his attention on the bemused Sentinels before him, the ones who had no possible defense from the *sceleratus vis.* "Feed me what I need."

"No," Dolan said, his voice raspy from blood in his throat, from strained vocal cords. "Carter, don't let him—"

But Gausto had gathered himself—and then quite abruptly stopped, looking over at Meghan with startled realization—understanding that Meghan, too, was gathering power. "You're—"

Make it count. Make it all count. Dolan lurched forward, out of no-longer-grasping hands, clawing to his feet—heading right back for Gausto. *Give her time…*

His stun gun was gone, lost in the scramble; he didn't need it. In a single staggering, stumbling leap he threw himself at the man, latched on, thought he was ready for the lash of the wards but shouted out again anyway, clutching on with every bit of willpower he possessed. Gausto shoved at him, snarling imprecations, his grasp on the *sceleratus vis* shattered and—

Give her time...

Dolan held on. *Flashing power, searing pain, violent surge of rejection* and there was Carter, coming in beside him. Dolan snarled wordlessly, warning him not to interfere again—but Carter only grinned back, brandished his stun gun and piled on, driving Gausto back against the wall again—untouched, and still trapped. Gausto struggled against them, his face inches from Dolan's, uncertainty flickering through the victory.

And the wards flickered.

"Meghan!" Gausto shouted, barely intelligible over the electric *zzzt* of the stun gun, the wounded cry of the wards...the noise of two men persevering beyond pain. "You can do better than this! Stronger! *As strong as it can be!*"

The wards snapped back into place, strong and thick, and Dolan only had time to realize he knew the look of them before they flung him away, he and Carter both landing in a heap, a fall broken by Ruger's sturdy form and Ruger's anticipation of the inevitable.

For a moment, Dolan only lay there. For a moment, he thought that's all he'd be able to do. The initial attack at the homestead, the combined effects of the *sceleratus vis,* the *Liber Nex* wards...profound, aching weariness filled his body. And yet...and yet...

A familiar feeling whispered up against him, caressing; his fatigue eased. He rolled to his side, found Meghan, blinked until his vision cleared. "Is that you?" he asked, words that barely made themselves audible. *Is it you?*

And she gave the tightest of smiles, defiance

wrapped up in silence, still sitting at the edge of the cot in her bloodstained shirt, the tensed muscles in her bare, bruised leg the only thing to give away her struggle.

Carter eyed them both, recognizing the undercurrent of something, but Ruger interrupted, pulling Carter to his feet and leaving Dolan another moment to himself. "I've lost score," Ruger said. "Who's ahead now?"

"The correct question," Gausto said, still breathing heavily from the onslaught but now smoothing his suit coat, adjusting his tie, smoothing back his already slick hair, "is 'who dies now?'" He pulled the vial from his coat, the one Dolan recognized from hard experience. "The answer, of course, is *all of you*."

Carter recognized the vial's significance as well. "Damn."

Gausto brandished the thing. "Now that my resources are...*expanded*...did you really think I'd let you walk away from here with information about the *sceleratus vis?* Once I know what you've done with the book—"

"The book?" Ruger gave Carter a puzzled glance. "We don't have the damned book."

Gausto glared at Dolan, who mustered a halfhearted shrug. "I lied. Sue me."

"Then you'll live somewhat longer than the others, if not much. It won't take long to get the truth from you." And he lifted the vial in a completely unnecessary dramatic gesture, focusing on it with a glower. "Support me, Meghan."

And Dolan thought he heard a whisper of response, a coyote's child leaping on her prey, jaws snapping shut. *You asked for it.*

Power surged through the room; Ruger and Carter barely had time to exchange alarmed expressions at the magnitude of it before Gausto loosed it at them—

And cried out in astonishment, recoiling from the vial—stiffening, quivering and slowly slumping to the floor, his expression dazed with incomprehension.

Hit with sudden understanding, Dolan laughed, short and hard—it was too much, and doubled him over in a cough. Carter grabbed his shoulder, shook it. "Straighten up, Treviño—what the hell—?"

Dolan cleared his throat, spat old blood and laughed again. "She did it. She did just what he asked. The strongest possible wards. Nothing gets in…*nothing gets out*."

Carter looked over at Meghan, brows raised. "Damn," he said. "You *are* your mother's daughter."

"He could always tell her to drop the wards," Ruger suggested, sounding very much like Briar Rabbit. *Go ahead, Gausto. Drop the wards. Do it….*

But Dolan was watching Meghan, listening to the bare whisper of her indirect thought, filtered through the earth to him. "I'm not so sure…" He looked at Gausto, who dragged himself up the wall to stand again, if unsteadily. "Go ahead, *Drozhar*. Ask her. Ask her if she can. Better yet, ask her why she *can't*."

Gausto's jaw worked, resisting the directive—but not for long. "Explain, Meghan."

Her voice, freed, rang clearly in the cellar. "You asshole. You told me to make it as strong as possible, and I did. That means the *aeternus*. Those wards are unbreakable. I tied them to *your* life."

"You—" Gausto struggled with her words, couldn't seem to understand them. "You—"

"You'll never touch anyone else again. Any power you use will bounce back on *you*. You *lose,* you freak—"

"Silence!" he shouted. "*You* are the ones to lose! I'm walking out of here—with *her*—and you can do nothing to stop me."

And Meghan instantly complied—but now Dolan could see the spark in her eye, the defiance. He caught that spark, held it…made it to his hands and knees, never releasing her gaze from his. *Fight it, Meghan. Fight it now!*

Success.

She'd taken what she'd learned in these scant days, taken the time Dolan had given her to prepare, and she'd woven the very wards Gausto demanded of her. And even if he still compelled her…he'd also given her access to the earth's power. To Dolan through that power…to her friends.

She reached for it, that pure connection to the land. Down through flagstones to the earth beneath, through the earth to Encontrados. Reached for the roiling purity of the power that welcomed her—recklessly, desperately opened herself to it. Hunting just enough to burn away the dark ugly bands tying her to Gausto…to free herself.

And *it burned.* It rolled through her like a tsunami, scouring and flooding *and it burned*—

Meghan screamed, a sound that cut through her from the inside out as her eyes rolled back and her body stiffened and jerked, and then she lost everything but the power and the burn and the power and the flood and the pure white incandescent flash that blinded her inside and out and left her lost and drifting.

Meg.
Wave upon wave of it, bright burning power...
Meghan, love. I'm here.
And the faintest flicker of sanity—
Meghan. Meg. I'm here. Come to me.
And the faintest flicker of self—
Meg. Come back to me.
Dolan?
Here, Meghan.
I can't—
You can. Come back to me, Meg.
Dolan? The bright haze thinned, dimmed to the reddish haze of wards...pulsing, alive...free.

Still here. A brighter spot in that haze, steady and comfortable. *Here, Meg. To me. I'll take you back.*

And suddenly she was there, beside that warm presence, and she was looking at the inside of her eyelids to boot, her back against the cot and her body still clenched and trembling, but Dolan's arm around her shoulders and his hand stroking back her incorrigible hair. She pried her eyelids open and found him close, half on the cot and half kneeling beside it, his face streaked with dried blood and his eyes haunted, and he, too, trembled from what they'd been through. "Dolan," she whispered, and he nodded, a barely discernible movement, his gaze still fastened on hers. She smiled, a mere exhausted twitch at the corners of her mouth. "Don't...call me Meg."

And he laughed, and he kissed her good and hard, and held her so close she could barely breathe—and that's just the way she wanted it.

Chapter 24

Dolan rested his head back against the low adobe wall that arched around the natural landscaping of Gausto's rented headquarters—*former* headquarters—and tightened his arm around Meghan's shoulders. Her head rested against his collarbone, where—with a little help from Ruger—she slept. Recovering from the day.

Captured. Tortured. Killed. Resurrected into slavery. Used as a power conduit…and nearly lost in a flood of it as she broke her bonds.

Yeah, busy day.

Ruger had brought her out here, carried her effortlessly while Dolan staggered along behind, and leaned her up against the retaining wall, even as he declined to ease Dolan's wounds. "You wasted the last healing," he'd said, actions belying his hard words as he helped Dolan sit on the narrow strip of grass bordering the short wall, where the low sun turned the shadows long. "Now you can do it like anyone else." But he'd hesitated long enough to narrow his eyes and give Dolan a careful eye. "Though we'll want a better look at you. Later. Right now, you just be here when she wakes up."

He'd cleaned up, at least—made use of washcloth and bathroom while Ruger worked on Meghan, so when she did open her eyes she wouldn't find the same blood-streaked horror that had confronted him in the mirror. And now, while Carter and his team cleaned up the house, removing all signs of the activity that had gone on there, Dolan sat out here on the grass with his knees propped up and Meghan tucked under his arm, floating in his own achy exhaustion.

Sceleratus vis. Just say no.

Meghan shifted slightly. Her hands, resting limply on legs folded to the side, moved—finding him. First his chest, then his thigh; she took a deep, slow breath and rested one hand there, detouring only to tuck her hair behind her ear in a futile gesture. "I would have been lost," she murmured. "I *was* lost. If you hadn't come for me—"

He said nothing. He briefly tightened his hold on her shoulders, and he kissed the top of her head.

After a long silence, she pushed herself up—still tucked in beside him, but more upright, leaning against the wall on her own. "I must have passed out. I guess I'm lucky I didn't pass *on,* when I broke Gausto's hold on me. We don't have any idea what he did to…to bring me back."

He looked away from her, not quite able to face that possibility so soon. But he admitted, "You're right. But if it was going to happen…"

"It would have," she said, trying to convince herself. "Dolan, your voice—!"

Gravelly, strained…the voice he'd been left after Gausto's handiwork. "It'll get better," he said, but then had to admit, "I think." And he kissed her forehead for good measure.

"Did it hold? What I did with Gausto's wards?"

Dolan grinned, and made no attempt to make it a nice one. "Steady as she goes."

She twisted around to look at the house, barely visible beyond the curve of the wall. "Where is he?"

"Gone."

"Gone?" She pulled away from him to look at him more completely, to take in their circumstances and their lack of company.

Dolan shrugged. "He's untouchable. We can't get in; he can't get out. He can't do anymore harm with the *sceleratus vis*…and Carter never meant to keep him in the first place. As the region's *drozhar,* he's pretty much got diplomatic immunity. He even took his men. One of Carter's team is escorting them out of the area."

"After all *that*—"

Dolan shook his head. "It's okay, Meghan. We got what we came for—we got more than what we came for. Gausto is neutralized, and he still has to face his sept's prince. And we have all of his materials on the *sceleratus vis.* Notes, history, formulas." In the background, footsteps approached. Silent to anyone else…loud enough to Dolan's ears. "Carter," he said out loud. "Maines."

Meghan stiffened slightly in surprise, and relaxed as the two came into view. Carter had a burnished aluminum briefcase; he set it on the driveway gravel and regarded them, more bemused than anything else. "I should probably say something official here," he said. "Admonishment, scolding…whatever. Truth is, Dolan's right. We have more than we came for. I can't work up any interest in picking apart the how of it. Except—" and he fixed his gaze on Dolan, light green and penetrating "—I want the location of the book. And I want it *now.*"

"Oh," Meghan said, waving the matter away as if it was of no consequence. "Doesn't everyone know that by now? It's at the outhouse. My mother put an illusionary ward on it. You'll find it masquerading as old-fashioned toilet paper."

Carter made a choking noise; Lyn Maines widened her eyes. "I knew I felt something!" she said. "I just couldn't pin it…" She stopped, shook her head. "Your mother was a woman of astonishing skills, Meghan."

Meghan seemed to absorb that for a moment, and then she nodded. "She was. I guess…maybe…she left me more than I thought."

"Speaking of that…" Carter said, and Meghan stiffened, her hand tensing on Dolan's thigh. He put his hand over hers, and sent silent reassurance.

Carter saw it all. "Ease up, you two. It's obvious that brevis made an inexcusable error in shutting Meghan out. We can't fix that now, but she does need training—not so we can use her, if that's not what she wants, but so she can stay safe and the people around her can stay safe."

"I can keep her safe," Dolan growled. It was especially effective with his current voice; it even widened Lyn's eyes slightly. Good.

"Maybe," Carter said, clearly not agreeing…but

leaving it at that. "Consider yourself invited," he told
Meghan. "Whenever you're ready. I think you'll find it
to be sooner rather than later, but it's up to you." He
caught Dolan's gaze. "And *you,*" he said. "I should retire
you from fieldwork immediately. Talk about a loose
cannon—" But he waved away Dolan's glower. "Not
yet. But I think you should come with her."

Dolan considered the words; they sounded more
like a suggestion than an order, and that didn't quite
fit. "To brevis?"

"I told you," Lyn said. "If you understood more about
what's been happening—"

But Carter silenced her with a look. "If he's interested, he'll come."

Dolan snorted. It hurt. "You think I'm that easy to
play?"

"It's been a while," Carter said. "Doesn't seem as
though you have any right to judge brevis if you don't
keep better track of us."

"I know what I need to," Dolan said, as hard as ever.
Brevis had a leak—the one that had renewed the Core's
interest in this area in the first place. Brevis had a
history of hesitating at just the wrong moment, leaving
its field agents hanging. Brevis had lost its focus, its
collective goal.

But when he eyed Carter, hunting deception, he
found only honesty. And Carter had joined his attack on
Gausto—*joined* him, not stopped him. Since his arrival,
he'd backed Dolan's intentions…even though it had
sometimes looked coerced. He'd still done it, when he
could have fallen back on brevis stuffiness and made
things worse.

If only he'd gotten here earlier…

Lyn watched him, giving him a strange and piercing look. A little bit hope, a little bit disappointment…as if he'd already largely fulfilled her expectations, and not in a good way.

There was something to be found out, there at brevis. What was behind Lyn's expression, for one. What was behind Carter's carefully tendered invitation.

As if he'd let Meghan go into that literal lion's den alone anyway.

Carter nodded, short and decisive, and picked up the briefcase. "We're just about done here. Plan is to take you back to the ranch, let you sort out your people…take some time to recover." He glanced at Dolan. "You've got a field report to file, but you can do it from there. Ruger also wants to spend some time with you."

Right. To see what he could glean of the taint of the *sceleratus vis.*

"Tell him to bring work boots," Meghan said, just a little too sweet. "All of our guests are working guests."

Carter grinned, an unexpected expression. "I'll do that." And he lifted his chin at Lyn, a little *let's go* gesture, leaving Dolan and Meghan alone again for the moment.

Meghan's chin went up. "If they think they can force me to—"

Easy, love. He sent it out between them, saw its impact. "I don't trust them, either, but…"

"There's *something,*" she finished for him.

"There might be."

At that they sat another moment or two, let the heat of the setting sun bake their aches and their exhaustion, taking the time to be aware of each other. Meghan turned to him, shifting over to her knees, and watching his face. Drinking it in, more like, as well as reaching out to rub a thumb over some spot on his cheek he must have missed. She said, "Will you? Come back to the ranch? Stay with me? Make sure I don't hurt them somehow?"

Dolan laughed. "Not a chance. Haven't you figured me out yet? I'm a selfish son of a bitch. I'm coming back to be with *you*."

Resignation, relief…annoyance. They crossed her face in quick succession, and she made a mocking fist. "I ought to—"

"Oh, God no," he said, holding up his hands in an exaggerated defense. "I'm done for the day. For the week!"

"For the year," she allowed, relaxing her hand. "Well, come here, then, and let me kiss you back into strength. Encontrados is waiting."

* * * * *

Look for Doranna Durgin's next thrilling
Sentinels romance, Lion Heart.
Available April 2010 only from
Mills & Boon® Intrigue Nocturne™.

*Mills & Boon® Intrigue brings you
a sneak preview of…*

Carla Cassidy's The Rancher Bodyguard

*Grace Covington's stepfather has been murdered, her
teenage sister the only suspect. Convinced of her
sister's innocence, Grace turns to her ex-boyfriend,
lawyer Charlie Black, to help her find the truth.
Although she is determined not to forgive his betrayal,
the sexual tension instantly returns as their
investigation leads them into danger…and back
into each other's arms.*

Don't miss the thrilling final story in the
WILD WEST BODYGUARDS
*mini-series, available next month from
Mills & Boon® Intrigue.*

The Rancher Bodyguard
by
Carla Cassidy

As he approached the barn, Charlie Black saw the sleek, scarlet convertible pulling into his driveway, and wondered when exactly, while he'd slept the night before, hell had frozen over. Because the last time he'd seen Grace Covington, that's what she'd told him would have to happen before she'd ever talk to or even look at him again.

He patted the neck of his stallion and reined in at the corral. As he dismounted and pulled off his dusty black hat, he tried to ignore the faint thrum of electricity that zinged through him as she got out of her car.

Her long blond hair sparkled in the late afternoon sun, but he was still too far away to see the expression on her lovely features.

It had been a year and a half since he'd seen her, even though for the past six months they'd resided in the same small town of Cotter Creek, Oklahoma.

The last time he'd encountered her had been in his upscale apartment in Oklahoma City. He'd been wearing a pair of sports socks and an electric blue condom. Not one of his finer moments, but it had been the culminating incident in a year of not-so-fine moments.

Too much money, too many successes and far too much booze had transformed his life into a nightmare of bad moments, the last resulting in him losing the only thing worth having.

Surely she hadn't waited all this time to come out to the family ranch—his ranch now—to finally put a bullet in what she'd described as his cold, black heart. Grace had never been the type of woman to put off till today what she could have done yesterday.

Besides, she hadn't needed a gun on that terrible Friday night when she'd arrived unannounced at his apartment. As he'd stared at her in a drunken haze, she'd given it to him with both barrels, calling him every vile name under the sun before she slammed out of his door and out of his life.

So, what was she doing here now? He slapped his horse on the rump, then motioned to a nearby ranch hand to take care of the animal. He closed the gate and approached where she hadn't moved away from the driver's side of her car.

Her hair had grown much longer since he'd last seen her. Although most of it was clasped at the back of her neck, several long wisps had escaped the confines. The beige suit she wore complemented her blond coloring and the icy blue of her eyes.

She might look cool and untouchable, like the perfect lady, but he knew what those eyes looked like flared with desire. He knew how she moaned with wild abandon when making love, and he hated the fact that just the unexpected sight of her brought back all the memories he'd worked so long and hard to forget.

"Hello, Grace," he said, as he got close enough to speak without competing with the warm April breeze. "I have to admit I'm surprised to see you. As I remember, the last time we saw each other, you indicated that hell would freeze over before you'd ever speak to me again."

Her blue eyes flashed with more than a touch of annoyance—a flash followed swiftly by a look of desperation.

"Charlie, I need you." Her low voice trembled slightly, and only then did he notice that her eyes were red-rimmed, as if she'd been weeping. In all the time they'd dated—even during the ugly scene that had ended *them*—he'd never seen her shed a single tear. "Have you heard the news?" she asked.

"What news?"

"Early this afternoon my stepfather was found stabbed to death in bed." She paused for a moment and bit her full lower lip as her eyes grew shiny with suppressed tears. "I think Hope is in trouble, Charlie. I think she's really in bad trouble."

"What?" Shock stabbed through him. Hope was

Grace's fifteen-year-old sister. He'd met her a couple of times. She'd seemed like a nice kid, not as pretty as her older sister, but a cutie nevertheless.

"Maybe you should come on inside," he said, and gestured toward the house. She stared at the attractive ranch house as if he'd just invited her into the chambers of hell. "There's nobody inside, Grace. The only woman who ever comes in is Rosa Caltano. She does the cooking and cleaning for me, and she's already left for the day."

Grace gave a curt nod and moved away from the car. She followed him to the house and up the wooden stairs to the wraparound porch.

The entry hall was just as it had been when Charlie's mother and father had been alive, with a gleaming wood floor and a dried flower wreath on the wall.

He led her to the living room. Charlie had removed much of the old furniture that he'd grown up with and replaced it with contemporary pieces in earth tones. He motioned Grace to the sofa, where she sat on the very edge as if ready to bolt at any moment. He took the chair across from her and gazed at her expectantly.

"Why do you think Hope is in trouble?"

She drew in a deep breath, obviously fighting for control. "From what I've been told, Lana, the housekeeper, found William dead in his bed. Today is her day off, but she left a sweater there last night and went back to get it. It was late enough in the day that William should have been up, so she checked on him. She immediately called Zack West, and he and some of his deputies responded. They found Hope passed out on her bed. Apparently she was the only one home at the time of the murder."

Charlie frowned, his mind reeling. Before he'd moved back here to try his hand at ranching, Charlie had been a successful, high-profile defense attorney in Oklahoma City.

It was that terrible moment in time with Grace followed by the unexpected death of his father that had made him take a good, hard look at his life and realize how unhappy he'd been for a very long time.

Still, it was as a defense attorney that he frowned at her thoughtfully. "What do you mean she was passed out? Was she asleep? Drunk?"

Those icy blue eyes of hers darkened. "Apparently she was drugged. She was taken to the hospital and is still there. They pumped her stomach and are keeping her for observation." Grace leaned forward. "Please, Charlie. Please help her. Something isn't right. First of all, Hope would never, ever take drugs, and she certainly isn't capable of something like this. She would *never* have hurt William."

Spoken like a true sister, Charlie thought. How many times had he heard family members and friends proclaim that a defendant couldn't be guilty of the crime they had been charged with, only to discover that they were wrong?

"Grace, I don't know if you've heard, but I'm a rancher now." He wasn't at all sure he wanted to get involved with any of this. It had disaster written all over it. "I've retired as a criminal defense attorney."

"I heard through the grapevine that besides being a rancher, you're working part-time with West Protective Services," she said.

"That's right," he agreed. "They approached me about a month ago and asked if I could use a little side work. It sounded intriguing, so I took them up on it, but so far I haven't done any work for them."

"Then let me hire you as Hope's bodyguard, and if you do a little criminal defense work in the process I'll pay you extra." She leaned forward, her eyes begging for his help.

Bad idea, a little voice whispered in the back of his brain. She already hated his guts, and this portended a very bad ending. He knew how much she loved her sister; he assumed that for the last couple of years she'd been more mother than sibling to the young girl. He'd be a fool to involve himself in the whole mess.

"Has Hope been questioned by anyone?" he heard himself ask. He knew he was going to get involved whether he wanted to or not, because it was Grace, because she needed him.

"I don't think so. When I left the hospital a little while ago, she was still unconscious. Dr. Dell promised me he wouldn't let anyone in to see her until I returned."

"Good." There was nothing worse than a suspect running off at the mouth with a seemingly friendly officer. Often the damage was so great there was nothing a defense attorney could do to mitigate it.

"Does that mean you'll take Hope's case?" she asked.

"Whoa," he said, and held up both his hands. "Before I agree to anything, I need to make a couple of phone calls, find out exactly what's going on and where the official investigation is headed. It's possible you don't need me, that Hope isn't in any real danger of being arrested."

"Then what happens now?"

"Why don't I plan on meeting you at the hospital in about an hour and a half? By then I'll know more of what's going on, and I'd like to be present while anybody questions Hope. If anyone asks before I get there, you tell them you're waiting for legal counsel."

She nodded and rose. She'd been lovely a year and a half ago when he'd last seen her, but she was even lovelier now.

She was five years younger than his thirty-five but had always carried herself with the confidence of an older woman. That was part of what had initially drawn him to her, that cool shell of assurance encased in a slamming hot body with the face of an angel.

"How's business at the dress shop?" he asked, trying to distract her from her troubles as he walked her back to her car. She owned a shop called Sophisticated Lady that sold designer items at discount prices. She often traveled the two-hour drive into Oklahoma City on buying trips. That was where she and Charlie had started their relationship.

They'd met in the coffee shop in the hotel where she'd been staying. Charlie had popped in to drop off some paperwork to a client and had decided to grab a cup of coffee before heading back to his office.

She'd been sitting alone next to a window. The sun had sparked on her hair. Charlie had taken one look and was smitten.

"Business is fine," she said, but it was obvious his distraction wasn't successful.

"I'm sorry about William, but Zack West is a good man, a good sheriff. He'll get to the bottom of things."

Once again she nodded and opened her car door. "Then I'll see you in the hospital in an hour and a half," she said.

"Grace?" He stopped her before she got into the seat. "Given our history, why would you come to me with this?" he asked.

Her gaze met his with a touch of frost. "Because I think Hope is in trouble and she needs a sneaky devil to make sure she isn't charged with a murder I know she didn't commit. And you, Charlie Black, are as close to the devil as I could get."

She didn't wait for his reply. She got into her car, started the engine with a roar and left him standing to eat her dust as she peeled out and back down the driveway.

© Carla Bracale 2009